Devya's Children Book 3:
Malia's Miracles

To Moriah,
    Welcome to the third adventure
featuring Jillian and Danielle.
Hope you enjoy growing with them as they
face new challenges.

                    ~ Julie C. Gilbert

Contact Information

Please watch the YouTube trailer
for Ashlynn's Dreams and Nadia's Tears.

Email questions and comments to the author
at **devyaschildren@gmail.com**.

Stay tuned to the Facebook page for news.
(https://www.facebook.com/JulieCGilbert2013)

(This book may be read without reading Book 1 and 2, but the series
would be better if read in order.)

Also by Julie C. Gilbert:
Short Stories
Ashlynn's Dreams Shorts: Helping Mr. Blairington and Other Misadventures

Young Adult Science Fiction
Devya's Children Book 1: Ashlynn's Dreams*
Devya's Children Book 2: Nadia's Tears

Christian Mystery
Heartfelt Cases 1: The Collins Case*
Heartfelt Cases 2: The Kiverson Case
Heartfelt Cases 3: The Davidson Case

* Available as an audiobook

Dedication:

To family and friends who have supported me all along:
William and Catherine Gilbert,
Jenny Shin, Laura Ginn,
Cara Guglielmon, Chrissy Guglielmon,
Lucas Dalenberg

Special thanks:
Timothy Sparvero, for awesome promotional materials
Kristin Condon, for bringing Jillian and Danielle to life

(Any remaining mistakes are my own, despite their efforts.)

Dramatis Personae
(Warning: may contain spoilers)

Dr. Carla M. Wittier – Jillian's old shrink lady
Dr. Stephanie Sokolowski (a.k.a. Dr. S.) – Jillian's new shrink lady

Jillian Blairington/Ashlynn – thirteen-year-old Dream Shaper
Danielle Matheson – Jillian's friend
Christy Roman – Danielle's friend
Dominique Roman – Christy's little sister
Susan Kilpatrick – cancer patient, Christy and Dominique's mother

Dr. Devya – researcher, creator of Devya's Children
Dr. Evelyn Carnasis – researcher, associate of Dr. Devya, mother of Jillian, Benjamin Connelly, and Aiden
Cora – associate of Dr. Devya, mother of Dustin
Dr. Karita Robinson – former associate of Dr. Devya, mother of Malia and Michio
Dr. Jessica Paladon – former associate of Dr. Devya, mother of Varick and Nadia
Maisha – cook for Dr. Devya

Devya's Children:
Varick – soldier
Nadia – thinker, Queen Elena, Naidine, Nadie
Ashlynn – dreamer, Jillian Blairington
Malia – feeler
Dustin – Devya's telepathist
Reeve – second dreamer, Benjamin Connelly
Michio – first nanomachine controller
Aiden – second nanomachine controller

Davidson Household:
Able Davidson – Marina and Malia's foster father
Carol Davidson – Marina and Malia's foster mother
Ann Duncan (Nee Davison) – Carol and Able's elder daughter
Joy Davidson – Carol and Able's younger daughter
Nicholas Davidson – Carol and Able's son
Marina Nardin – Carol and Able's foster daughter
Malia Ayers – Carol and Able's foster daughter

Summary: ITEM 1-130

Ashlynn's Dreams includes the first seventy-two items which detail how Jillian Marie Antel Blairington comes to know she has the unique ability to shape dreams. During those adventures, she forges a strong friendship with her babysitter, Danielle Matheson, who gets kidnapped as a means of controlling Jillian's behavior during the Dream Shaper training.

   Nadia's Tears covers items seventy-three through one hundred and thirty which follow Jillian's efforts to awaken Nadia from a coma and Danielle's efforts to keep Christy Roman safe and out of trouble. In Nadia's dreams, Jillian meets her sister at various stages of life, including the emotionally wounded Nadie, the fierce Naidine, and the wise Queen Elena. After helping Jillian get to Nadia, Danielle tries to concentrate on school but gets drawn into Christy's troubles. Jillian succeeds in waking Nadia just in time to rescue Danielle and Christy.

Prologue

ITEM 131: Carla Wittier's fifth letter
Item Source: Dr. Carla M. Wittier
To Dr. Stephanie Sokolowski:
I apologize for the condition of this journal entry. After the trouble I had last year with the break-ins, I went on a shredding frenzy. Although I realized the mistake at the time, I have only recently found time to put the story to rights. It made me smile and miss being Jillian's "personal shrink lady," a feeling I'm sure you can relate to these days. Her honesty is always refreshing.
Regards,
Carla M. Wittier, Ph.D.

***

ITEM 132 (formerly ITEM 10): Jillian's ninth pre-kidnapping journal entry
Item Source: Dr. Carla M. Wittier
Some places beg to be explored, even when Nana and Momma say they ain't fit for kids. I told y'all that I'd explain about Mr. Thomas Kremel's creepy old place, but I got all distracted with other stuff. It's located one heck of a long hike behind our house. It actually ain't much more than a mile, but you can't see it from our house 'cause there's a bunch of hills and fat trees in the way.

My own personal shrink lady, Dr. Wittier, says sometimes adults got good reasons to tell kids to stay away from a place. I sorta promised her I'd try not to get into any real dangerous situations, but this trip took place long before I met Dr. Wittier. She's real sweet for an old lady, and though she ain't as old as Nana, she's almost as smart in world wisdom 'cause it's her job to be that way. Nana says shrink ladies are money-leeching ninny heads, but Dr. Wittier's different. She talks with me for free 'cause she expects to learn something from our conversations. I like talking to her 'cause, unlike most adults, she actually listens when I tell her things.

Dr. Wittier says I gotta keep introducing myself 'cause someday she might get my stories published so lots of people can read 'em. I'm only explaining that 'cause I don't wanna come across as what Nana calls a fluff-headed fool. That said, I am Jillian Marie Antel Blairington. Writing that out by hand sure does take a while. Dr. Wittier said I could use a pen name, but Nana says I ought to be proud of who I am, long name and loud spirit and all.

Anyway, back to what I meant to tell y'all. I first explored the old Kremel place on a dark autumn day when I was a little kid. I meant to go to Jimmy Denson's house to play, but I got lost 'cause I'd only been there twice before and never the back way. Also, I was coming from Nana's house, which is six houses farther down from mine. Momma was working, Daddy was out with some friends, and I was supposed to be at Nana's. Only since Daddy didn't actually drop me off and Nana wasn't expecting me, I figured I could go to Jimmy's for the day. His momma said I was such a pleasure to have that she'd welcome me any time, any day.

I think it was partly the sudden storm clouds that came up, but the trees behind Nana's place seemed much scarier than the ones behind our place. I ran so I could get to Jimmy's as fast as possible. I know that ain't the smartest thing to do when the skies are fixing to dump a few billion raindrops on yer head, but there wasn't much else I could do at that point.

A loud crash made me stop running. I listened real close and caught a faint whistling noise. Nana says I got a dangerous sense of curiosity. Once I heard that whistling sound, there was nothing nobody could do to keep me from searching for the source. The whistling sound came again, only this time it was half a whistle and half a mournful moan. For a moment, I thought somebody might be in pain, but then I remembered Nana saying that the wind could do real good people impressions.

I may have been more adventuresome as a kid, but I wasn't stupid. My steps slowed to a fast walk as I neared the whiny noise. It's a good thing I'd stopped running since I almost smacked into the side of the old Kremel place anyway. I didn't know what it was at the time 'cause even though Nana had told me about it she'd never explained how to find it from her house.

I walked around the whole thing. It didn't take long 'cause it was a dinky little place. I started to walk around it again. Just as I reached the far side from the door, a crash of thunder made me jump and lightning lit up everything. I knew it was gonna rain any second and that if I didn't wanna get soaked I had to get into that shack real quick. Fortunately, there was an old window hole a little higher than me. I reached up and climbed in. Looking back's a heap clearer than the moment, and Nana was right to say I oughta be grateful there wasn't glass in that window. I scrambled into the rickety old shack just in time to stay dry.

It's pretty dumb to go touching things in strange places, especially creepy old places, so I looked around the room without touching anything. The place was filthy. Nana woulda had a fit looking at so much dust gathered in one place. She twitched when I told her about it. I could tell she wanted to go back and give the place a good scrubbing. It's probably just as well that she didn't go back and dust 'cause there ain't nobody there to appreciate her fine work, unless ya count the critters skittering across the walls and floors. I hadn't expected to go exploring, so I didn't have proper jars to capture 'em in.

Right off, I noticed that the whistling came from the front door key hole. I didn't weigh much more than a fat sack of farm fresh potatoes so the floor didn't have cause to complain, but that floor moaned and groaned as I explored the room. There wasn't much to explore, except an old wooden table with one broken chair. When I got close to the table, I read P. Kremel carved into it. I tucked a little mental note away to ask Nana about P. Kremel. Nana knows almost everything about everyone, even long dead people.

The storm outside didn't last long so I figured I oughta get back before the storm's big brother or momma came to drown me. Besides, exploring alone ain't half the fun as with a friend.

Two steps from the front door, the floor quit holding me. I screamed and threw out my hands to catch myself as a rotted board gave way and dumped me forward. The door approached awfully fast then my left hand hit the floor with a loud smacking noise. A sliver of a second later, my head thunked against the door, and I took an unexpected nap. It was probably a merciful thing 'cause my wrist ached something awful when I woke up. Every second or so a wave of pain flowed up my left wrist and back down again. I cried and wished I was home. My head hurt too, but since my wrist hurt more, I didn't mind the headache.

I scrambled to my feet. My left ankle, which the floor had pretty much swallowed, was a mite tender, but it wasn't broken. I could tell 'cause I could walk on it with only a limp and a shot of tolerable pain. I say tolerable 'cause it was minor compared to my wrist.

The rain had stopped for good and the afternoon seemed perfect as I left Mr. Kremel's old, crumbling place. The birds were having a singing contest so the slow walk back to my house was rather pleasant. I first made it back to my house and then limped on over to Nana's 'cause that's where I was supposed to be anyway. I knew she'd have some nice tea to warm me head to toe. She examined my wrist as I explained how it got hurt. After poking it gently, Nana said it wasn't broken but would be sore for a few weeks. Then, she wrapped the wrist mummy-like, gave me blackberry tea, mini strawberry scones, and an earful on exploring dangerous places.

Chapter 1
Healing Nadie

ITEM 133: Jillian's sixty-fifth post-kidnapping journal entry
Item Source: Jillian Blairington

I've fallen way behind in my life accounts 'cause there hasn't been much to note. Days come and go without much fuss, which I suppose can't be too bad. I mean excitement tends to translate to life-threatening experiences around here, so peaceful normalness is a nice change.

About the only real struggle right now has been Malia's work with Nadie. The first time I got invited to their shared dream, I thought I'd done something by accident. Darkness covered everything, but it wasn't a scary darkness like being alone in a strange place. Something felt familiar. Usually a dream belongs to one person, not two, but I sensed Nadia and Malia equally in control of this dream.

Not wanting to interrupt, I prepared to withdraw, but Nadia's voice came from the air behind me. "Please stay, Jillian. Your Gift is making this possible. We would be honored by your presence."

Before I could ask Nadia to explain, my unspoken wish for clarity changed the dream. Tiny lights like in a movie theater lit a path from me to an oversized chair that held two figures. One figure reached out and waved for me to come closer. I imagined a tall lamp like the one Momma and my New Daddy bought for the family room appearing right next to the chair and had it shine on its lowest setting.

The new light revealed Malia curled up on the chair with Nadie clinging to her like a blanket. I hadn't seen the three-year-old version of Nadia since the meeting in the throne room where many past and future versions revealed themselves. As I approached the pair, I noticed Nadie stayed awfully still for a little kid.

"She's asleep," said Malia. She craned her neck back to look down at the child.

"She's dreaming she's sleeping?" I asked, confused.

Malia grinned, nodded, and gently ran her right hand down Nadie's silky, golden hair. The grin slowly faded as Malia closed her eyes and rested her chin on Nadie's head. "These sessions are helping, but they're hard for her."

"What sessions?" I barely refrained from glancing around like the answer was hiding in a dark corner nearby.

"It was your idea that I help her," Malia reminded, chuckling.

"Oh, right," I said, feeling kinda dumb for having forgotten that conversation. "Is she all better?"

"She may never be completely better," Malia admitted, "but she is much improved since you last saw her." A far-off look came into Malia's expression, but she blinked it away. "Would you like to talk to her?"

I shrugged but shook my head. "Let her sleep." I leaned closer to study Nadie's face. A lock of shorter hair curled over her left cheekbone, framing her eye. She had her right thumb jammed into her mouth, and her left hand gripped Malia's shirt. "She looks peaceful."

"She is, now that the nightmare comes only sporadically," Malia commented. "She has you to thank for that."

"She woulda outgrown it in a few years anyway," I said, knowing it to be true 'cause I'd tracked Nadia's major dreams since early childhood. The nightmare was actually a very specific, painful memory about losing one of our brothers during a training exercise. I hadn't deleted it completely, 'cause Nadia still wanted to remember. Instead, I messed with the frequency and intensity that Nadie felt each time it came up.

Dr. S. is looking at me with the shrink lady version of the Evil Eye, so I probably ain't making much sense. I discovered this aspect of my Gift while trying to soothe my baby brother's dreams. When I concentrate real hard on one person, I can pre-load a dream for 'em. That got me thinking maybe I could do the opposite too and stop a dream that keeps coming up. Nadia agreed to let me try, and I had some success blocking the dream that used to haunt Nadie constantly.

The task of blocking that dream took a lot longer than spotting and replacing scary dreams Isaac might have, but he's just a baby.

Besides, Nadia's more complicated than any person I know, so it shouldn't surprise me that her dreams differ from other people.

The natural dreams Nadia usually has consist of scenes from her memories. She once explained that everybody takes in a whole lot more than they process. The explanation goes a long way in explaining why people tend to dream strange mixes of folks they know, things they've done, and places they've seen.

Nadia doesn't always dream as herself though. At times, the dreams can be attributed—that means something like assigned—to specific past or future versions. It must be strange to meet future versions of oneself. To help Nadie, I simply took some common dreams from the seven and eight-year-old versions of Nadia and set it up so that the recurring nightmare got replaced three out of every four times it tried to play.

"Burying the pain isn't the same thing as outgrowing it," Malia said, breaking into my thoughts. "Nadia can be too practical at times. Her answer to the problem was to confine it to one portion of her past: Nadie."

"You saying this is her fault?" I wondered, not quite sure where Malia wanted to go with that comment.

Malia shook her head. Her long, dark hair hung down far enough to rustle with each of Nadie's calm breaths. "Not at all, though I suppose that argument could be made. I'm saying we are stronger together. Our Gifts complement each other. I grew up with Nadia and never knew how to help her until you came along, so thank you."

"You're welcome," I said, feeling kinda embarrassed. "But you woulda figured it out eventually."

"I'm not so sure. I was different then, more self-absorbed and unsure of myself." Malia adjusted her hold as the child slowly woke up. Brushing the hair off Nadie's face, Malia leaned down and kissed the girl's cheek. "Feeling better?"

"Better," Nadie confirmed, mumbling because of the thumb.

"Look who's here." Malia grabbed the girl's wrist and tugged until the thumb popped free. Then, she rearranged the child's limbs so Nadie sat facing me.

"Hello, Jillian," greeted Nadie. Leaning back against Malia, Nadie blinked at me slowly, showing off her beautiful, long eyelashes. Dried tear streaks ran down to her chin, but her expression held none of the deep-seated grief I'd come to expect from her. "Thank you for coming to see me."

The formality from a kid so young made me smile. "Did ya have a nice cry?"

"Yes. Malia holds me when I cry," replied Nadie. "She is comfortable."

"I'm glad." A thought struck me. "Will you go away forever when she finishes healing ya?" My tone conveyed concern. I didn't want Nadie to go away for good. It would be like losing a part of Nadia.

Nadie shook her head back and forth quickly in a manner that reminded me of Aiden and Michio. It makes a body wonder why their eyes ain't bouncing around their skulls like pinballs. It must be a kid thing. They've got no fear of hurting their necks. "I will stay. You might need me."

I couldn't think of what I'd need from the ghost of a past version of my sister, but I didn't think hurting her feelings would do much good. I also remembered Nana's words about never dismissing people 'cause they're young, inexperienced, or not particularly known to you. So, I nodded.

We chatted long into the night, but I didn't mind. It was like a sleepover, only Malia, Nadia, and I weren't even in the same states. Malia lives in Pennsylvania, I live in the money sign state next door, and I don't even know where Nadia is at the moment. One would think that might disturb me, but I've come to accept a lot of things since meeting my siblings.

Chapter 2
Malia's Adventures

ITEM 134: Jillian's sixty-sixth post-kidnapping journal entry
Item Source: Jillian Blairington

I feel old. Not physically so, but internally old if you know what I mean. Worry sure can age a body. I've gotten much better with not worrying about other people's business, honest. My adventure into Nadia's dreams taught me a whole heap about what I can and can't control.

On sound advice from Nadia, Nana, and Dr. S., I've laid aside my worry about the schemes Dr. Devya must have cooking up in his super-smart head. His plans for the future may or may not involve me, but seeing as worrying can't give me greater insight into his thoughts, I gotta trust Nadia's word that he's behaving himself for now. As Nana says, one simply can't control all the crazy in the world.

Momma and Isaac still worry me a fair amount, but I'm starting to understand Momma's feelings a little better. Isaac's growing like a weed. He'll be a year old in a few short weeks. I feel bad about missing much of his life, but Nadia needed me with her for much of the last year. Time moves on whether one's ready for it to do so or not. Summer's hurtling toward its inevitable end, and I've just finished catching up on the school work I missed while I was helping Nadia.

About the only one in my family who doesn't worry me is my New Daddy. Mr. Jeffrey Michael Blairington is a swell man. He works hard. He loves my momma, me, and Isaac lots. I can tell 'cause his eyes brighten and he smiles whenever he holds Isaac or talks to me. He's the sort of man who drops whatever he's doing to give a person his full attention. I wish I had that quality.

Danielle doesn't have exactly that trait, but she's got a similar heart. She and my New Daddy are the kind of people who go far out of their way to help people in need. Back when she got kidnapped with me, Danielle proved to be brave and emotionally strong. Her love grew even stronger in the midst of uncertainty and pain. She never once blamed me for her troubles, even though my existence is essentially what got her into that mess. More recently, she risked her life to save Christy Roman from some poor decisions. Danielle always finds ways to be a blessing to those around her. It goes far beyond politeness. If she were a few decades older, she'd make a fine Nana-like figure.

Nana worries me 'cause she's getting on in years, and she seems to be running out of steam. It's sorta like a car slowing down as it nears the end of its life. Odd things break down, and one spends more time trying to fix stuff than actually enjoying the car. Last time she was up here, Nana said she might not be able to travel for a while 'cause she needs a hip replacement surgery. Momma, Isaac, TJ, and my New Daddy are going down to visit her this week and help her during the recovery.

Although everything in me wants to go with 'em to visit Nana, I need to concentrate on the other side of my family right now. The other side is of course Devya's Children: Varick, Nadia, me, Malia, Dustin, Reeve (that's Benny Connelly), Michio, and Aiden. Dr. Carnasis has arranged for Nadia to visit with Malia soon. I haven't seen either Nadia or Malia for months, though we talk nearly every day in dreams or head conversations. Danielle and I are bringing Michio with us, and Varick's gonna meet us at Malia's new place.

This is a special time for Malia and her new family. I don't know much about 'em, but Nadia assures me the Davidson family members are about as good as people get. Carol and Able Davidson have raised three children, two girls and a boy and decided to take on the responsibility of two more girls, my sister Malia and a Russian girl named Marina Nardin. The adoption is the main reason for the huge celebration.

Having Malia home safe and sound is another reason to rejoice. I'm told she recently returned from some rather distressing adventures helping to rescue some trafficked children from people bent on selling 'em for a profit. Nadia purposefully kept me ignorant of Malia's danger, and though I understand why she handled the situation that way, I'm a little miffed at her. Sure I had summer school work to concentrate on, but that hardly compares to knowing I might have been able to help Malia some way. I hope she doesn't think I abandoned her.

Malia has arguably the hardest Gift to bear. Varick gets to learn how to fight. Aiden and Michio get to build complicated things. I can shape dreams. All these Gifts seem straightforward and simple compared to Nadia and Malia. Nadia at least has the advantage of understanding things on a larger scale. Dr. Devya and Dr. Karita Robinson designed Malia to feel emotions very strongly and change 'em to whatever she wishes. I think they were going for a possible emotional therapy, but they got so much more.

Dr. Devya doesn't value Malia's Gifts as much as Nadia's. This hurts Malia. It's a complex issue. Even though Dr. Devya doesn't treat her right, Malia craves his approval. I guess that's a side effect of having grown up in his various scientific compounds. Nadia struggles with similar feelings, but her logical mind helps her deal with those feelings. Emotions are Malia's life, so they have a greater impact on her. She can trick herself into not feeling the hurt, but she usually lets it happen as it will.

My Gifts aren't valued as much as Nadia's either, but I don't give a fig one way or the other. I was raised up with healthy doses of proper affection by Nana and Momma. Besides, Nadia's Gifts *are* more valuable than mine, but then again, so are Malia's Gifts. I think Dr. Devya's problem is that he doesn't understand Malia and that scares him. People react weird when something genuinely frightens 'em.

I won't claim that my training is always easy or comfortable, but I certainly didn't have to learn what everything felt like. My first real encounters with Malia's training came in Dr. Devya's dreams while I was doing Nadia a favor. I'll never forget those images. Later, I saw more in Nadia's dreams, but I'll leave it to Malia to explain her training if she feels it's necessary. I'm happy she's begun writing to Dr. S. and Nana even if it ain't quite on a regular basis.

The party should be unforgettable. I met the Davidsons' elder daughter—FBI Special Agent Julie Ann Duncan—back when Danielle and I escaped from Dr. Devya's compound. The only boy, Nicholas Davidson, recently finished college. I forgot to ask Nadia about what he studied or what he's gonna do, but I guess I could ask him when I meet him in a few days. The younger daughter and middle child, Joy, will soon marry an FBI agent named George Baker. The preparations for the Davidson-Baker wedding is a third reason for the gathering.

Danielle's gonna drive me to this little shindig 'cause I can't drive, and she's more than earned the right to visit with Nadia, Malia, and the rest of my siblings. I'm glad this trip will give us more time to spend together 'cause sooner than I'd like, Danielle will be busy with college stuff. She's going to move into her dorm at The College of New Jersey a few days after we get back. I'm gonna miss her something fierce. She's not going far, but college is a whole different world. Things aren't going to be the same between us, and that makes me sad. Malia once told me joy is a choice, so I will try to choose joy in these special moments with my friend.

The only ones who will miss our reunion are Benny, Dustin, and Aiden. Benny's got his own life and adoptive parents who love him dearly. As much as possible, all concerned parties are trying to keep him ignorant of his Gifts. Dustin could have joined us, but his momma—Cora—is afraid we'll corrupt him with our wild ways.

Aiden's not coming as a guarantee that Nadia will return when the time comes. Much as I like to pretend we're a big, happy family, things like that shove reality in my face. Aiden is in no more danger than usual I suppose, but it ain't right that Dr. Devya feels he's gotta threaten Aiden to control Nadia. She gave her word to return. That ought to be enough. I wonder if anything any of us do or accomplish will ever be enough for Dr. Devya. The man's got some serious trust issues. Nadia or Malia could help with that if he'd let 'em.

Chapter 3
Road Trip

ITEM 135: Danielle's thirty-sixth letter
Item Source: Danielle Matheson
Dear Dr. S.,

    I am so, so sorry for yet another letter drought. This is why I'm a terrible blogger, no consistency. Thankfully, this delay had nothing to do with catching up on school work. Despite my less than stellar performance during senior year, I successfully met all the requirements of my high school and the state of New Jersey to earn my diploma.

    There's so much to talk about that I don't know where to start. Guess I'll just pick up where I was last time and go from there. I had to cheat and re-read my last email to you to even know what I was talking about way back then.

    Calvin (Dillan Greenfield) and I ended up attending the prom together. I wore a lovely royal blue dress because he insisted we match and I didn't want to make the guy suffer through a purple tie. We've exchanged a fair number of texts since then, but I'd venture to say he's way more invested in our relationship than I am. It's not that I don't like him, but I'm afraid we don't have a solid enough foundation to successfully weather the next four years of college-induced separation.

    Graduation was lovely. Thanks again for the card. (I don't count my thank you letter as an official communication, so again, I apologize for being a lousy correspondent.) The weather was surprisingly gorgeous for an outdoor ceremony, despite my cynical predictions. The speeches were tolerably short if not life-changing in their inspiration. The school officials even managed to call all 597 names of the graduates in a timely fashion. A few of the more idiotic graduates attempted to blow up inappropriate dolls, but the chaperones were literally waiting on the sidelines with keys in hand to deal with the offensive things. Mom, Dad, Katy, and Jillian beamed at me from the stands. Dylan made himself a useful distraction by pulling funny faces every time mom wasn't paying attention.

Thank you also for the recommendation letter. I'm sure that helped with the admissions decision, given my mediocre finish to senior year. Your friend on the faculty threw in a few good words on my behalf as well. It really is about who you know in this world. I'm not ashamed to rely on such for something like this, and I'm looking forward to meeting lifelong friends in college. I don't know much about my new roommate, except that her name is Karen and she has a sister named Ellie. Karen and I have exchanged about three emails to date. I get the feeling she's dealing with a lot right now, but I'm sure I'll find out more when we move into our dorm. I can't believe that time's flying up so quickly.

Did Jillian tell you about our pending road trip? We're headed out to Fairview, Pennsylvania to visit Malia and her new family. I'm not sure if she was adopted yet or is going to be while we're there. I wonder if Malia will change her name. I imagine that could be tricky.

Mom's already getting misty-eyed, but she's being a trooper about handling my last minute moving details since I won't be here to do so myself. She and Dad are going to take Dylan and Katy along on the college preparation shopping trip. That should be an interesting Walmart excursion. I'm sure to get plenty of chips, candy, and junk food, depending on how much freedom my parents give Dylan and Katy. Dylan has promoted himself to unofficial food master. I'll probably end up with enough fruit rollups to cover the walls of my dorm twice over. There are worse fates.

With Mr. and Mrs. Davidson's permission, I invited Christy Roman to come with us on our road trip, but she decided to spend more time with her mom. I offered because I thought she could use a break from the constant worry, but Nadia told me Christy's mother is getting worse. I thought about staying to lend some support, but I already promised Jillian I'd take her to see Malia and Nadia. Much as I hate to admit it, there's not much I can do for Christy's family.

When I last wrote you, Christy and I were returning triumphantly, having scored a victory against some human traffickers. Varick even surprised Christy with a large gift of money to go towards treating her mother's cancer. Since that time, we've ridden a tide of good will and hope as the community rallied to help Christy and her little sister, Dominique, cope with the day-to-day details while their mother fights for her life against the disease. Now, sadly, the hopes are fading.

I haven't spoken with Christy in a few days, but I've called and left a few messages to let her know I'm thinking about her. Nadia told me Susan Kilpatrick—Christy's mother—now has metastatic breast cancer, which is basically the worst kind you can have because that means it's moved from the original site to other parts of the body. I don't understand much of the technical details, but I gather moving cancer is bad. Christy hasn't told me how bad it's getting, but I'm sure she will when she's ready.

If I had more courage, I would ask Jillian and Nadia to help Christy's family more directly, but that would be unfair. The more I learn about Devya's Children, the more I'm convinced that letting anybody know about their powerful Gifts would be a massive mistake. Nadia no doubt knows my feelings on the matter, but she also knows better than I do what manner of trouble could arise if they managed to pull off a miracle and save Christy's mother.

Although I won't ask Jillian for help, I've spent days of my life wrestling with the issues. On the one hand, Jillian or one of her siblings must have the ability to cure the cancer. I think Michio's Gift was always meant to allow him to heal diseases, but he's young and relatively untrained. On the other hand, I know enough about human nature to understand that the world isn't ready for these children and their Gifts. It tears my heart to pieces to know that I can't in good conscience encourage any supernatural effort to save Christy's mother.

My moral high ground quakes and crumbles when I think about it being my mother. Is it worth the risk to several lives in the hopes of saving one? The practical side of me admits that Jillian and her siblings have only a slim chance of saving Susan Kilpatrick anyway.

I need to go pack. My car has a fresh tank of gas. I have printed instructions of how to pump gas in uncivilized states that don't have attendants to do that for you. We have plenty of Dylan-approved snacks. I have my GPS primed and Mapquest directions as a backup. So, why do I still feel unprepared for this trip?

The Contrite, Inconsistent Correspondent,
Danielle Matheson.

***

ITEM 136: Jillian's sixty-seventh post-kidnapping journal entry
Item Source: Jillian Blairington

Today, I'm trying out the belated birthday gift Malia and Nadia gave me. More specifically, Queen Elena delivered news of it in the dream Nadia had last night. It's a computer program that lets me write using my thoughts. Not quite sure if I like it enough to use exclusively, but it sure does come in handy when taking a road trip. At first, I found it strange to have to think *delete, delete, delete* every time I wanted to get rid of something, but I discovered that if I had the intent to delete something, it would still work.

It's been a morning full of surprises. Momma had to go in for the early shift at ShopRite today, which woulda worked out well 'cause Danielle and I wanted to get on our way before any morning traffic.

If you count this program as the first major surprise, the second surprise was meeting Varick at Danielle's house. He'd parked his motorcycle in the center of the driveway so we couldn't miss him. Momma let out a small gasp as Varick's shadowy figure materialized before her headlights as we pulled into Danielle's driveway.

"Varick!" shouted Michio. He waved madly with both arms.

"What's he doing here?" Momma wondered, voicing the question I was opening my mouth to ask. Her surprised tone told me why she wasn't scolding Michio for shouting.

"I dunno," I answered, even though the question wasn't really directed at me. I glanced back at the car seat holding Isaac to see if I needed to help him sleep 'cause of the racket. He was still sleeping soundly. "I'll find out," I added, opening my door and hopping out.

"I'm here to make some deliveries and escort you on your journey," Varick said, before I could repeat the question for him. Setting his helmet on the motorcycle seat, he sauntered up to meet me wearing a knowing grin. "Nadia sends her greetings and an apology for not warning you I'd be here."

The slam of Momma's car door was followed quickly by her greeting. "Good morning, Varick. It's so nice to see you again." She walked around the car and opened the side door to get Michio out.

"Good morning," Varick responded, neatly stepping around her. "Here, let me get him out for you."

"Hi!" shouted Michio in a manner that reminded me of Aiden.

"Hush, Michio," I scolded. "You'll wake Danielle's neighbors. It's too early to be shouting."

He smiled big and heart-melting-like.

His noise brought Danielle to the door, looking like my little brother had just awakened her.

"Hi!" Michio called in a slightly softer tone. At least he tried to control the volume, even if he was still lousy at it.

"Hey, little man. Are you ready for the road trip?" Danielle held out her arms and accepted Michio from Varick.

Michio nodded so hard I thought he'd shake himself loose from Danielle's hold.

"Question is: are *you* ready?" Varick asked. His eyes took in Danielle's bleary eyes, unkempt hair, and pajamas.

"Late night?" asked Momma mildly. She'd freed Isaac's carrier from the car and hauled him up to the front door. He would spend the morning with Danielle's momma.

Danielle shrugged. "Short night. I forgot my father needed to be at the airport this morning for his trip to Texas. He hired a limo company to take him, but that means crisis management fell to me and Mom when Dylan tumbled out of his bunk bed this morning."

"Is he all right?" Momma wondered.

"He's fine," said Danielle. "Mom sent me a text a few minutes ago saying Dylan dislocated his shoulder. The doctor is sorting him out now, but it might be a few hours before we can get on the road."

"Should I call out of work?" Momma inquired.

Danielle waved dismissively. "Don't worry, Mrs. B., I'm on Katy duty for a few hours. I can watch Isaac, too. We'll get on the road as soon as my mom gets back from the hospital."

"I help!" declared Michio.

"Michio, what did we talk about the other day?" asked Varick. His voice held what I considered to be an undue amount of warning.

Michio looked ready to cry. "No help."

I worry about how easily he slips into baby-talk, but I suppose it ain't the worst flaw he could have.

"Help with what?" I asked. It should have been obvious, but I chalk the slowness up to the early hour.

"He needs to be careful about using his Gift in public," Varick reminded us, instinctively lowering his voice.

That made sense, but I didn't think he needed to be mean about it.

"Sorry," Michio said, still wearing a sad face.

"Wanting to help people's not the problem, little man," Danielle assured him. "Varick just wants you to be safe, and for now, safe means keeping secrets, okay?"

Momma put down Isaac's carrier and moved close enough to give Michio a quick hug and kiss. "Be a good boy and mind Jillian and Miss Danielle, ya hear?"

Michio again nodded, solemnly this time. "I hear good."

That got a chuckle from everybody except Isaac who was still sleeping. After a semi-awkward farewell, Momma prepared to set off for work, but before she could drive away, Varick stepped up to the driver's window and tapped on it. When she lowered the window, he said a few words I couldn't hear and handed her an envelope. She tried to refuse, but he said a few more words to convince her. Though I can't be certain, I'd bet my last dime the package contained money for the trip down to Georgia.

While we waited for Danielle's momma to return from the hospital, Varick rummaged around in the refrigerator and found some eggs to scramble for breakfast. Danielle showed him where to find bacon and bread. Soon, we had a hearty breakfast awaiting us. Danielle made coffee for herself and Varick and poured orange juice for Michio and me. Katy joined us right in time for food, though she was distracted by Isaac. He'd woken up and was sending out a steady stream of baby babbles lest we forget him.

We finally started our journey a little after eleven. Danielle's Momma arrived just after ten, but it took us over an hour to exchange stories, assure Mrs. Matheson we'd be fine, and pack the car.

Varick spent the trip driving his motorcycle a few car lengths behind us. I decided that an escort could either be seen as creepy or sweet. Danielle said we should assume sweet since her car didn't have the power to lose Varick and there was no point since he knew where we were headed.

The trip took a lot longer than Mapquest had estimated, but that's partly 'cause we had to stop a lot to use the facilities, eat, or let Michio run off some of his energy. I used Danielle's cell phone to call Malia and let her know we'd be really late. I just didn't know how late.

Chapter 4
Dangerous Test

ITEM 137: Danielle's thirty-seventh letter
Item Source: Danielle Matheson
Dear Dr. S.,

Our crazy late start coupled with frequent stops, including two meal stops, a delay so Varick could do his hero thing, and an even longer delay for me to recover, resulted in us arriving at the Davidson house insanely late.

For a long time, I've known Varick's Gifts and training revolve around fighting, but until today I had not really seen him in action. It's like he's got some Spidey sense that alerts him to trouble. Today, trouble came as a pair of mostly drunk college-age delinquents.

We had stopped at a rest area along Route 80 so I could get fuel for my car, food for my passengers, and stretch my legs. Varick taught me how to pump gas. All right, so he mostly did it by himself while explaining what he was doing. I could probably fumble my way through the process now. He's a decent teacher in that respect.

As Varick and I walked back to my car having paid for the gas, I noticed two young men talking to Jillian. She held Michio, and her body language spoke her unease. For his part, Michio perched on Jillian's left hip and eyed the pair carefully. The guys must really have been out of their heads to bother hassling random people in a rest area, especially a girl holding a small child. It's times like these I understand my mother's frequent exclamations of *what's this world coming to?* and other cries of dismay.

My first instinct was to freeze and my second instinct involved running forward and shouting, "Hey! What's going on?" The instincts collided, leaving me lurching forward and coughing from choking on the words.

Varick simply walked toward Jillian at a slightly elevated pace. "Need help?" His casual tone immediately made the young men bristle as if their masculinity had been challenged.

"Maybe." Her response had the clipped quality inherent of suppressed anger combined with frustration. If we were in a more private area, Jillian would have simply dealt with the problematic pair herself, but knocking them unconscious via her Gift wasn't exactly a first-tier option.

Arriving next to Jillian, Varick gave the young men a sympathetic smile. "You probably want to walk away now, mates."

"Who's gonna make us?" asked the taller of the pair. He threw in a profanity-laced insult for good measure.

"This here's a free country," drawled the shorter, stockier challenger. "We can go wherever we want and do whatever we want."

"I agree," said Varick. "I'd just prefer that *wherever* wasn't here and *whatever* didn't involve bothering my sister."

By this time, I'd finally unstuck my feet and staggered over to the confrontation happening next to my car.

"You should join us, man," said the taller drunk. "We can all have a bit of fun." The taller one looked up and spotted me. "You could do so much better than him, sweetheart. What you need is a real man who—"

"Varick, if you ain't gonna do something soon, I will," Jillian interrupted. She adjusted her hold on Michio and whispered something in his ear.

He nodded eagerly and let her put him down. Before I could do anything, the little rascal ran up to me, snatched the keys, and darted for my car, hitting the unlock button as he went.

The bothersome young men howled with laughter. I glared at everybody, including Jillian for prompting Michio to steal my car keys.

"Danielle, get in the car with Michio," Varick ordered. "Jillian and I will handle this."

Normally, my stubborn nature would demand I ignore such an order, but the situation was too weird to argue. I could barely think straight let alone correct the nuisances on their false assumption that I was "with" Varick. As I sidestepped to get around the pair, the tall guy stepped with me and caught my arms in a strange parody of a ballroom dance.

Varick made his move then. I don't recall him moving, but he must have because the tall guy's hands suddenly released me. Within a second, the guy was on his knees with his right arm twisted up behind his back and his left bracing himself.

With a cry like an enraged bull, Short and Stocky drew a switchblade from his pocket, clicked it on, and charged Varick. In one smooth motion, Varick released the taller guy's arm and shoved him down. The man collapsed as if Varick's shove had made him go boneless. Meanwhile, Varick met the new assault. He caught the guy's knife hand and disarmed him with a quick move I could barely follow. The man's forward momentum sent him crashing into Varick and flung them both in my direction.

I yelped and jumped back, but I couldn't get far enough to avoid the pair completely. Just before I would have been bowled over, Short and Stocky passed out and flopped onto his stomach like a beached baby whale. I winced in sympathy for the man's gut and shot a shaky, grateful smile Jillian's way. She nodded and returned the grin.

"You leave! You leave or I call police!" shouted the man working the gas station.

"We should go," Jillian said, letting her urgency show.

Varick shook his head. "We don't want the police involved. They probably have Danielle's license plate and my motorcycle plates on camera. We'd do best to calm the owner down." After dragging the unconscious pair over to some pumps and propping them up, Varick tucked his hands in his pockets and sauntered over to the distraught man.

Dazed, I watched as Varick slipped the gas station guy a few bills. It's amazing how quickly money can soothe people. The man didn't look ecstatic, but the cash certainly improved his mood. It took Varick about ten minutes to convince the man to do nothing besides get a few large cups of coffee prepared for the troublemakers.

We got on the road a few minutes later, but I couldn't concentrate on driving, so we made yet another stop to grab sodas and process.

The Road-Weary Driver,
Danielle Matheson.

***

ITEM 138: Jillian's sixty-eighth post-kidnapping journal entry
Item Source: Jillian Blairington

26

I find that a lot of random trouble coming my way has its root in Nadia. I ain't cross with her for that, but I wish she gave me more than ten seconds warning. Varick and I handled the two out of sorts fellows fine, but I think the incident shook Danielle. She oughta be real familiar with strange happenings by now, but I guess that's a feeling that comes with time.

As I caught sight of the would-be troublemakers, Nadia's voice addressed me in my head. *Would you like to right some wrongs before they can be committed today?*

"It's all right by me," I replied.

"Hi!" Michio called. He waved to the air next to me, which probably held an avatar of Nadia that only my little brother could see.

Seizing the swinging hand, I said, "Now ain't the time to talk out loud to Nadia."

"But she's over there," Michio argued, pointing with his other hand toward where he'd been waving.

"That's not the real Nadia. We'll see her tomorrow but right—"

"Well, now, what have we here?" asked one of the men. He stood a head taller than his grungy companion.

The taller man is Tucker Gilroy, Jr. and the shorter one is Lester Michael Hunt, Nadia supplied unprompted. *They came to rob the station, but lost their courage for that sort of crime.*

"I think we found us a young lady looking for a good time," piped up Lester.

"Looks like she already had a good time a few years back," crowed Tucker. That set 'em both laughing.

"Seriously?" I muttered at Nadia. "Don't they know I'm not even fourteen yet and Michio's four?"

I altered their perceptions, Nadia admitted. Her initial thought was positively slow for her, but the next one came with the more familiar pace. *If their attentions did not fall upon you or Danielle, they would merely have fallen upon the next unfortunate young lady to arrive at this rest area.*

"Swell," I murmured, shuddering to think what illusion Nadia had placed over Michio and me. "Next time, warn a body."

I shall try. Let Varick handle the situation.

Varick arrived on the scene right about then and exchanged a few words with the drunks. When words didn't look like they would get the men to back down, I sent Michio to fetch the keys from Danielle so he could get to safety inside the car. As the men turned their attention to Danielle, Varick subdued Tucker with a few quick moves. Lester tried to tackle 'em both, but I made him and Tucker take a forced nap. The timing was important 'cause I had to knock 'em out as Varick did something that could make a man keel over.

That incident only took a few minutes, including the time it took Varick to bribe the gas guy into not calling the police. However, Danielle needed more time to think and not drive. Since I couldn't take over the driving and Varick had his motorcycle, we had to let her take her time. Knowing all this, Varick led us to a McDonalds and herded us inside.

We got Michio an apple juice box and a small thing of fries. The rest of us had fountain drinks. Varick chose root beer, Danielle had regular coke, and I had iced tea. For a while, we sat there sipping our drinks and minding our own thoughts. When Michio finished his snack, Varick swept him off to the play area, leaving Danielle and me a perfect opportunity to talk.

"What just happened?" Danielle wondered at last.

I was gonna answer her question, but Nadia told me to let her talk for a while before speaking.

"Who were those men? What were they thinking? That was a major highway rest area. People don't get accosted by drunks in the middle of broad daylight!" Danielle's ramblings varied in speed as her level of indignation—that means something like outraged, righteous anger—changed. She drew a few quick breaths to calm herself, but they didn't work. "It's pretty obvious what they wanted. We could have been hurt. *You* could have been hurt."

I don't think it occurred to her that given their ages, she made a more likely target than I did. Then again, Nadia was messing with their perceptions, so who knows what they actually saw.

"We weren't in real danger, Danielle," I said as gently as I could. "Varick was there."

Danielle's gaze shifted to watch my older brother as he entertained Michio. Varick wouldn't win any body-building contests, but Nana would say he carries his muscles well. His short blond hair lent him a clean cut air. The jeans and sturdy black riding jacket fought the innocent look, but his eyes reinforced the initial image. Today, Varick's eyes were a pretty shade of deep blue. Apparently, he can flip his eyes to green as his emotions or will dictate.

"Varick won't always be there," Danielle pointed out. Her eyes added the next question a few seconds before she voiced it. "What will we do then?"

"We ain't exactly helpless," I said, keeping my smile small so she wouldn't think I was making fun of her.

She suddenly looked like she was fighting tears. Danielle ain't exactly the weepy sort, so that told me this conversation was about more than what had almost happened.

Before I could ask what was really on her mind, Danielle blurted, "Nadia offered me a job." Her eyes said the admission relieved and surprised her.

"Doing what?" I asked, hoping the caution in my voice didn't come across as disapproving.

"I hate feeling helpless," Danielle declared.

I squinted at her, not quite sure we were on the same conversation. "What's one got to do with the other?"

"When I was helping Christy and Marina, I felt like my life was actually making a difference. You, Nadia, Malia, and the others have Gifts that can help people any time, but I'm just me." She took a deep breath and tried to smile. "I'm not making much sense, am I?"

Shrugging, I asked, "What's Nadia want you to do?" I kinda knew I wouldn't like the next words out of Danielle's mouth.

"She wants me to be her representative, an assistant of sorts."

Frowning mightily, I asked, "Are you gonna do it?"

"I don't know," Danielle whispered. "I feel like today was a test, and I failed it miserably."

"You did fine," Varick contradicted.

"Where's Michio?" I asked, alarmed to have him out of sight.

"Here!" called a cheerful voice from the floor.

I leaned over to see Michio clinging to Varick's left boot.

"I'm not sure I can do it. I'm not brave enough," Danielle said, sounding tired.

"Bravery comes in time," Varick explained. "Only strength of heart can't be taught. You've simply got to have it, and you do."

"Then why did I want to run away?" Danielle challenged.

Varick's voice slipped into teacher-mode. "We all want to run away. Only fools seek conflict. What matters is that you *didn't* run when you saw trouble. That was the test, and you did well."

Danielle closed her eyes and nodded that she'd heard Varick. "Thank you. I just need a few more minutes and we can continue." She rose from her seat and headed toward the restrooms.

"Let her go," Varick murmured. "She has a lot to think about."

"What's to think about?" I demanded.

"Accepting Nadia's job will change everything," Varick answered.

My heart lurched. I'm not sure what expression I wore, but Michio sensed I was upset. He crawled up next to me and gave me a hug. I clung to him, letting my fear for Danielle tighten my grip. I always knew she could face danger 'cause of her connection to me, but I'd never expected Nadia to purposefully involve her. The realization cut as deep as any betrayal, though for the life of me, I couldn't decide who to blame or what to fear.

Chapter 5
Is Danielle All Right?

ITEM 139: Jillian's sixty-ninth post-kidnapping journal entry
Item Source: Jillian Blairington

We pulled up to the Davidson house around ten-thirty, but the place was plenty busy despite the hour. I think they had every light in the house lit up to welcome us. As soon as we parked, the front door opened and people poured out like coins from an upturned piggy bank.

"You're late," Malia scolded as she embraced me. She stepped back so I could see the bright smile that told me she was glad we'd made the trip safely.

"Nadia's even later than we are," I observed, glancing about to make sure I wasn't unknowingly fibbing.

"She'll meet us tomorrow at the courthouse," Varick promised, walking around me to help Danielle with the bags. A moment later, he set Danielle's suitcase down long enough to pick up Malia and swing her around like she weighed nothing, which ain't far off from the truth.

When Varick set Malia down, I spotted a long cut along her right forearm. "What happened to your arm?"

"It's a souvenir from my recent adventures," answered Malia. "Don't worry about it. Michio can heal it later if I wish. Come meet my new family."

Welcomes, introductions, and hugs went round and round for several minutes. Finally, Mrs. Davidson herded the lot of us into the house so we could have some refreshments while we continued meeting, greeting, and catching up.

Once everybody had a tall glass of sweet iced tea in hand, Mr.

Davidson cleared his throat to get our attention. "I know I'm supposed to leave the speeches until tomorrow, but I wanted to formally welcome you to our home." He paused like he wasn't sure what else to say then grinned and raised his glass. "So, welcome."

Everybody followed suit and murmured agreement. After a brief moment of silence in case he had more to say, small conversations broke out all over the room. Danielle got to chatting with Mr. and Mrs. Davidson. Varick held Michio and struck up a conversation with Marina Nardin and Nicholas Davidson, and Malia pulled me aside into a room off the kitchen.

It took us a few minutes to work past the pleasantries, but finally, Malia asked, "Is Danielle all right?"

I poured some iced tea down my throat to drown the rising silly surprise. I really should remember that one of Malia's Gifts can be defined as emotional perception, at least that's what Nadia says. "I think so. Why? What do you sense about her?"

"Not much," Malia replied. "That is why I am asking. She doesn't usually keep her feelings locked up quite so ... thoroughly."

It struck me that Malia doesn't talk like a normal eleven-year-old, but I kept shut on the issue 'cause it's what Nana calls a useless point. Besides, the same thing could be said for me, but I talk the way I talk. Analyzing ain't gonna make it different. My gaze wandered back to the kitchen where Danielle conversed easily with Malia's soon-to-be adoptive parents. One would never guess from her expression or demeanor—that means how she acts and what her body language tells the world about her—that Danielle had any worries on her mind.

Realizing I'd not answered Malia's question, I shrugged and said, "I guess she's just worried about starting college."

"No. That is the nervous energy that lies beneath the surface," Malia informed me. "There's something else, something heavier weighing upon her. Has she acted strangely of late?"

I thought of her blue spell after the almost fight at the gas station and the words traded in the fast food place. Part of me wanted to spill everything about the choices facing Danielle and her intense worry over Christy's momma, but I didn't think I should. "You'd best be asking her about that, but wait until after tomorrow."

One of Malia's eyebrows conveyed a question.

Leveling my best impression of Nana's stern face, I said, "This is supposed to be a happy time for you and your second family. You ain't allowed to worry until after the party."

"All right," Malia agreed with a grin. "But tomorrow night, I shall call a council of war to discuss Danielle. Nadia can tell us more anyway." The grin changed into a slight frown. "What shall we talk about, if not anything to do with worries?"

"I dunno," I answered, scrambling to find an appropriate topic. "Nana says girls preparing for parties like to talk about clothes." I shrugged. "Guess we could do that. Momma made me pack a dress. I ain't over fond of 'em, but they have their uses. Are you gonna wear something special tomorrow?"

Malia's grin sprang back to life but it looked a mite embarrassed. "Mrs. Davidson helped me pick out a very nice party dress. You can see it now, if you'd like."

"Sure," I said, trying not to shrug lest she think I didn't care.

We threaded our way through the kitchen and found the staircase to the second floor. Along the way, I noticed lots of little decorations that gave the place a very cozy, country feel.

"Nana would like this place," I commented.

"She does," said Malia. "Mrs. Davidson just got an iPad and wanted to learn how to take pictures, so I showed her how by taking a tour of the house. We emailed some of them to Nana."

A wisp of jealousy tried to grow into a choking fog inside me, but I squashed it 'cause Nana woulda called it mean-spirited foolishness.

Midway up the stairs, Malia stopped suddenly and faced me. "I hope you don't mind that we've kept in contact."

Forcing a smile, I said, "Guess I wasn't quick enough covering that, but don't mind me. Nana ain't mine to hog."

My assurance satisfied Malia enough so that she continued up the rest of the stairs and led me down the hallway to her bedroom. The walls had been freshly painted a nice creamy white color with a border of purple flowers running along the top and bottom of all walls. The curtains were a deep purple color that matched the rug dominating the center. The rug was simple yet elegant. It looked like someone had taken a giant paintbrush and added ribbons of gray and lighter purple on top of the solid, sturdier purple that made up most of the rug. The bits of wood that showed out from under that rug appeared freshly polished, and the rest of the place looked neat as a hospital room. I was almost afraid to enter.

Even though the dress was in plain sight, it didn't immediately jump out at me 'cause it blended in well with the rest of the room. A mess of tiny white spots dominated the top of the dress, looking like stars cast in the velvet canvas of the night sky. That description came from Nadia, of course, but since I can't do better, that'll have to do. The straps were thin enough to show off one's shoulders yet do their job and keep the dress where it's supposed to be. A swath of the same cloth making up the rest of the dress ran around the center, cinched at one side by a pretty flower that had a hint of white in it. The rest of the dress flared down in a half-dozen wavy ruffles that reminded me of cake icing.

"I take it you like the color purple," I said, glancing around.

"I like a lot of colors, but this one seemed suitable for the room and reminded me of Nadia." Malia moved farther into the room and gestured toward the left wall. "It was previously pink, as it had belonged to Joy. I would have happily kept it the same, except that Mr. and Mrs. Davidson insisted I make the space my own."

"Are ya ever gonna call 'em 'mom' and 'dad'?"

An expression I couldn't read crossed Malia's face. "I had not considered the question."

"I think they'd like you to," I noted, trying to keep my voice soft. It wasn't really my business.

"I agree, but I'm not sure how I feel about doing so." Malia's expression said she was well aware of how odd that sounded coming from her. "I have never really called anybody 'mother,' except Dr. Robinson, yet she never felt like a mother."

"Does Mrs. Davidson feel like a mother?" I wondered.

"Yes," replied Malia without hesitation.

To me, that settled the matter. If someone felt like a momma, they oughta be called momma. I couldn't understand Malia's hang up over the title 'cause I'd long ago started referring to my various sets of parents as Momma, Second Momma, and so forth. Still, Nana would be proud at how well I kept my opinion to myself. Malia probably sensed it anyway given her Gifts, but I can't help that. I turned the conversation to a different topic altogether and we chatted for a while about how we'd spent the summer so far.

Before long, Mrs. Davidson came up to tell us we ought to get ready for bed since tomorrow would be a long day. It's the sorta thing one expects a momma to say. I'd have to corner Danielle tomorrow and see if she'd help me get Malia to really accept her second family.

Chapter 6
Malia Gets a Second Family

ITEM 140: Danielle's thirty-eighth letter
Item Source: Danielle Matheson

Dear Dr. S.,

I appreciate your concern for me, but it's been a good day. I'd rather not wrestle with my demons right now. Once I sort a few more details, perhaps I'll send you an itemized list of concerns.

The weather was uncooperative to say the least, but that didn't detract from the festivities. The morning dawned with a cool, misty feel to it, and as soon as the sun truly hit its stride, that turned into a hot, muggy, gross feeling. I went for a run with Malia. We invited Jillian and Marina, but they both rolled over and groaned, which I took as a polite refusal.

By the time we finished our jogging tour of the neighborhood, we were both soaked with sweat. Malia probably could have done another three miles, but she had mercy on me and offered to quit early. She even pretended to be tired so as to not hurt my feelings. I had just enough time for a quick shower before breakfast preparations got full into their swing. After much convincing, Mrs. Davidson let me help set the table.

Breakfast consisted of large stacks of blueberry pancakes and plenty of bacon and sausage. Jillian purposefully avoided the sausage, but fared well against three good-sized pancakes. She's been avoiding sausage links since getting back from Devya's new lab, wherever that is. I asked her about that once, and she said it had to do with a strange dream about TJ trying to eat a few thousand sausage links. Her loss.

Those sausage links were delicious.

Jillian has some weird dreams when she doesn't apply her Gifts. Did she tell you about the one with the tiny flies? Talk about creepy. I had the privilege of experiencing that one myself because she used it in an experiment to see if she could transfer dreams—feelings and all—to somebody else. It worked very well. Imagine a few million miniature flies slipping in through the screen windows of your house and diving for you. Then, imagine you can't move. Everything in you wants to scream, but you know that will just let them get inside you. The dream was worse than that, but I see no reason to bother you with the rest.

How did I get off on that tangent? My mind seems to want to dwell on creepy things tonight, which is rather a shame since aside from the weather, the rest of the day proceeded pleasantly.

After breakfast, Malia and Marina slipped upstairs to put on their party dresses. Both dresses looked great on their respective wearers, but I'm partial to Marina's gown.

Generally, flowers on dresses disturb me, but this dress definitely gets a pass on that account. It had one strap for the left shoulder that sported two pale green flowers with wispy ribbons hanging off the bottom one like freshly cut vines. The center part looked like a painter's expression of stormy seas done in green. Three more flowers like the ones on the single strap balanced the dress by occupying the space around the right hip. Delicate, transparent cloth flowed down from the flowers. The deep green color was lightened by being placed over a white dress. The whole dress gave the impression of new life thoughtfully wrapped.

Malia and Marina's entrance into the room stopped all conversation. I felt underdressed in my dress slacks and simple blouse.

"You both look gorgeous." Mrs. Davidson's statement summed up everybody's thoughts.

My gaze landed on Mr. Davidson. A faint smile lightened his otherwise serious expression. His eyes were shiny with a glowing pride similar to what was in my father's eyes when I graduated.

The only one wearing a scowl was Nicholas.

"What's that look for?" inquired his sister. Joy Davidson had arrived a little after breakfast, while the girls were upstairs changing.

Nick—as he insisted we call him—heaved a sigh. "I'm just thinking about all the snot-nosed high school guys I'm going to have to beat up over the next few years."

"I help!" offered Michio.

36

That declaration got a laugh from everybody and broke the spell that had kept us in place, reluctant to leave this cozy room or the company of these good people. We piled out to the cars. By prearrangement, Malia and Marina went with Mr. and Mrs. Davidson in a silver Mercedes and the rest of us crammed into a blue minivan driven by Nick. Joy's fiancé would meet us at the courthouse.

Joy offered me the shotgun seat, but I declined, knowing it would be more amusing to have her near her brother. I was right. They reminded me of an older version of Dylan and Katy. I idly wondered who would win a bickering contest, Joy and Nick or Dylan and Katy. My brother and sister have youthful enthusiasm on their side, but the Davidson siblings have a few more years of life and a bigger vocabulary. They should make a reality show like that.

We arrived at the Erie County Courthouse late because Nick wanted to try a new shortcut, even though his sister and the British GPS lady protested loudly. Michio cheered both sides, while Jillian and I withheld our opinions. Nick quickly found a parking spot, but we had to walk a ways to actually get into the building.

The sky chose that moment to open up, so we waited a few more minutes for the worst of the rain to subside. Finally, we decided to brave the rain. Nick gallantly took Michio from me as we made our mad dash to the courthouse.

When we finally burst into the assigned courtroom, the judge leveled a longsuffering look at us. The amount of people present surprised me. We got a good, long look at them as we shuffled down the aisle toward the section reserved for close family and friends. A man leaned over and shifted a baby carrier to make room for us, and a woman gently tugged a gawking toddler closer for the same reason. I didn't recognize the family until the woman smiled and nodded at me. They were Carol and Able's oldest biological child, Julie Ann, and her family. I will always remember Special Agents Ann and Patrick Duncan since they met Jillian and me soon after our first experience with Devya.

I thought the ceremony would start right away, but nothing happened. My heart beat faster in nervous anticipation. Jillian and I exchanged puzzled glances.

Before I could ask either Agent Duncan what was wrong, the judge leaned forward and intoned, "Do you have the release papers from Mr. Nardin?"

Mr. Davidson cleared his throat. "No, Your Honor, but our

lawyer is—"

The courtroom door opened and a blonde woman swept in. "Please forgive the delay, Your Honor. I have the requested papers."

Blinking stupidly, I stared at the young woman. She didn't look familiar, but the voice—British accent and all—definitely belonged to Nadia.

The judge waved the woman forward and carefully pored over the papers she handed him. My gaze slid sideways to Jillian. She had a hand clamped firmly over Michio's mouth and whispered fiercely in his ear. I'm glad she was thinking fast because if it had been up to me, Michio would have raced forward and tackled Nadia's ankles.

If you want the full ceremony, you'll have to rely on Jillian. The Honorable Judge Jacob P. Sheridan may have been good at his job, but he was what Jillian would call very, very longwinded. In my defense, I roused myself at the most important parts.

As the key players rose to sign the appropriate papers, the judge smiled. He looked slightly pained like his face wasn't used to the expression, but his rich voice filled the small courtroom with heartfelt emotion. "I feel like I should start this ceremony with, 'Dearly beloved, we are gathered here in the sight of God and these witnesses.' " He paused to let the polite chuckles fade. "Though I shall spare you that, the statement holds truth. It is a privilege to stand here with you and witness the beautiful growth of this family. Carol and Able Davidson have requested that their other children come forward and stand with their new children."

That took a little doing because Agent Duncan's son didn't want her to put him down. Joy and Nick exchanged embarrassed looks then moved to flank Malia and Marina, respectively. Finally, Agent Patrick Duncan successfully freed his wife from their son's grasp. The boy fussed until a warning look from his mother made him mind. Seconds later he was all smiles, which I'm betting has something to do with Malia.

Once Judge Sheridan had everybody's attention again, he said, "As a family court judge, I have seen a wide variety of couples looking to expand their families, good people all, but this situation is unique. Rarely do we see a distinguished couple raise three children to adulthood then turn around and say, 'Let's do that again.' Yet, here we are gathered for such a momentous occasion. Since you would rather hear from them than me, I shall now invite them to say a few words."

Mr. and Mrs. Davidson walked hand-in-hand over to the

microphone set up in the center and turned to face the crowd.

Mr. Davidson leaned into the microphone first. "We wanted to take a brief moment to thank our faithful friends and extended family for joining us today. Our lives are truly better for your presence." He stepped back, indicating an end to his speech.

When Mrs. Davidson switched places with her husband, she adjusted the microphone to a better height. "We also wanted to extend special thanks and welcome to our two new, beautiful daughters." She stopped speaking to compose herself then continued in a hoarser tone. "Children don't usually get to choose their parents, but you have chosen us, so thank you. Whether you take our name or not won't change our commitment to love you and finish what your birth parents started when they gave you life. On the lecterns, you'll find two copies of the paperwork, one with your names changed and one without. No one needs to know which you choose at this time, but before you sign, I'm going to exercise a long-established mother's right and embarrass the other children." She waved Ann, Joy, and Nick forward. "Would you like to say a few words?"

Though clearly surprised by the opportunity, Ann Duncan squared her shoulders and took her mother's place behind the microphone. "When Mom told me she and Dad wanted to adopt you, my first thought was to ask her how many crazy pills she had swallowed that morning." After an appropriate pause, she continued, "But as I got to know each of you better, I began to understand."

"Mommy!" screamed Ann's son.

"Hi, Joey," Ann responded, waving to the little boy. "As you can see, we are still a crazy family, but I know we're all better off now that you're a part of us. Welcome home, dear sisters."

A smattering of applause rose then faded. Nick and Joy both stepped forward next. After a few glares and a friendly elbow or two, they used rock-paper-scissors to settle their differences. Nick put out rock and Joy put out paper. Joy flashed the audience a triumphant grin and fist pumped in victory. Nick wrinkled his nose in an exaggerated petulant expression then bowed deeply to his sister and ceded the microphone.

"Sisters are so much more fun than brothers," Joy declared. "I can't wait to arrange a girls' night where we can swap secrets, get our nails done, and plot ways to terrorize the menfolk in our lives. Welcome to the home team." She flashed her fiancé a smile.

When Nick finally stepped up to the microphone, he found it

down around mid-chest. After moving it to a comfortable height, he cast a sympathetic look at Special Agent George Baker. "I would like to say that any man nice enough to marry Joy must be a saint, but that's a line of thought for another day. Today, I want to thank these two fair young ladies for easing my burden as the youngest child. I'm looking forward to having brotherly duties such as busting feather pillows over your heads and chasing away would-be suitors." He cleared his throat. "Seriously, welcome. You are now a part of the tribe." He delivered his last line in a passable impression of C-3PO.

Without much more ado, Mr. and Mrs. Davidson walked over to the two lecterns and spent a few minutes carefully signing each of the papers. Next, Malia glided to the left lectern, and Marina gracefully made her way over to the right one. Each girl sifted through the papers, chose a set, and solemnly signed. As they almost simultaneously set down their pens, the courtroom exploded in applause and every person capable of leaping to their feet did so.

Next to me, Jillian smiled in a satisfied manner that made me sure Malia had signed the paper to accept Davidson as her last name. All of Devya's Children ended up with the surname Ayers. Accepting Davidson would be a good sign of Malia's willingness to integrate herself with her second family.

The Pleased as Punch (and too full of punch to move) Witness,
Danielle Matheson.

Chapter 7
A Real Home

ITEM 141: Malia's second letter
Item Source: Malia Karina Davidson
Dear Dr. Sokolowski,

Thank you for the thoughtful letter and generous gift. The outpouring of support has been very strong. I needed to employ my Gifts just to keep on even emotional ground. Jillian insists that I let myself fully experience these emotions, but I would rather store them for later analysis. That may sound cold and unfeeling, but it is simply what I've been taught to do for years. I am trying a little each day to let myself experience the natural fluctuation of emotions that regular people feel, but it is a slow retraining process.

It may seem that I am overly concerned with names, but I find them a convenient focal point. When you reach the conclusion of this letter, you will no doubt notice that the signature ends with Davidson. Accepting this surname makes me no less an Ayers, for I am still an "heir to a fortune" like all my siblings. Like Jillian, who was first called Ashlynn Annabel Ayers, I simply have two identities, two families, two lives to reconcile. After consulting with my new mother, Nadia, and even Maisha through Nadia, I have chosen the name Malia Karina Davidson. While not terribly inventive, the name is true to who I have been and who I am now.

The name changes for Marina were a little more extensive. She laid aside her former name of Marina Petrovna Nardin and chose to become Marina Zara Davidson. She kept her first name for the obvious reason of having spent the last seventeen years answering to it, but I think the meaning of "from the sea" is fitting. Metaphorically, we have both been plucked from a sea of circumstances that once ruled our lives. When we learned that we could change anything we wanted about our names, Marina seemed troubled, so I had a long talk with her. She didn't mind her name, but I could tell it pained her to remember the father who rejected her so thoroughly as to sell her to strangers. When Nadia suggested Zara, a name meaning "princess" and "to blossom," I immediately knew that Marina would love the hopeful symbolism contained therein.

I apologize for ignoring your initial inquiries about my experiences with Ryker. For a fuller picture of the man, you'd have to ask my new sister, Ann, or her husband, Patrick. Having a nephew and niece to dote on has been neat, but calling Ann my sister still sounds strange to me. I suppose that's only natural since it's been official for about half a day.

Incidentally, Michio is having a grand time getting to know Ann and Patrick's son, Joseph. Although I stand by the decision to let Aiden stay with Dr. Devya and the scientists, I regret the continued separation between Michio and Aiden. Their Gifts are so similar, and I know Michio misses Aiden. We all do. I could manipulate his emotions until he forgets to be sad, but that would fail to solve the problem. A touch of sadness and longing is a good thing. It reminds us to cherish what we have and motivates us to actively pursue meaningful relationships.

While I'm not ready to share my heart on all the Ryker matters, I will say that I have no regrets about what transpired. I do not have a death wish, nor am I one who craves trouble or pain. I'm not ashamed that I needed to be rescued. The role of damsel in distress is actually far more familiar to me than that of heroine. In Ryker's clutches, I got to be both simply by being present at the right time and place, offering a few words of comfort, and subtly using my Gifts as they were meant to be used.

In answer to your question about feeling like a heroine, I would argue that heroism comes down to choices made by ordinary people placed in extraordinary circumstances. People often have the wrong idea about what makes a hero or a heroine. My brother, Varick, fits the stereotypical mold of a hero. He's physically strong, decently handsome, and trained to deal with people intent on evil. Daring rescues and disarming foes are both a matter of course for him. Nadia's Gifts let her work through others to accomplish great feats of goodness, but the very nature of her Gifts precludes acknowledgement. The same goes for Jillian's Dream Shaping Gift. Ann and Patrick have a job as FBI agents that often demands they be heroes, but they would be the first to claim ordinary status.

Now, I have a few questions for you. When does helping somebody become meddling? Is meddling truly a bad thing? Is it not a lack of "meddling" that allows evil and injustice such a foothold in this world? Jillian's friend, Danielle, feels very troubled. It's difficult to explain, but a burdened soul feels heavier than a carefree one. Even my new mother noticed the signs of distress. Jillian agreed to discuss it tonight, but I wanted your impressions as well.

The adoption ceremony was beautiful. We got to hear a few words from each member of our new immediate family. Even Nadia came to offer her congratulations in person. Really, it was her victory, for she orchestrated nearly every detail, including placing Marina and me with the Davidson family. We could not talk like we did in the old days, but Nadia's effort to be there meant a lot to me. Not even the presence of her two minders could ruin the experience, though I must say I felt Aiden's absence rather acutely—intensely, that is.

Jillian says I sound too much like Nadia, using big words and too much formality. She is correct, though Cora and Dr. Carnasis have probably shaped both our speech patterns. Truth be told, I miss them as well. Until Mrs. Davidson came along, Cora and Dr. Carnasis constituted everything I knew about a mother figure. At their feet, I learned to crawl, then walk, then talk, and express myself in more than childish fits. For all their faults and moral shortcomings, I am grateful for having known them. Bitterness is by nature an easy emotion to cling to but one that sours the soul, as Maisha would say.

Nick has made it his life's goal to make me laugh. He claims I am too serious. While I feel too much to ever take life quite as cavalierly as he does, I appreciate his efforts. He bought me a whack-a-mole mallet from eBay and told me it would encourage good behavior in rotten little middle school boys. His gift to Marina was a can of mace and a key chain with a whistle to go with the used car our new parents bought her.

Some of the guests were mildly offended on my behalf for the seeming disparity in gifts we were given, but they don't understand that gifts are more about fit than monetary value. Although I'm almost twelve, I would have little use for a car for several years. Mom and Dad offered to get me any pet I'd like, within reason. Snakes, lizards, and mice were stricken from the list of possibilities. I understand their desire for giving me a companion to grow up with, but keeping track of my siblings is more than enough to occupy me.

The gift I wanted most was the presence of my siblings. For the most part, that was granted in full. Dustin didn't want to come. That saddens me, for I feel the tenuous relationship we had slipping away.

Mom and Dad still wanted to get me something tangible, so I requested a bicycle. I'm proud to say I thought of that one on my own. I would happily have asked for nothing, but few would understand that my family means more to me than possessions. They would either pity me for a girl who doesn't even know enough of the "good" things in life to ask for them or despise me for having false humility. If I were to truly lack in a basic need, such as food, clothing, or shelter, I might have a different outlook on possessions, but things come and go.

People come and go, too, but they leave a stronger impact upon me. Every person I've ever read with my Gift feels slightly different, even identical twins. Jillian and the rest of the siblings from my first family feel brighter and more intense than other people, but I think that comes from knowing more than the general public. Danielle's inner aura for lack of a better term has grown brighter since I first met her. I'm pleased that this change indicates emotional growth, but part of me shares Jillian's fears that Danielle's association with us will put her in grave danger.

You probably think that is a foolish, crippling notion. Hypocritical too, seeing as I have just linked my life closer to a family of good people. Time and again I must force myself to remember that I cannot control the world. My identity as a child born in one of Dr. Devya's labs may one day endanger people I love, but letting that knowledge dominate my thoughts, dictate my actions, or control who I become would be pointless. Evil and innocence collide every day.

I do not claim to know all of my Gifts, but the ones I do know tell me I'm meant to ease emotional burdens. In a way, each of Devya's Children was designed to fix something. Varick handles specific tasks, Nadia creates and executes large-scale plans, and Jillian guards the sleeping masses. I touch the bridge between mind and matter. I'm not sure what Dustin's purpose is besides allowing Dr. Devya to know himself better through their close mental link. In terms of rebuilding something broken, Dustin may have the hardest task of us all. Michio and Aiden take healing and building to new heights and depths.

The thing I fear most right now is the idea of starting school.

It's more than anticipating first day troubles of finding classes, meeting teachers, making friends, and avoiding bullies. I find any place with a large gathering of people disturbing because there are too many emotions confined to one place. Dr. Devya's labs always had a lot of people, but most of them were adults—scientists or guards—who kept their emotions wrapped up tightly. Middle grade students lack that skill. Nadia tries to show me how to better close out such feelings, but those lessons are proceeding slowly.

Thank you for listening to my wandering thoughts. I will update you as I learn more.

Yours respectfully,

Malia Karina Davidson

Chapter 8
Two Strange Exits

ITEM 142: Jillian's seventieth post-kidnapping journal entry
Item Source: Jillian Blairington
Seeing Nadia enter the courtroom made me wanna leap off my seat and smother her with a hug. Malia glanced over at me, and I felt her Gift at work, calming my excitement enough to think. I'd almost forgotten that Nadia was playing the part of a young, ambitious lawyer working for the Davidson family. Both Malia and Nadia had warned me about the arrangement, but Nadia striding down that center aisle sure made a powerful picture.

Even without Malia's Gift, I felt Michio's attention fix on Nadia. Before he could wave, I wrapped him up, covered his mouth with a hand, and whispered, "It ain't time yet, Michio. Nadia don't want people to know who she is today. We gotta keep her secret."

He mumbled something against my hand.

I couldn't make out words, but I sensed it was a question. "Say that again real quiet-like in my ear," I instructed.

Michio brought his lips to my right ear, and asked, "Stealth mode?"

I winced 'cause Michio's idea of a whisper could be heard three rows up and two rows back. "That's right, Michio, stealth mode."

He dutifully mimed zipping his mouth and tossing away a key, shifted position on my lap, and settled down to watch the proceedings.

The adoption ceremony thing passed kinda quickly, but I didn't pay it much mind 'cause I was anxious to get it done. The party arranged for afterward would give us more privacy and a chance to catch up. Besides, I wanted to pay more attention to how people reacted, especially toward Nadia.

I spotted her minders right off. They posed as a couple there to support the family, but their alert eyes darted everywhere. Not rightly sure whether they were bracing for an attack or an escape attempt, but they looked more than prepared for either situation. I doubted they had managed to smuggle a gun into the courtroom, but seeing as they worked for Dr. Devya, I also doubted they entered weaponless.

Varick leaned over and spoke softly. "Don't worry. Today they are her protection."

The words didn't comfort me 'cause they implied that Nadia's minders were sometimes guards rather than guardians. I know it's simply the way things are for my sister, but I won't pretend I like it.

The explosive cheers that swept through the courtroom brought me back to the present. I smiled 'cause Malia had told me she was gonna sign the one that changed her name, and I was happy she'd found a solid second family. Now, I just gotta get Varick and Michio to take on second families. I highly recommend 'em. People like us need every bit of loving support we can get. Nana would say that's true for everybody, but I ain't worried about everybody right now, just my brothers.

Anyway, we made so much noise that the judge had to use his gavel to restore enough order so he could close the ceremony. The sound of the final gaveling immediately made everybody stand.

A hundred side conversations broke out, but Mr. Davidson fought his way to the microphone long enough to invite everybody over for some light lunch and cake. He closed by saying, "We'd hoped to accommodate guests on the lawn, but I think God wants us to be cozier today. You're still welcome to join us as we officially welcome our two new daughters."

"You're a brave, brave man," called a man to my left.

"Brave's got nothing to do with it. That's called crazy," declared another man.

"We prefer the term 'adventurous,' and anyway, if you want to join us for lunch, grab directions from Joy or Nick in the back," said Mr. Davidson. "Kids are always good for cheap labor." He winked at the crowd and stepped away from the microphone.

Nick and Joy rolled their eyes at one another, but then, Joy pulled a stack of quarter sheets from her giant purse and handed half to her brother. They exited the row and marched toward the double doors leading out of the courtroom. Gradually, the crowd quit congratulating the family and filed out. Not everybody needed directions, but I'd say about three-quarters of the people accepted 'em.

Since my ride was busy handing out directions, I wandered around, meeting people and exchanging the usual pleasantries. Michio had scampered off to play with Joseph Duncan. I let him 'cause I figured he couldn't get into too much trouble in a room packed with adults. Soon enough, I found myself next to Nadia.

Smiling politely, Nadia thrust her right hand out to shake. "Tania Kaverin of Harding, Kaverin, and Dunsque. You must be Jillian. It is nice to finally meet you. Malia has spoken of you often." She sounded serious, but her eyes laughed at me.

"Ain't you kinda young to run a business?" I wondered, shaking her hand. I had to concentrate on the task, so I wouldn't throw my arms around Nadia.

"Oh, I do not run the business, I simply work for them," Nadia replied. "My father, Eric Kaverin, is the name on the label so to speak."

The minders moved close, doing a great job of pretending to be absorbed with their own conversation, but they didn't fool me. They used meaningful eye contact and small gestures to convey their impatience. I sensed something was wrong.

"Excuse me, but I think these people have a question for me. Perhaps we shall meet again someday." Nadia moved off to talk with the couple.

"Are you coming to the party?" I asked, hoping I sounded polite instead of desperate.

"I do not know," Nadia answered. "I had planned to, but it looks like something may have come up."

I couldn't tell what they said to her, but she nodded and frowned. Thankfully, Nadia spoke in my head before my curiosity could best my self-control. *I apologize for the swift exit, Jillian. I must return, but I will try to make the council of war tonight.*

The couple fell in behind Nadia as she bolted for the exit.

"What's up with her?" Danielle inquired, keeping her voice low so only I could hear the question.

I shrugged and wished Nadia would explain further. Unfortunately, my Gifts for making things happen my way only work in dreams. "Maybe Varick knows," I guessed.

He didn't, but he also didn't seem disturbed by Nadia's abrupt exit. "Maybe Malia knows more," Varick suggested.

48

I woulda charged right up to Malia and demanded what she knew if Danielle didn't talk sense into me first. "Let Malia have this time with her family. We can grill her later."

Contrary to Danielle's prediction, every time I tried to get near Malia, another stranger came over and struck up a conversation. She shot me sympathetic looks but graciously entertained the guests.

I thought it might be easier when we reached the Davidson house, but I think it actually got worse. Finally, I quit trying. Instead, I grabbed a drink, filled a plate with food, and found a relatively peaceful corner to sit down and eat. That's where Varick found me. Nana says that if you're close enough to people you can read 'em like billboards. Varick's face told me nothing, but the gentle way he knelt beside me said I wasn't gonna like what he had to say.

"You're leaving, too," I said, thinking of what fitting bad news could further darken the day. I usually ain't so gloomy, but the pounding rain wasn't helping my mood. I stared down at my potato salad like it had caused this mess. Stabbing a chunk of potato with a plastic fork, I tapped it on the plate like it was a drumstick.

"There's a problem at the lab. Nadia needs me."

"You ain't gonna tell me about it, are ya?"

A brief shake of his head was the entirety of Varick's answer.

Sighing, I said, "Go then. Be safe. Tell me about it when ya can." Speaking those words, I got a real clear picture of what Momma must feel like when she wonders what I've gotten up to.

I probably shoulda seen Varick off, but I was too mad at him for abandoning Malia on her special day. A feeling of melancholy swept over me, but I fought it so nobody would sense something amiss.

The phrase "alone in a crowd" finally made sense to me. That got me thinking about the future. Part of my anger with Varick sprang from fear for him. He's always rushing off to complete this mission or that, and he ain't even a full-grown man.

Life's short enough without seeking trouble. My inability to say goodbye bothered me. The family that raised me might be normal, but my other family is another matter altogether. Trouble has a bad habit of finding us.

Chapter 9
Job Opportunity

ITEM 143: Danielle's thirty-ninth letter
Item Source: Danielle Matheson
Dear Dr. S.,

Since Malia's up late tapping away on her computer, I figure I may as well join her and share one of my burdens at the same time. I need the practice typing on my iPad anyway. At the risk of sounding old, I prefer desktop computers, then laptops, then these newfangled things with tiny, fake keyboards. I like the feeling of real keys beneath my fingers. My parents complain that I've worn away the letters on the family's computer keyboard. I can't help it if the paint on those things is so lousy.

Perhaps I'll make this letter short and actually try holding a conversation with Malia. She happens to have the ability to soothe emotions after all. Why waste good, old-fashion genetic engineering? Sorry, that would be the cynical side of me coming out again. The lack of sleep made me do it.

Nadia's job offer came to me in a dream. I sure hope nobody ever hacks this email and reads that because they'll either write me off as a nutcase, or worse, they'll want to lock me up to study. Jillian could help me recall every detail of the dream, but I remember enough to attempt a retelling.

I found myself back in that alley behind the horrible place where Christy and I helped rescue Marina.

Christy was on her knees pleading with me to do something, but for several moments, I couldn't figure out what she wanted.

Finally, her words reached me. "Save her! Please! She's all I have! We need her!" Gesturing frantically, Christy continued, "She's right there! Save her!"

My head whipped in the direction she indicated, and I saw Christy's mother being dragged away by strands of smoke. I tried to move toward her, but my family held me back. Dylan and Katy each anchored one of my legs. My father gripped my right arm, and my mother's hand clamped over my mouth. At first, I fought hard, trying to shake them off without hurting them. Their grips only tightened, but as soon as I stopped fighting, they let go. I collapsed to the ground and shivered, trying to ignore Christy's continued cries for help.

As my sanity started running off, the dream froze and Nadia appeared. "Forgive the intrusion, but that did not seem like a pleasant dream. I have a proposition for you. Will you hear it?" She reached out and helped me stand up.

I cleared my throat but didn't feel confident enough to arrange words into sentences, so I simply nodded.

"You did well in saving Marina and Christy." Nadia held up a hand to forestall my response. "I know you would deflect praise to others, but your humility does not change the facts. Would you consider a more active role in saving others?"

A dozen questions clogged my throat for a few horrific seconds, but I finally managed to choke out a request. "Define active role."

"I seek an assistant, Danielle," Nadia said. "As Jillian has probably explained, I am bound to stay with my father for a few more years. I do not wish to wait that long to embark upon my most challenging missions. Varick and Jillian will help as they can, but I need someone willing to endure the indignity of hosting my mind." She smiled at the expression my face acquired. "I need someone to work with me as you did in speaking with Marina the first time."

"Why me?" I know it was a stupid question, but I'm human enough to occasionally need verbal validation. The feelings rushing through me blended outrage at the suggestion, fear of what might happen, and excitement at the prospect of really making a difference.

"You are perfect for the part," Nadia declared in her usual *hold-nothing-back* tone. "You are physically fit, intelligent, courageous, and kind. In addition, you are willing to work with others, and you already have an innate desire to make things better for those around you."

"How could I help?" I asked, embarrassed by her glowing

51

review.

"There are several ways in which this could work. The simplest and most logical of these pathways would have you acting for me on any mission that requires more direct control," Nadia explained. "I am certain your parents wish you to finish college. That is a great path, but should you seek a more active role earlier, I will see that your financial obligations are met."

"Are you trying to bribe me into quitting college before I begin?" I asked, stunned at how un-Nadia-like that sounded.

"Not at all," Nadia assured. "I apologize for poor wording. We would not be having this conversation if I thought money held any sway over you. I am merely pointing out that you can do anything you want with your life. I have the means and desire to fully support you in whatever decision you make. American society says college holds the key to a good job which will in turn lead one to happiness. I am saying you have more options."

Her answer quenched my outrage, but I was still tongue-tied.

Sensing my hesitation, Nadia added, "Take your time. I do not require an answer right now. Talk to your parents or Jillian if you like, but please be cautious if you speak to others."

"What makes you say that?" I asked, even though my expression made the question redundant.

"Father does not know I am making this request, and he cannot know until you are certain of your response." Nadia self-consciously tucked a lock of golden hair behind her right ear. Her gaze rested on the ground. When she spoke again, it sounded like she was talking to herself as much as to me. "He would probably find the idea too tempting to let the choice be made voluntarily."

"Meaning, what exactly?" Even as my dream-self voiced the question, I had a very good idea of what she was implying.

Nadia's blue eyes snapped up and bore into me, filled with defiance, resignation, and understanding. "Power is power." Nadia took three steps away, drew in a slow breath, and faced me again. "If Father knew there was a way to make me more effective, he would not hesitate to exploit that option. You were here long enough to know how he operates. Your family and friends would become chains to you, as mine are to me."

"How can—"

She didn't even let me finish. "Please understand, Danielle. I am not saying I view those I love as obstacles. Rather, my love chains me to their fate. I would not like to see that become your future unless you choose that of your own free will."

"You're saying taking this job would endanger my family," I concluded, just to make sure I was getting the whole message.

"I am saying that is a possibility," Nadia confirmed. "I can only speak for myself, but I am certain my siblings feel the same. We are going to change this world, hopefully for the better. No world changer has ever succeeded without making enemies. Our very existence threatens established thinking. Danger and great good are inextricably linked. If you join us, you will share both in triumphs and trials." Nadia covered the few steps between us and reached out her right hand. She waited until I had grasped her hand before saying, "Think carefully. I will respect any choice you make. Thank you for your time. Now, rest."

I slipped effortlessly into a nice, deep sleep, the sort I'm avoiding right now. Nadia must have somehow employed Jillian's Gift for making people sleep soundly. She gets more tricks in her mental arsenal every time I meet her. I find that fascinating and terrifying.

Life was so much simpler when people just told me what to do and where to go. I don't really mean that. I like having choices, but they shouldn't be so darn hard to make.

Working for Nadia would never be boring, but I'm not a huge fan of danger. I should be happy somebody thinks my life could be useful, so why am I so conflicted? Are my feelings caused by cowardice or caution?

The Indecisive One,
Danielle Matheson.

Chapter 10
Council of War

ITEM 144: Jillian's seventy-first post-kidnapping journal entry
Item Source: Jillian Blairington

Malia's promised council of war started off a lot smaller than she'd intended. My avatar appeared in a nice conference room at the appointed time. The long, brown table looked freshly polished, and the black leather chairs looked comfortable but not too comfortable. The room felt emptier than it was thanks to the nameplates marking places for Varick, Nadia, and Michio.

"Would you like me to get Michio?"

"That's not necessary," Malia replied. Standing at the head of the table, she picked up Varick's nameplate and rubbed her pointer finger across the name. When she placed it on the table again, it read: *Malia Davidson*. The one that had said *Malia Ayers* now read *Varick Ayers*. Tapping her fingers on the polished wood, Malia added, "But you might want to see if Danielle will join us."

The suggestion surprised me 'cause I knew we planned on discussing her. I guess I could have argued with Malia but following her suggestion seemed easier. In a moment, Danielle appeared in one of the chairs lining the table's left side, across from the empty places for Varick and Nadia. A nameplate materialized before her.

"Thank you for coming," Malia said, speaking equally to Danielle and me. "Please be seated."

Glancing down, I saw a nameplate appear in front of me. Though I couldn't read it, I assumed it spelled out my name. Curious to know which name Malia had chosen to place there, I picked up the nameplate. It read: *Jillian Blairington*, but a second later it switched to *Ashlynn Ayers*. I grinned and sat down as bid. "Are Nadia and Varick coming?" I asked, taking their nameplates to be good signs.

"They may join us later, but we'll have to start without them," answered Malia.

"Why are we here?" Danielle's eyes wandered the room, noting the many tasteful, battlefield paintings adorning the walls. "What is this place?"

"This is a war room, a place to safely discuss plans of action," Malia explained. "We are here to ask you how we can help."

"With what?" Danielle's tone said the question was spoken by reflex.

"You are burdened," Malia pointed out. She settled into the large chair at the head of the table. The bulky chair looked positively throne-like holding Malia's skinny frame. "What weighs upon you?"

I imagined large, ornately carved armrests springing from the chair, just 'cause I could. Malia might be hosting this dream, but I still had more control over it than she did.

"There's nothing wrong with me," Danielle protested.

Conjuring a glass of water, I slid it over to Danielle. People tend to talk better once they have a good glass of water. I added a lime as it touched her hand. She nodded silent thanks.

"Burdens do not have to spring from us to affect us," Malia stated. "And shared burdens become easier to bear."

"I guess I've got a lot on my mind," Danielle said, skipping around the point.

"Such as?" I prompted. Though I've never exactly been known for my patience, I really wished Danielle would open up to us. My Gift didn't quite cover a wish like that, but I wondered why Malia didn't use her Gifts to get answers.

"Take your time," encouraged Malia. "You are not obligated to tell us anything. We are simply here to help as needed."

Danielle sipped at the cool water and toyed with the glass, sliding it back and forth between her hands.

"Are you worried about Nadia's job offer?" I asked, needing to speak in order to avoid busting something.

Tilting her head to the side and biting her bottom lip, Danielle thought for three seconds then shook her head. "No. It's not that. I've decided to give the job a trial run next summer. Nadia has already accepted my proposal as a good compromise."

"Then—"

"Peace, Jillian. Give her time."

Frowning, I imagined a tall glass of water with lemon for myself. I squeezed the life out of the lemon then conjured another to sit prettily on the side. A crazy part of me said I ought to suck the lemons to pass the time. I squashed that notion.

"Christy's mother," Danielle whispered at last.

Malia nodded slowly, like she had known that all along.

The subject didn't surprise me, but I found Danielle's hoarse tone unsettling.

"She's gotten worse," Danielle continued, not meeting my gaze.

We'd known for many months that Christy's momma had cancer, and Nadia had told me a few more details. Still, the knowledge didn't seem enough for Danielle's strong reluctance to talk about the subject.

"I don't wanna sound mean, but why's this eating you, Danielle?"

My question made tears pool in Danielle's eyes. I quickly imagined a box of tissues appearing right next to her. She snatched one and dabbed at her eyes, sniffling to hold back a tide of emotion.

"She does—and does not—want to involve us," Nadia answered, appearing behind the seat reserved for her.

"You can't get involved!" Danielle yelled. She strangled the poor tissue in her hands.

"Somebody better start making sense," I muttered. I added a silent promise to turn the lot of 'em into toads if they didn't cooperate.

"We are already involved," Nadia said. "I have given the matter much thought."

Hope and fear crossed Danielle's face. "It's dangerous."

"I think I understand," said Malia.

"Good. Then you explain," I snapped.

Instead of speaking, Malia waved at Nadia to continue.

"Jillian, the situation with Susan Kilpatrick is rapidly changing for the worse," Nadia explained. She managed to sound sympathetic even as her words rushed out. "In short, conventional medicine has failed, and her doctors are recommending a move to hospice care. Danielle knows we may be able to intervene but does not wish to endanger us."

"Is that right?" I felt my frustration drain away.

Swallowing hard and finishing the rest of the water, Danielle nodded agreement with Nadia's summary. She still looked miserable, even with the story out in the open.

"Can it be done?" wondered Malia, as the silence grew to an awkward point. "Can we save her?"

Nadia gripped the shoulders of her chair hard with both hands then let go. "I must leave now, but in answer to your questions, yes, I believe we have a good chance of saving the lady. I will explain more at a later time. Farewell." Practically before her goodbye reached our ears, Nadia disappeared.

We stayed a little longer to trade theories and convince Danielle that she needn't feel guilty on our behalf, but Nadia's exit sorta sucked the life out of the council meeting. Finally, we gave up, agreeing that rest mattered more than guessing what kind of plan Nadia had dreamed up.

Chapter 11
Annual Report

ITEM 145: Jillian's seventy-second post-kidnapping journal entry
Item Source: Jillian Blairington

Despite my earlier words to Varick, I had no intention of waiting around for him to tell me about the problem Nadia needed help with at the lab. He can be a pretty lousy communicator when he gets busy, but I suppose that goes for anybody.

As soon as the meeting with Malia, Nadia, and Danielle ended, I searched for Varick's dreams. Since I couldn't find 'em, I figured he must still be awake. I next searched for Nadia, and again, I found a whole lot of nothing. As I resigned myself to natural sleep, I felt the tingling sensation I link to a real world event getting sucked into my dreams. It took many months of practicing with my Gifts to connect the feeling to that kind of event. These glimpses into places I ain't supposed to be able to see used to scare me, but this time, I felt relieved.

The perspective started out all wrong, like looking up from the floor. I saw a pair of heavy, black army boots, a few fancy pairs of men's shoes, and a navy colored set of what Momma calls prove-a-point pumps. Since this was now technically part of my dream, I changed the view so that I could watch more than the feet.

The lab looked like most of Dr. Devya's labs, except that this one seemed to have more space up front. I didn't have proof, but I made the assumption 'cause one of the fancy pairs of shoes turned out to be his. The pumps belonged to Dr. Carnasis, who wore a simple, elegant navy suit with a skirt that came to her knees.

Her customary lab jacket was folded up and draped across her arms, which she kept crossed to go with her less-than-pleased expression. The army boots belonged to Varick, who stood quietly near the front of the room. If he hadn't been breathing, I woulda thought him a very nice mannequin. The two other pairs of men's shoes belonged to people I'd never laid eyes on before.

Nana says it ain't right to judge men based on looks, but Malia and Nadia claim that instincts exist to tell us innate truths. These men in their dark suits and gloomy ties looked like trouble. I didn't like how their critical gazes lingered on Varick.

"The tests went well today." Dr. Carnasis spoke with the slowness that says one is quickly losing patience. "That should be enough for your report."

"One or two good results do not answer for every anomaly," answered the scary man standing closest to Dr. Carnasis.

"The nanomachine controller is still too unpredictable," pointed out the other scary man.

"He is a child," Dr. Carnasis said with that same sense of strained patience.

"Aiden's progress is very close to the projected path," Dr. Devya noted.

"But he's still behind," argued Scary Man One.

"And Nadia is far ahead," Dr. Carnasis rejoined. "Projections are by their very nature, guesses. It's not an exact science."

"Even so, his fainting episodes are troublesome," said Scary Man Two.

Dr. Devya waved the concern away with casual contempt. "We are addressing the problem."

"How?" challenged Scary Man One. "Your emotions project threw off her shackles and walked away, and the only reason the soldier dutifully returned is because he feels a blind sense of loyalty to the mind project."

It took me an extra second to translate his stiff speech into normal names, and I didn't much care for his dismissive attitude. At least Dr. Devya and Dr. Carnasis tried to refer to us by name.

"Where are the other projects anyway?" Scary Man Two's question brought me back to the dream.

"They are receiving training elsewhere," Dr. Devya replied.

Scary Man One smiled tightly. "You shouldn't lie to us, Dr. Devya. I don't think you understand how serious the matter has become. A poor annual report will get you shut down for good."

"That would be a mistake," said Dr. Carnasis. "Nadia alone is proof that our methods are successful."

"Your past genetic engineering success is not in question. Your current competence and continued relevance are both in question," droned Scary Man Two. "Many scientists would kill for these contracts, and in many other professions, so many failures would not be tolerated."

Scary Man One picked up the lecture. "In the past few years alone, you've misplaced three of your major projects and lost control of a fourth. The most valuable project nearly died mysteriously. Your security has suffered serious breaches, and two of your scientists turned traitor. Do you know what that tells me?" He paused for Dr. Devya or Dr. Carnasis to answer. When they said nothing, he continued, "It tells me it might be time to clean house."

Dr. Carnasis's eyes stabbed into Scary Man One with anger I'd only ever seen her level at Dr. Devya. "Threats are not in your best interests, Sanders, especially useless, vague threats. Your bosses were told from the beginning we required a free hand with all the projects. A little free-thinking on the part of these children is hardly cause for concern."

Mr. Sanders's expression lost the fake good humor. He stepped very close to Dr. Carnasis. Her heels gave her a few inches, but Mr. Sanders still towered over her. "That free-thinking is going to get one of them killed, and that—" He broke off mid-threat as Varick grabbed his shoulders and yanked him back a step. His surprised cry turned into a strangled, angry noise.

I hadn't even seen Varick move, but now he stood behind Mr. Sanders looking calm as can be, despite the fact that Scary Man Two's gun was pressed against the back of his head.

"Varick." Dr. Devya spoke the name as a warning. "This is hardly necessary."

"Release him," barked Scary Man Two.

"I'm not even touching him," Varick said, speaking normally.

"Put that gun away, unless you want him to use it on you," snapped Dr. Carnasis.

In the second it took Scary Man Two to process the warning, Varick twitched his head left, reached up, seized the man's wrist, and squeezed until the gun dropped. Mr. Sanders spun to face Varick, but Varick was already moving. He snatched Scary Man Two's gun out of the air with his left hand while his right pulled the gun off of Mr. Sanders's belt. He pointed each man's gun at their gut for a tense second before letting the weapons loop harmlessly on his pointer fingers. The men retrieved their guns and reluctantly put 'em away. Their cheeks flamed with humiliation.

"This is precisely why I told you to leave the weapons at the entrance. Do you believe me now?" Dr. Carnasis sounded weary and stern at the same time.

"You do not understand these children," said Dr. Devya. "Until you do, you will never control them."

"You're not controlling them either," retorted Scary Man Two.

"This isn't over," Mr. Sanders muttered.

I don't know if they had more to say or what Dr. Devya and Dr. Carnasis said after that 'cause my dream ended about there. I say about 'cause it lingered, focusing on Varick's troubled face. Since this wasn't his dream, I couldn't feel his emotions, but his eyes looked worried and angry. I wanted to stay and find out what was upsetting Varick, but an unseen force pulled me toward another dream.

Chapter 12
Dreaded Phone Call

ITEM 146: Danielle's fortieth letter
Item Source: Danielle Matheson
Dear Dr. S.,

Last night does not fall on my list of top ten most restful nights experienced. As I finally fell asleep, Jillian invited me into a meeting already in progress. If I had known she was going to explore my mental and emotional burdens, I'd have skipped the little session. While I appreciate her concern, I hate the whole situation.

Here's the circular path of why I feel so guilty. I know I've been over this in previous letters, but I have to lay it out again in the hopes that writing it down will scrape it off my spirit.

My gut tells me that it might be possible for Jillian or one of her siblings to concoct a plan that saves Christy's mother. At this point, that and a straight-up Biblical miracle are the only options left to the family. That self-same, non-helpful gut instinct also tells me that Nadia, Malia, Jillian, and the rest would drop everything if they thought they could help, even if the odds aren't in their favor.

Miracles, even hush-hush ones, are terribly hard to keep secret. I can't think of a single scenario wherein Christy's mother gets healed, everybody accepts the miracle without asking *why* or *how*, and the family lives happily ever after in blissful anonymity. That could be a flaw in me, but pessimism is awfully close to realism.

This really shouldn't bother me. I mean Nadia's Gifts make it child's play to pull these concerns from my mind. At the risk of sounding egotistical, my guilt springs from my personal connections to

Christy and Jillian. Nadia's been monitoring the situation because she knows that I'm deeply concerned. Jillian's a part of Nadia's family, and the friendship we formed because of the kidnapping affair has led Nadia to share those concerns. Without those personal connections, this would be one more misfortune in a sea of tragedies making up the memory archives Jillian spoke about seeing in Nadia's dreams. So, if the children decide to give this miracle thing a go and something goes wrong, it's inherently my fault.

Here I sit in the Lehigh Valley Hospital hiding behind the flimsy shield of this iPad while Christy and her little sister, Dominique, stew in their despair a few feet away. To keep sane, my mind plods back over the day and idly marvels at how much can change within a few hours thanks to the most mundane things, like a phone call.

As mentioned previously, I did not sleep very well last night, but breakfast with the Davidson family went a long way in lifting my flagging spirits. Ann and her family had stayed the night in a nearby hotel, but they drove over to partake in the morning meal. Nick had crashed on the living room couch. Joy had shared her old room with Malia and Jillian, and I'd occupied the floor in Marina's room. (Probably the other reason my sleep wasn't exactly restful.)

Christy's phone call came after breakfast, while I was doing towel drying duty for the dishes. I'd volunteered for the position to get a chance to chat with Joy. She's a veterinarian's assistant, and I'd also heard she had run afoul of evil minded people once upon a time. Morbid curiosity made me want to compare notes and battle scars. Having actually been knocking on death's door for a time, Joy wins in the category of "most harrowing experience."

Joy chuckled when she heard Christy's ringtone. "Is that 'The Imperial March'?"

"It's a long story," I said, nodding confirmation. I dried my hands on the damp towel and picked up the phone to check the caller ID, even though the theme told me the caller's identity. Force of habit, I guess. My thumb hovered over the button to reject the call.

"Go ahead and answer it," Joy said, sensing my hesitation but misinterpreting it. "I'm almost done here, and besides, it's about time you got back to being a guest instead of conscripted labor. Thanks for the help."

Now lacking a good excuse to ignore Christy's call, I slid my finger over the accept button, and said, "Hey, Christy, what's up?"

Silence greeted me.

"Christy? Are you there?" My heart thudded with anticipatory dread. Stumbling over to the kitchen table, I pulled out a chair and dropped into the seat.

Sniffles disrupted the silence.

"Okay. Okay, take your time. I'm here when you're ready to talk," I babbled.

A few more sniffles came over the line. Then, a voice I hardly recognized as Christy's spoke. Her words came out haltingly at first, then quickened to a frantic pace, and finally, dropped into bleak nothingness that could hardly be heard. "I'm sorry. I-I didn't know who to call. I know you're away, but I can't do this alone. I don't know what to do. My mother's dying."

At first, I was speechless. The announcement released a bunch of emotions, some of which made me blush at their cruelty. It occurred to me that if Christy's mother died, the miracle debate would become moot. A crushing wave of guilt squashed that thought flat, but I couldn't deny the odd relief it had provided. A burst of anger at the circumstances broke through my self-absorption. Christy needed me.

"Where are you?"

Christy mumbled a response that she was at the hospital with her mom and sister.

While Christy was answering reflexively, I pumped her for more details. Then, I asked Nadia to fill in some other details, which she did almost instantly. Christy's mom had been scheduled for a move to hospice care but had gotten worse before the move could take place. Her doctor didn't think she'd survive a move now. Christy's aunt and uncle, whom she didn't particularly like, had come to help with funeral arrangements. That certainly hadn't won them Christy's favor. While I know details are important, I agreed with Christy that not waiting for her mother to even die was extremely callous.

When she caught on to my intent, Christy protested, "Don't come. Enjoy your vacation. There's not much you can do here anyway."

That hurt, but I know Christy wasn't thinking clearly. Clamping down on the urge to tell her to shut up and let me help her, I said, "You and Dominique need a friend right now. I'll be there tonight." Sensitivity never was my finest attribute, but I have my moments.

"You will?" Christy's tone held a dose of heart-breaking vulnerability.

"Of course, I will," I promised. "Let me make some

arrangements. I'll call you back when I have a plan."

As I ended the call, the enormity of the task before me threatened to overwhelm my senses. Letting my phone clatter to the table, I stared at it until I sensed a presence hovering behind me.

"Would you like some help?" asked Malia, sounding absurdly polite.

Of course, I wanted help. I had about a zillion plans to make and zilch in the energy reserves. No words would come, but I nodded.

Malia's small hands landed on my shoulders and my mood began shifting. I'm not saying I immediately felt like all the problems in the world had vanished. The change proved far more delicate than that. I felt calmer, more in control of my thoughts. The tasks before me still seemed huge but surmountable.

"Thank you," I murmured, when Malia's hands fell away. My gaze shifted to Joy who was studiously scrubbing at the dishes.

"It's all right. She knows about my Gift," Malia said. "I told the family when the idea of adoption first arose. They needed to know in case something like this came up."

"I see," I lied.

"May I come with you?"

Swallowing idiotic surprise at the question, I opened my mouth to talk some sense into her.

"My mother has already given permission for me to go with you, as long as you agree to the arrangement," Malia continued.

"How did you know I was going?" I demanded. I didn't know I was going until about two seconds before this conversation.

I expected her to say Nadia had told her, but Malia simply smiled. "Your emotions told me just now, but Jillian warned me of the possibility early this morning, which is when I sought permission to accompany you."

"Don't you want to continue celebrating with your new family?" I tossed the question out there as a last-ditch effort to deter the child. I didn't have the heart to say she couldn't come. She probably knew as much or more about the situation with Christy's family than I did. It wasn't my place to ban her from helping.

"I would like to, yes," Malia admitted, "but I need to be with your friend's family in case Nadia thinks of a way for me to help."

"It's gonna be a tight squeeze in the car," Jillian declared, entering the kitchen holding Michio's left hand.

"What makes you think you're coming?" The question came

out harsher than I'd intended.

"We help," Michio replied.

I shook my head in a combination of disbelief and resignation. "Guess I'd better go pack."

"I packed for ya," Jillian said.

"Nick is loading car," Marina added. Her Russian accent stamped finality on the statement.

It would have taken an extreme force of nature to change the plans set in motion, so I went with them. I took a few moments to confirm with Mr. and Mrs. Davidson that Malia indeed had permission to go. On impulse, I invited Marina to join us, but I was grateful when she declined in favor of helping Joy with some wedding plans. Between luggage and passengers, Jillian's comment about the car being a tight squeeze would hold true without a fifth person.

I called Christy to relay the important details while the Davidson family pitched in to prepare some sandwiches and snacks for our new road trip. Nick handled the jigsaw puzzle of packing my car. I was about to go help him when it occurred to me to call my parents and Jillian's parents about the change in plans. Joy hopped on the computer long enough to whip up directions to the hospital and an address to feed my GPS. You'd think the preparations would exhaust me, but I felt oddly charged and ready to face the day. While I could attribute the feeling to Malia, it's more likely the sense of purpose gave me new energy.

We stopped only once for a brief stretch and a bathroom break. Jillian and Michio napped most of the way, but Malia kept me company as we tackled the long drive. She only dozed off once and briefly at that.

I'll tell you about our welcome at the hospital later. I need to recharge the old iPad and get a drink. It's going to be a long night.

The Helpless Friend,

Danielle Matheson.

Chapter 13
Maisha Puts Her Foot Down

ITEM 147: Jillian's seventy-third post-kidnapping journal entry
Item Source: Jillian Blairington
What I thought was another dream turned out to be more of a daydream for me. Over the past few months, Nadia and I have experimented with sharing our Gifts. Our experiences helping Danielle proved that Nadia could tap into Gifts given to Malia and me. Nadia discovered this particular application of her Gift by accident, and she doesn't use it much 'cause it can be dangerously distracting. Essentially, she connects our minds so I can hear and see what she does. She lets me flip the scene a few different ways if I don't like a particular view, but usually, the view she chooses turns out to be the best. It takes some getting used to, but it sure can be informative.

Jillian, I do not have much time to explain, but if you listen and observe closely, you may soon understand.

A complicated control panel lay before me, and hands that looked like they ought to be mine but really belonged to Nadia flew across the panel, punching in lots of commands. I had to concentrate on relaxing so I wouldn't mess Nadia up by distracting her.

An ear-splitting alarm started blasting, but Nadia silenced it with a few more commands. "That is not good," she muttered.

"Hurry, honey," rumbled a powerful voice I instantly recognized. "Varick's distractions ain't gonna keep them security boys busy for long."

I flipped to a different view so I could see Maisha standing next to Nadia, strangling a fluffy green towel. She's definitely the sort of

67

person who wears their emotions on the outside. Right now, she looked mighty anxious.

"That is why I requested your presence," Nadia replied, sounding far too calm for the situation. Her frantically tapping fingers were a better indication of her haste. "You may have to finish this part on your own."

"Don't speak such, Miss Nadia. You ain't going nowhere," Maisha vowed.

Nadia kept giving the computer commands at a speed that rivaled how quickly she usually speaks, but she turned her head enough so I could see the half-smile. "Mr. Sanders and Mr. Smith may disagree with you, Maisha. They are already displeased with Father, and they understand how much he values me."

Twisting the towel like she wanted to wring water from it, Maisha declared, "Dr. Dean loves ya, honey. He just ain't sure how ta share that with anybody, even Dr. Evie, and theys been friends a long time."

Maisha's words surprised me 'cause most of the time I've known 'em Dr. Devya and Dr. Carnasis have been flat-out arguing.

"That is true—"

The sound of something crashing into the door cut Nadia off.

"Varick has been captured," she announced, looking grim. If possible, her fingers moved faster across the keys. "They are coming."

The heavy thing banged into the door again and again. I didn't know how much pounding the door could take, but nothing could stand that level of abuse for long. I chose to ignore the pounding noise 'cause it was giving me a headache, and I wanted to concentrate on Nadia and Maisha's conversation.

Maisha peered up toward the door then fixed her gaze on Nadia again. "You gonna have ta get the precious little'un yourself, Miss Nadia." She draped the green towel over Nadia's right shoulder. "I'm gonna have me a chat with Dr. Dean and his guests."

"Stay with me, Maisha," Nadia pleaded. "Please. I cannot do this and keep you safe."

"Don't you worry about me, Miss Nadia," said Maisha. "The Good Lord gonna guard me 'til it's my time, an' if this be that time, then you's be wasting yer breath arguing." She gave Nadia's back a friendly pat and lumbered over to the bottom of the stairs.

As Maisha reached for the railing, the door burst inward with a loud crash. Three men rushed in with Dr. Carnasis close on their heels.

Two security men followed Dr. Carnasis, each holding tightly to one of Varick's arms. My older brother looked mad enough to snap the cuffs holding his arms behind his back. Dr. Devya hurtled down the stairs but stopped short of crashing into Maisha. Mr. Sanders and Mr. Smith—the guy I'd been calling Scary Man Two—halted a step behind Dr. Devya. Dr. Carnasis stopped two paces behind Mr. Smith and Mr. Sanders. Seeing the traffic jam, the security men bringing Varick along didn't bother starting down the stairs.

Dr. Devya held his hands out in a calming gesture. "Maisha, this isn't—"

"Get out of the way," barked Mr. Sanders.

"No, suh. This is where my foot goes down. I ain't letting you anywhere near Miss Nadia until you's a good sight calmer."

Mr. Sanders drew his handgun and aimed it at Maisha's face.

"I wouldn't," Dr. Devya warned, sighing.

"How did you idiots get government jobs?" asked Dr. Carnasis.

"What's to worry about?" Mr. Smith wondered defensively. "The boy wonder's not going to interfere."

"Varick is not your problem," explained Dr. Carnasis.

Now, Jillian!

Once that thought sank in, I put myself into a light sleep and let Nadia tap my Gift. Together, we sifted the minds in the room, selected Mr. Smith and Mr. Sanders, and dropped 'em both into a deep sleep. Maisha pulled Dr. Devya off the bottom step as the government men collapsed. Mr. Sanders fell forward and slightly left, stopping against the wall near the bottom step. Mr. Smith fell backward and woulda slammed his head on the stairs if he hadn't fallen into Dr. Carnasis, who instinctively caught him and eased him down.

"Nadia is your problem," Dr. Carnasis finished, trying to shove Mr. Smith's dead weight off to the side so she could stand again.

"You two gents should probably collect your bosses and leave before they hurt themselves," Varick advised the security men guarding him.

"What happened?" demanded one of the security men. He let go of Varick's arm and inched back.

"They fainted," said Dr. Carnasis, despite the fact that she knew exactly what Nadia and I had done. She knelt next to Mr. Smith and gently tapped his face with her palm to awaken him.

His head flopped in the other direction.

"If I didn't know any better, I'd say they was struck down by the Good Lord Himself," exclaimed Maisha, fanning herself with her right hand. "Land sakes, what a sight!"

"Nadia, please awaken our guests," instructed Dr. Devya.

"No more guns," Nadia insisted, keeping her back toward the action. Most of her attention remained on the control panel.

"Agreed," said Dr. Devya.

Jillian, please have Malia sleep for a moment. Do not worry. She knows this is coming as I have requested her help.

Since Nadia usually has good reasons for her requests, I reached for Malia and made her take a light nap. I didn't bother telling Danielle what we were doing 'cause I wasn't real clear on the details. Once connected, I felt Nadia reaching through me to Malia. A feeling of intense cold charged through my mind, freezing my brain. Mr. Sanders and Mr. Smith both woke up coughing and shivering like they'd emerged from icy water.

Thank you, Malia, thought Nadia. *Jillian, you may let Malia wake up now.*

"Where are our weapons?" demanded Mr. Smith.

"They were removed for your safety," Dr. Carnasis informed. "Varick has them." She gestured up the stairs toward where my brother, now free from the handcuffs, busily removed the bullets from the guns.

The security men lay moaning on the ground, attached together by the handcuffs that had once been on Varick. I didn't do anything to 'em. That was all Varick.

Leaning down so only the security men could hear, Varick said, "Stay down and out of whatever comes. You can collect the weapons later." With that promise, Varick chucked the empty guns outside the door in one direction and littered the lab floor with loose bullets.

"Varick, you are making a mess," Nadia scolded.

"This is going into the report," declared Mr. Sanders.

"What exactly are you going to report?" asked Dr. Carnasis. Her right eyebrow jumped upward to emphasize her question.

"Broke lab door, entered room, dropped unconscious, lost weapons," suggested Varick.

"Would somebody please get Maisha a lab stool?" Nadia requested.

All eyes turned to Maisha who looked kinda pale. "I's all right, honey. My heart jus' got a good workout is all. I be fine in a minute."

Dr. Carnasis pushed past the government men and fetched a

lab stool for Maisha. "Sit here and rest." She set the stool in a place where Maisha could lean against the wall and helped her perch on it.

"Thank you, Dr. Evie. That's right kind of ya," said Maisha. "Now that I's settled, maybe y'all would tell me why you is busting down doors."

"It was locked," Mr. Sanders muttered. "But that doesn't matter. I demand to know what's going on here."

"I'm sure Nadia will tell us soon," Dr. Devya noted wearily.

"You should know!" shouted Mr. Sanders.

"This is just the sort of blatant—"

Mr. Smith's rant got interrupted by a baby's cry.

Mr. Smith, Mr. Sanders, and the security guys flinched. Dr. Devya and Dr. Carnasis fixed tired gazes on Nadia and the neon green bundle she held. Maisha's eyes brightened, and she appeared suspiciously recovered from her mysterious weakness. The baby continued wailing, commanding everybody's attention.

"What is that?" Mr. Sanders spat through clenched teeth.

Eyeing the empty pod, Dr. Carnasis chuckled. "*That* is your doing, Sanders."

"How?" His temple throbbed with irritation.

Mr. Smith began nodding slowly. "Ah. This must be the child who failed the tests yesterday," he explained to his partner. Upon receiving only a dark glare, he continued, "The one we marked for termination."

"All this. Today. Everything," sputtered Mr. Sanders. "This was to save that sabotaged, useless, scrap of—"

"That chile is gonna bless some family in need of blessing," Maisha declared. "You ain't got a right ta call anybody useless. It ain't that baby's fault Dr. Victor thought she'd be better off without Miss Nadia's Gifts."

The baby cried throughout Maisha's speech, as if she knew the mean old government men didn't like her.

Nadia let the baby wear herself out, and then shifted the bundle so everybody could see her. "This is Anastasia."

"What happened to calling her Renee?" Varick asked.

"Renee means 'reborn.' Anastasia means 'resurrection.' Though the meanings are similar the second name includes a stronger element of loss before renewal, and that is her story," Nadia replied.

"Have you chosen a middle name?" Varick pressed.

"What does it matter?" wondered Mr. Smith, throwing up his

71

hands in frustration. "She's useless."

Varick and Maisha scowled at the man.

Nadia ignored him. "If Father does not object, Cora and I would like her second name to be Adira, meaning 'strong, noble, and powerful.' Do you object, Father?"

Dr. Devya shook his head.

"Anastasia Adira Ayers," murmured Varick. "It is a good name. May I hold her?"

As she handed Varick the baby, Nadia said, "Father, I know you will not tolerate her presence here for long, but I have a family ready to welcome her. Will you let Varick take her to them?"

"He has tests to complete," argued Mr. Sanders.

"You need more proof of his abilities?" Dr. Carnasis asked, truly stunned.

Dr. Devya didn't answer right away. Movement ceased for a moment as everybody waited to see what he would say. Finally, Dr. Devya nodded and relief rushed through the room like a breeze.

Dr. Carnasis left Maisha's side and slowly approached Varick. "Give her here. I will see that she gets washed, fed, and prepared for the journey."

At this point, Nadia let me slip out of the dream. I figured I'd peek in on the goodbye later, but for now, the dream gave me plenty to ponder.

Chapter 14
Don't Let Them Take Me

ITEM 148: Danielle's forty-first letter
Item Source: Danielle Matheson
Dear Dr. S.,

Hospitals are sad places. The last time I spent a significant amount of time at a hospital, Grams was getting major heart surgery done. She made it through, but the ordeal stressed my family out for weeks. The young doctor treating her had come very close to saying "what's the use of such an expensive surgery on an old lady" without actually uttering something that stupid. My mother is not a violent person, but I think if that doctor had stuck around much longer she would have strangled him with his own stethoscope. Thankfully, an older doctor with better bedside manner patiently explained the risks in the proposed surgery. Grams died a few years after that surgery, but I wouldn't trade those extra years for anything.

Cancer wards are probably the saddest sections of hospitals. It's not like hopelessness seeps out of the walls, but I can't imagine working in a place where many of the patients you interact with will die within the year, if not days or hours. Guess that rules out nursing as a career choice, not that I ever considered it as a serious option for me. I don't have the right disposition.

Katy would do fine as a nurse. I think she got all the compassion genes. She's always begging to go to the local veterinarian hospital so she can visit with the sick animals. She's not old enough to be an official volunteer, but mom has a friend who lets Katy linger in the waiting room to see the pet comings and goings. My kid sister has a way with animals, old people, and babies. She's forever chattering about her "work." Most of the regulars know her by now, and some let her play with the animals. You'd think Katy would stick to the cuddly things like puppies, kittens, chinchillas, and baby rabbits, but the kid positively gushes over mice, rats, lizards, and even snakes. Snakes! I could use some of that compassion right about now.

We arrived at the hospital like conquering heroes. Christy almost cracked a few of my ribs with the force of her hug. She thanked me about a dozen times then blurted out the whole ordeal, most of which I already knew. The part about Christy's mother being moved to a private room was new to me. My pessimistic side pointed out that solicitous hospital staff probably meant an approaching end. Whatever their reasons, I was grateful for small favors. The hospital has no restriction on family visiting hours, but I'm not sure that applies to family friends.

When Christy finally ran out of steam, introductions went around. Jillian and Michio didn't say much. They just read and re-read some children's books a kind nurse dropped off in the room. Malia sat down between Christy and Dominique and has hardly moved since. Things settled into an uneasy silence, punctuated only by the soft, regular beeps of a machine attached to Christy's mother. I, of course, wrote you my first rambling email of the evening.

You may ask yourself what blessing has warranted the boon of a second missive tonight, and I'll happily explain that I need to tell you the newest crisis or go crazy with despair.

We just met Christy's aunt and uncle. I usually don't judge people on first impressions, but the situation warrants an exception. I believe I've mentioned the silence lingering over the room. As uncomfortable as the silence could be, having it shattered so abruptly disturbed me.

"Christy, who are these people?" demanded a middle aged woman. "What are they doing here? This isn't a day care center. It's a hospital. Show some respect." Even though she was addressing Christy, her critical gaze landed squarely on me, then darted over to Jillian and Michio, and finally, swept over Malia.

Christy's shoulders jumped, and Dominique froze.

Malia reached over and brushed Christy's left arm before hovering near Dominique.

Scrambling to stand and whirling to face the newcomers, Christy said, "Aunt Sophie, these are the friends I told you about."

"Well, make yourself useful and introduce us, girl," grumbled the man who had entered the room a step behind the fierce woman. He looked like the poster boy for the phrase "grumpy man." Wisps of graying brown hair sprang up haphazardly across the top of his head. Broad, bushy eyebrows rose above beady eyes. Big ears framed his face. These features could describe any normal man, but the scowl looked like it had been perfected over a long time.

"I'm Danielle," I offered. "That's Jillian and Michio, and Malia's standing by Dominique." I gestured in the proper directions as I made the introductions.

"I wasn't talking to you," muttered the man.

Shooting me an apologetic look, Christy said, "This is my aunt and uncle, Sophie and Phillip Pendleton. Aunt Sophie's my mom's older sister."

"And I'd like to visit with my sister in peace," declared the woman.

"No." Dominique spoke softly, but one could hardly miss the conviction behind her short protest. She'd sat still in her seat to this point. Now, she twisted around and glared at her aunt and uncle.

"Wait until you're our ward, girl," said Uncle Phillip. "We'll teach you to respect your elders."

Without warning, Dominique burst into tears and bolted from the room. Christy cast a dark look at her uncle and took off after her sister, catching her just outside the room.

Jillian, Malia, and I exchanged questioning looks that asked: *Should we go after them?*

"Let's visit the cafeteria," Malia suggested. "It was nice to meet you both." She nodded politely to each and slipped past them, headed for the door.

Looking triumphant, the unpleasant pair moved to the seats recently vacated by Christy and Dominique, mentally dismissing the rest of us.

I crossed the room to scoop Michio off of Jillian's lap so she could stand.

"Food?" Michio asked.

"That's right," Jillian confirmed. "What would you like?" She continued casually questioning Michio as we made good on our escape from the room's toxic atmosphere.

We found Christy, Dominique, and Malia tucked in a side hall leading to some storage closets. Actually, Dominique's muffled sobs betrayed their private spot. I stopped but sent Jillian on with Michio. We hadn't eaten in quite a while, and it would have been unfair to the little guy to renege on the promise of food.

"Don't … let them … take me!" cried Dominique, sobbing into her sister's shirt. It took her several breaths to get the whole statement out between gasps.

The plea tugged at my heart and demanded I pay attention in case I could somehow help. The brief brush with Aunt Sophie and Uncle Phillip convinced me the idea of them raising a child was bad news.

"Please, Christy. They're mean. They hate us."

"Shhh," Christy murmured. "Don't speak like that, Domi."

I felt awkward witnessing this private moment between Christy and Dominique, but Christy waved me over. Malia had settled a short distance away from the Romans. I sat down a few steps into the passageway, completing our fire hazard of a people triangle.

Picking up on my concern, Malia leaned toward me and whispered, "We should have privacy for a few more minutes."

When Dominique finally calmed down, Malia convinced her that a drink and a walk would be good for both of them. I thought the kid might refuse, but Malia can be very persuasive.

Alone at last, Christy and I had absolutely nothing to say to one another. For a minute or two, Christy organized her thoughts, and I tried to contain useless phrases of comfort. I'd met people lacking in social graces before, but her aunt and uncle radiated malevolence.

As if she were tracking my thoughts, Christy said, "They're something, aren't they?"

"What's their problem?" I demanded. "That level of anger at the world doesn't spring from thin air."

Sighing, Christy leaned her head back against the wall. "I don't know everything, but they weren't always like that. They lost their son in a pool accident, and I think they had a few miscarriages after that." She shrugged. "My mom would know more, but she only woke up twice today." She paused to battle some rising sobs. A few tears slipped past her guard and plummeted down her cheeks. "The doctor says she could go at any time."

Taking hold of Christy's hand, I murmured, "I'm sorry." Meanwhile, my mind buzzed with partial plans. I argued with myself over letting Christy know any of the possibilities. At this point, there was no definite plan, only blind hope that Nadia would tell us what to do. It occurred to me that I'd been setting almost divine expectations of the girl.

"What do I do?" asked Christy, breaking into my thoughts.

"About what?" I shot back. She really had lost me.

The story poured out of Christy like a late-breaking summer storm. "My mother is dying. What will I do about my sister? Dominique's ten. I'm seventeen, and I don't turn eighteen until November. No court is ever going to give me custody of her, when there are two adults willing to take on the job."

"Why would they want her?" I asked. They really didn't seem overly fond of the child.

"Duty; government aid; to prove they can. I don't know," Christy admitted. Her expression grew even more pained. "I take that back. There could be another reason."

What reason? I pinched my leg to keep that question in.

"They can't have her," Christy protested weakly, sounding like she was addressing herself more than me. "She'll be miserable, and I'll probably never see her again."

"Why wouldn't you see her?" I wondered.

Sure, dear Aunt Sophie and Uncle Phillip could win grump-of-the-year awards, but that didn't mean they were outright cruel.

Elbows propped on knees, Christy plunked her head into her hands, and moaned, "You don't understand my family."

Only through great effort did I hold in a demand for an explanation. I knew one was pending. I just wanted it five minutes ago. See, my parents taught me those horrible lessons about patience and tactfulness.

When Christy's misery finally gave way to an expression of deep embarrassment, she stopped clutching her head, and said, "My mother hasn't always been the cheerful, soccer mom type she shows the world. She's struggled with depression for a long time. When she's headed for a downturn, she gets emotionally needy. When she gets emotionally needy, she can get sort of free with her attention to men, if you know what I mean."

"Oh," I said. "That must be the home trouble that had you sleeping over my house for two months when we were kids." I couldn't believe I hadn't made that connection ages ago. Kids really can be blissfully ignorant.

"Dominique's really my half-sister," Christy said, lowering her voice. "My parents fought a lot, but they worked out their differences in time for my father to adopt her just after her birth. A few weeks later, he had a heart attack and died. Few people know. I don't even think Domi knows."

"How did you find out?"

"When mom's cancer took up most of her attention, I started handling the bills and stuff. I found some legal paperwork hidden in her room. A lawyer sent a letter to my mother telling her that Dominique's father had passed away and left her a legacy to claim on her eighteenth birthday."

"You think they're after the money?" I asked, feeling like I'd been dropped in the middle of a soap opera. *How would they even know about it?*

"I don't know," Christy answered. "Thirty thousand dollars is a nice surprise, but it's hardly worth a fight. Domi would probably throw the money at them if it would make them go away." In response to my expression, she continued, "I didn't tell her about it yet because it wouldn't mean much to her, and she's a long way from eighteen."

There wasn't much more to say after that. Maybe my dad will know someone who can help with the custody thing. My rumbling stomach made polite conversation impossible, so I convinced Christy to accompany me down to the cafeteria. She had no appetite but picked at a sandwich for my sake. I devoured a cheeseburger and an apple to offset said cheeseburger.

After the meal, we trooped back up to the room to resume the vigil, hoping against hope not to meet Aunt Sophie and Uncle Phillip again.

Christy's Sounding Board,
Danielle Matheson.

Chapter 15
Dustin's Confession and Gift

ITEM 149: Jillian's seventy-forth post-kidnapping journal entry
Item Source: Jillian Blairington

The nice nurses at the hospital did their best to comfort and protect Christy and Dominique. One brave lady even asked their aunt and uncle to leave 'cause they were upsetting the girls. Their aunt started to pitch a fit, but I think Malia put a stop to that. Not rightly sure what she did, but instead of finishing a threat to report the nurse to her supervisor, Aunt Sophie grabbed Uncle Phillip's arm and stormed out.

I spent most of the evening pretending to read books to Michio. Instead, he was quietly telling me about some of the projects he wanted to work on. He likes building things. He thought it'd be fun to build a set of swings out of toothpicks. I like building things well enough, but that sounded odd to me. As the night wore on and Michio wore out, I tucked him into the empty cot next to Christy's momma. Malia and Dominique soon joined him, and Danielle suggested I do the same. They looked comfortable, but that tiny cot sure was crowded. Three bodies, even skinny kids, are enough to tax any cot.

I offered to help Danielle sleep, but she said she wanted to stay awake a little longer. Christy had already slumped forward against her momma's hospital bed and cried herself to sleep. Accepting Danielle's wishes, I curled up on one of the blankets a nurse had brought for us to share.

While deciding between a natural sleep with normal dreams and a working sleep to make sure Christy and Dominique got some rest, I accidentally fell asleep and had the decision made for me.

It had been quite some time since I left my body to experience a dream. That probably sounds silly since dreaming doesn't usually involve the body. Maybe I just think of this type of dreaming as being out-of-body 'cause it's like watching something like a fly on a wall, since there's no avatar of me to control. For a long time, I'd been afraid to do that sort of dream walking 'cause one of the first times I did it I got somebody in big trouble.

This dream belonged to Nadia. I could tell 'cause it felt like some of the dreams she stored in the crystal chandeliers. She's gotten pretty good at summoning me to specific dreams.

I noticed the baby on the lab counter right away. Anastasia was sleeping on her back in a carrier with one tiny arm free from the cloth wrapping her up like a burrito. She wasn't much bigger than a burrito either. If she could keep her balance, I think TJ would be a perfect steed for her. I pushed the nonsensical thought aside to focus on the white disc covering most of her forearm. A wire ran from the disc up to a machine that I assumed checked her heart rate and other life signs.

Do not concern yourself with the machine, Jillian. The scientists only want to know if she is healthy enough for Varick to move.

Before I could question Nadia about anything, Dustin entered the room and leaned back against the door. The nervous glance he shot around the room told me he probably wasn't supposed to be there.

"What are you doing here?" Varick's voice held an even mixture of amusement and challenge.

If I'd had my body, I woulda reacted like Dustin who jumped and hit his head against the door. Rubbing his sore head, Dustin turned to Varick and frowned. "You expected me to come."

"Of course, we did," Varick said.

"We?" Dustin repeated, rubbing his head again. "Oh. Hello, Nadia. You might as well show up so I don't feel quite so barmy talking to the air."

Nadia appeared in the room behind the carrier, one hand gently resting above the baby's head. She kept a faint, white aura around herself to show she wasn't really there. "Hello, Dustin," Nadia said, returning the greeting. In response to his questioning look, she added, "I may not enter your mind, but I can hear your unguarded thoughts." She gestured to the baby. "Besides, Varick and I felt drawn to her. Why should you not feel the same?"

"Father won't like it," Dustin said, taking a few steps closer to Nadia and the baby.

"Father doesn't like a great many things," Varick noted.

"Anastasia is not like us, but she is still our sister. Father has already been by to make his peace," said Nadia.

Dustin looked at Nadia like she'd told him he was gonna learn to fly tomorrow. I honestly couldn't tell if she was lying to him or not. Nadia's got a rather complicated view on the subject of lying. She'll never do it to purposefully hurt someone, but if it's somehow safer to indulge in a lie, she's all for it.

"Varick will have to leave soon. You should speak the words you came to say. We will give you some privacy if you like." With that, Nadia let the avatar disappear.

Varick looked like he didn't want to leave, but he nodded to Dustin and strode toward the door. "I'll return when you're finished," he promised. "You know how to reach me."

Dustin crossed the remaining space separating him from the carrier like someone walking over hot coals. He glanced around again like he felt my eyes upon him. I brought my consciousness down to a level where I could see his face and found him very close to tears. Tentatively reaching forward to brush a finger down Anastasia's right cheek, Dustin sucked in a shaky breath. "Nadia?"

"Yes, Dustin. I am here," spoke Nadia's voice.

Sniffling and drawing in a bracing breath, Dustin asked, "Do you know what I did?" His soft, haunted voice filled the empty air above Anastasia.

"I believe so," Nadia replied.

"I let this happen," Dustin confessed. "I knew what Dr. Parris wanted to do, and I kept silent."

"Do you know why you did so?" Nadia inquired.

"I wanted to see if I could," said Dustin. Tears fell down his face. "I knew he didn't want to hurt her. He only wanted to remove her Gift. I've never had a secret to keep in my whole life. Not one like this. Father sees almost everything. I just—I'm sorry."

Silence answered him.

"I'm sorry," Dustin repeated.

Nadia's voice rang with compassion and sincerity. "Dustin, I am not a higher power, nor the wronged party. It is not my place to forgive you, but Anastasia will never know what she lost. She has nothing to fear, and you, in turn, have little to regret."

"I could have stopped him," Dustin said. "He tried to kill you."

"He tried to kill us all," Nadia clarified. "But if you had said something, Father would simply have killed him and your conscience would have a different burden to bear."

"I feel like I stole her Gifts," Dustin whispered.

"Perhaps, in a way, you did, but the past is gone," Nadia said. "Make amends and learn from the mistake. That is all anybody can ask of you."

Dustin said nothing for a long time. Finally, he asked, "Can I have that privacy now?"

"As you wish, Dustin. I am here when you need me."

I felt I should leave Dustin to his confession, but curiosity made me stay. It took him a long time to work up the courage to talk to Anastasia. When he finally spoke, I was glad I stayed 'cause it let me see a new side of my brother.

Picking up the baby's tiny hand, Dustin said, "I'm sorry, Anastasia. I wish I could go back and say something that would let you keep your Gifts. I wanted you to stay. Everybody's leaving, and nobody understands. Nadia tries, but she's always busy. I wanted someone to talk to." Tucking a hand into his pocket, Dustin pulled out a bracelet made of many brightly colored woven threads. Quickly folding the thing six or seven times, he placed it onto Anastasia's wrist. "I hope your new folks don't just throw this away. Maisha gave it to me, but I want you to have it. Bracelets are more of a girl thing anyway, and maybe one day you'll wonder who gave it to you and think of me."

Chapter 16
The Glove Box Surprise

ITEM 150: Danielle's forty-second letter
Item Source: Danielle Matheson
Dear Dr. S.,

Congratulations, you're the beneficiary of the bountiful hours of downtime to be had in a hospital. My wakeup call came nice and early this morning in the form of Malia gently tapping my arm and calling my name.

"Hmm?" I asked, barely waking up enough to yawn, check if I'd been drooling, and stretch my shoulders.

"Good morning," Malia greeted, sounding amused yet in a hurry. "I need your full attention very soon, Danielle. May I help you wake up?"

I think I groaned a little, but I managed to nod. Malia took hold of both of my hands and flooded me with a feeling like crisp, cool water dousing my face and arms. Behind the bracing cold feeling, she tucked elements of alertness, purpose, determination, and hope. "That was really amazing. Thank you," I gushed, trying not to sound like a pre-teen fan of a boy band.

Acknowledging my thanks, Malia said, "Nadia and I have a plan, and we all have a part to play. Will you hear it?"

"Of course," I affirmed, tightening my hands around Malia's tiny paws as I sat up straighter. "What is it? How can I help?"

"You need to set up a prayer chain and inform a few of the nurses of our goals. No details, of course. Tell them we need some privacy to pray for a miracle." The soft, very British way Malia

83

pronounced "privacy" struck me as charming.

Alarm shot through me, but I quickly fought it down. "What happens if we succeed? Isn't that going to cause a lot of publicity?"

"The right publicity can be a good thing," Malia said, squeezing my hands one last time then letting them drop into my lap. "Nadia or I will explain further details as necessary."

"What will everybody else be doing?" I wondered, casting my gaze over the slumbering people strewn around the room.

The room looked like a scene from a refugee camp. Michio and Dominique Roman slept soundly on the hospital cot. Dominique's right arm had draped around Michio, pulling him close like a big teddy bear. Jillian's feet stuck out from behind the cot where she'd thrown down a blanket for the night. Her right foot twitched from time to time, telling me she must be mid-dream. Christy's mother still lay corpse-like in her bed, and Christy sprawled half-in, half-out of the chair she'd occupied all night.

"We're a lively bunch," I muttered.

Smiling faintly, Malia explained, "Jillian is training in a simulation Varick set up, and Michio is resting. I haven't told Dominique and Christy of our intentions yet. You're much better suited to that task, but it can wait. Jillian will keep them resting until the appropriate time."

It struck me again how very Nadia-like Malia could sound, but I refrained from commenting because I know how much little sisters loath being compared to their siblings. Instead, I asked, "How much do I tell them?"

Malia's expression turned pensive, and she didn't reply right away. She took a moment to stare at Christy and then Dominique, studying their even breathing. At last, she answered, "As little as possible. The less they know, the safer they'll be."

"Do you expect trouble?" I didn't want to ask that question. I know I expected trouble, but Nadia, Malia, and even Jillian can access greater knowledge than I can. Thus, they can anticipate troubles far more accurately than me.

"It's hard to say," Malia replied. "If we fail, it's best they know only that we tried to save their mother. If we succeed, it's best they know it only as an act of God, for it will be in either case."

Her explanation surprised me, though I'm not sure why. Surely, kids born in a lab had the same opportunity to believe in God as anybody. My surprise identified a disturbing prejudice I'd clung to

84

unknowingly. Its revelation shook me. To distract myself, I asked, "What should I do first?"

"Get dressed, get money, buy food, eat something, talk to the nurses, tell Christy, and then make your phone calls," Malia instructed. "When the others awaken, I will see that they eat well."

"Get money from where?" I questioned. "How did you know I needed money?" This unexpected trip had cut deeply into my cash reserves. I'd made the observation the previous evening when we were in the cafeteria, but I'd pushed the inconvenient thought off, thinking I'd track down an ATM eventually. One day, I will learn not to ask stupid questions that usually have their answer in Nadia.

"I felt your concern last night," Malia revealed. "You hid it from Jillian and the others, but not me. As to your first question, the answer is in your glove box. Varick thought we might have some extra expenses."

My mouth opened to question her further, but I firmly shut it. Bobbing my head in acceptance, I went to the corner where we'd dumped our stuff and dug out my purse. "Would you like to come with me to the car?"

"Yes, it will be good to move. We will likely be in this room for a long time."

For some reason, the very practical answer made me laugh. After changing to a fresh pair of khaki shorts and a slightly wrinkled T-shirt, I double checked that I had my car keys and waved Malia out the door. She glided along the hallways leading back to the elevator with sure steps that made me marvel at the energy inherent in youth. Katy would have been skipping, but the smooth, even gait fit Malia well.

As the elevator reached the ground floor, Malia grabbed my hand in a painful grip. "I should stay here."

"What's the matter?"

Malia frowned in a way Jillian would describe as "mightily."

The elevator chimed its annoyance with our hesitation and hissed its doors shut.

"The emotions are wrong. The men out there are looking for someone." Malia's free hand shot toward the elevator controls and depressed the button to keep the doors shut.

"You think they're looking for you?" My tone made it a question.

"Maybe." Malia shook her head and frowned toward the ground. "This could complicate the healing."

"Why would anybody be looking for you?"

Malia's expression cleared, like she'd wiped a slate clean. "We can consider that question later. For now, I will return to the room. If you're willing, please retrieve the money from your car and purchase enough food for everybody."

I'm not sure what the kid would have done if I'd refused, but the thought never crossed my mind. Malia doesn't rattle easily, but whatever she'd felt had obviously upset her. I zipped out of the elevator like a stone from a slingshot and quick-stepped it all the way to my car. The early morning sun made the few cars in the lot shiny. A leisurely stroll enjoying the fresh air would have been nice, but Malia's sudden worry dashed any sense of casualness about the errand.

Pressing the unlock button a half-dozen times, I flung myself into the passenger seat then locked the door with the button on the side panel. Feeling marginally safer but still edgy from high adrenaline, I stared at my glove compartment for several seconds. It looked perfectly normal. Slowly, I reached for the latch and let the box swing open, expecting to see an envelope or something.

Nothing seemed different.

The bulky paperweight the car manufacturers think you'll actually read sat on top of my current and expired insurance papers. The package holding the jumper cables lay partially buried under the insurance cards. I peeked into the booklets first, but finding nothing, I picked up the jumper cables. Feeling slightly foolish, I undid the string on the black bag. A roll of used bills had been tucked into the center, held together by a thick rubber band like some gangster's ill-gotten gains.

Plucking out the bundle with two fingers, I let it swing down into my palm and closed my fist around it. Slipping off the rubber band, I quickly counted the money. All told, the roll consisted of five hundred and thirty-two dollars. It seemed like a strange number to me, but the money might as well have been a million for the giddy way it made me feel. At the very center of the roll, I found a white envelope. I stuffed sixty dollars into my wallet, creased the rest of the money, stuffed it into the envelope, and shoved the package into the bottom of my purse. Then, I headed for the cafeteria.

Not knowing exactly how much to get, I ordered three sausage, egg, and cheese sandwiches, two bacon, egg, and cheese sandwiches, and one egg and cheese sandwich. Christy, Jillian, and I could probably finish a sandwich on our own. Malia and Dominique would likely split one, and Michio would probably quit after three-quarters. If my calculations were correct, that would leave us with a spare sandwich in the hopes Christy's mother woke up enough to eat something. Because I didn't know when I'd get out again for lunch fixings, I added half a dozen bagels, two blueberry muffins, a half-dozen water bottles, three apple juices, and a round of orange juice for everybody.

"That's a lot of food," commented the kid who rang up the order. "Are you planning on feeding an army or staying for a month?"

"Hopefully neither," I answered.

He smiled shyly. "Would you like me to have someone bring the order to a specific room?"

I considered accepting the offer, but a memory flash of Malia's concern made me hesitate. "No thanks, just double bag everything, and I'll take it myself."

"You sure? It's no problem. I can probably help you myself. I'd have to ask my boss though."

"Thanks for the offer, but I'll be fine," I insisted.

Halfway to the elevator, my aching arms yelled at me for not accepting the kid's help, but I pressed on. Reaching my destination yet not having a free hand, I kicked at the door. Jillian answered it and relieved me of the heavier burden.

She grunted when the full weight landed on her, narrowly missing her feet as it thumped to the ground. "What'd ya pack in here? Bricks?"

"That's all the drinks," I replied.

Malia came over to help Jillian.

Christy rushed to take the remaining bag from me. "We were getting worried," she whispered so only I could hear. "Malia told me what she felt on the elevator. She said you'd explain the rest."

"Let's eat first," I suggested.

"I need to know now, Danielle," Christy declared, planting her feet more firmly.

If I wanted to get past her, I'd have to shove her out of the way. Sighing, I said, "Let me feed the children and you and I can chat in the restroom." I know that doesn't sound like a glamorous arrangement, but the restroom really did provide the most privacy one could get in the hospital suite.

The food delivery took about three seconds because Malia offered to finish the distribution. The arrival of a nurse delayed our conversation about ten minutes more, but Christy finally hauled me into the lav and locked the door.

"Start talking." Christy leaned back against the door so I'd get the message that I wasn't leaving until she got some answers.

Message received, I told her as much as I dared. "You're going to have to trust us."

"Who's 'us'?" Christy demanded.

This was not a great start.

"The less you know the better. We want to save your mother, but we're going for a miracle here so secrecy is very important."

"Why?" My friend sounded dazed, but I figured I'd better try to kill her curiosity before it caused problems.

Reaching out to hold Christy's shoulders, I started on a fine speech. "There's no guarantee they can win here, but if they do and people find out what they're capable of, their lives will be ruined." I let that sink in for a second before forging on ahead of the obvious question forming on my friend's lips. "Miracles don't sit well with most Americans, Christy. They'll ask 'how,' just like you want to. The answer will lead them to those children, and that *cannot* happen."

"They can heal her?" Christy asked, confirming my fear that she probably hadn't heard much beyond that possibility.

"No one can know they're even going to try!" I hissed, tightening my grip on her shoulders. "Not even Dominique. Promise me you won't tell a soul!" It took massive effort not to shake her to stress my point.

"I promise," Christy murmured, stunned by the force behind my words.

An idea popped into my head. "Do you remember Nadia from our previous experience?" I waited for her to confirm, then continued, "If you want to help, there may be a way, but you'll have to understand that if Nadia feels the need, she'll suppress the memory. Also, you have to follow my instructions without question, no matter how strange they seem. Do you agree to those terms?"

"Yes," Christy answered instantly. "I want to help."

"Good. Now, let's go eat. We've got a lot of phone calls to make after breakfast."

The renewed sense of hope did wonders for Christy's appetite. She polished off a sausage, egg, and cheese sandwich and ate the reject bacon from my sandwich. I had wanted the egg and cheese sandwich, but Michio had consumed the whole thing while Christy and I were plotting in the restroom. So much for my careful food consumption estimates.

When we finished eating, I explained the phone calls I wanted Christy to make and made a few of my own. Malia spent most of the time sitting with Dominique by the sickbed. Jillian and Michio bounced around the room building a strange nest of blankets behind the far cot and dozing on and off.

There's a lot more to tell, but I need to take a nap.

The Pleasantly Sleepy One,

Danielle Matheson.

Chapter 17
The Caratran Captives Part One

ITEM 151: Jillian's seventy-fifth post-kidnapping journal entry
Item Source: Jillian Blairington
After witnessing Dustin's strange confession, I slept normally for about four hours. Just as I would have woken up naturally, Nadia summoned me to her throne room. That's the space in her mind where she and I meet to chat. I guess we don't really need a place like that, but I sort of got used to it while trying to wake her from that weird coma she fell into almost a year ago.

Queen Elena rose from the throne as I appeared below the dais steps. I like that word: dais. It's one of my favorite words 'cause it's strange, cute, and functional, just right for describing a platform thingy that holds a throne. I probably shouldn't pick favorites with people, but I like this version of my older sister. Queen Elena might not always be cheerful, but she carries a sense of grace and beauty about with her like an invisible cloak.

The dress she wore caught my attention 'cause it wasn't blue or green or even purple. The plain creamy color would have looked downright bland if the load of tiny gems decorating the bust and center didn't liven it up with a pleasing mixture of oranges, reds, pinks, and whites. The dress also went straight toward the ground without flaring out like it wanted to take up six feet in every direction.

"Nice dress," I commented. That probably ain't a good way to start a conversation with royalty, but Queen Elena understands me a whole heap better than most people. She knew it was my way of saying, *What happened to the other one?*

"Thank you, Jillian," said Queen Elena, letting an amused smile lighten her expression. "Naidine and I are expanding our wardrobe colors."

"What's wrong with your usual colors?" I asked.

"She has agreed to don more than blue and black clothes, and I have agreed to wear less green and purple," Queen Elena explained. "It is a small step we must take to reconcile our differences."

"Why would y'all need to do that?" The question slipped out before I could stop it even as my Nana-sense told me it was impertinent.

"It is in both of our interests to be unified. As time moves onward, Nadia will likely come to emulate one or the other of us, and so we must be close if we wish to maintain our identities."

"Why can't she keep ya both, like now?" I didn't mean to sound whiny, but I think it came out that way. Not sure what my expression said, but I was going for something to repeat the question.

"Change is a part of growth," spoke the queen. To my surprise, she swept down the stairs and drew me into a tight hug. When she released me, she said, "Do not worry for either of us. The question of Nadia's future personality pales in comparison to the needs of the moment. Right now, I have a task for you."

As she spoke of a task, my eyes automatically flicked up to make sure her crown had all its jewels. Thankfully, the thing sat where it's supposed to on her head, nestled on top of the braids wrestling her long, golden strands of hair into order. At least Queen Elena hadn't given up on the fancy way of keeping her hair. My friend Jimmy Denson, who has met Queen Elena in some dreams, said her hair makes her look very queenly.

Tracking my thoughts, she laughed softly. "I promise it is not another task to fix the crown. Varick has prepared a simulation for the coming healing of your friend's mother. I told him I would ask you about it first, though I know your answer."

"What's gonna happen?" I really meant to ask if she thought we could succeed, but it seemed kind of rude, seeing as our plan would likely come from her.

A distant look crept into Queen Elena's pretty blue eyes, and I glimpsed the stress hiding there. "I do not know." Her lips twitched in a tiny shadow of a smile. "Those words are more common to me than you expect, Jillian, but do not take them as precursors to defeat." Her voice grew stronger as her conviction showed through more clearly.

"Our task is difficult, not impossible. Michio should be able to perform the actual healing. Malia and I will guide him through the process. Danielle will liaise with Christy, Dominique, the nurses, and anybody else necessary. Malia had a suggestion which I am currently investigating. We may need your help with implementing her plan. For now, you must prepare to troubleshoot problems that arise, and keep the patient and workers in the correct levels of sleep."

"How will I know what level to keep 'em at?"

"Malia and I will help you with those decisions," Queen Elena said. "Varick is waiting now, will you go to him?"

"I will go," I answered, dropping to first one knee then both as the dream deepened through its changes.

Bowing my head, I closed my eyes to let the throne room fade as Varick's dream drew me in. My ears let me know when I got to my destination. The music, a heart-pounding quick theme, made me throw my avatar's body flat on the ground and burn half my blue bar—that's the magic one—on an energy shield. The stingy part of me regretted what would probably turn out to be a waste of good magic until three red energy beams glanced off the top of the shield.

Rolling onto my back, I opened my eyes and took quick stock of my armor, equipment, and weapons. The simple pair of dark trousers held up with a belt and the black long-sleeved shirt made me modify my "armor" terminology. It felt strange to even think of the clothes as a uniform. Calling it "light armor" would pretty much insult all other such armor. The situation didn't bother me as much as the realization that my only equipment item was a book of matches and my sole weapon turned out to be a rock.

Varick had dumped me into some desperate situations before, but I usually had more than a rock for defense.

"The Chosen One of Terabane is never truly defenseless," spoke the disembodied voice of Sonia, local goddess of wisdom. She's the narrator in each of Varick's *The Immortal Warrior* games. Sonia's voice is actually Nadia, but her speech patterns and advice are unique to her character. I've never played the actual video game 'cause I don't think my parents would much approve and it's way more lifelike in dreams.

More energy beams peppering the deck by my prone body prompted me to move. Rolling to a kneeling position, I strengthened the energy shield and whipped out the matchbook. Ripping out three matches, I lit and released 'em in quick succession, imagining 'em turning into tranquilizer darts that would seek the people targeting me.

My magic bar crashed well into the red zone, but three startled yelps followed by thumping noises told me I'd downed a few enemies. Two more red energy beams splashed across my shield, making it shimmer a warning of coming failure. Lacking the magic to do anything fancy with the rock, I huddled behind my shield and peered toward the origin of the last two shots.

Another two beams zipped out, lighting the grim face of a young soldier in a fancy blue uniform complete with matching cap. Clutching the rock hard, I wound up like my Old Daddy had taught me and hurled it like a fastball right at the man's face. The soldier ducked instinctively, making my rock bounce off his cap. The blow dazed him enough to let me tranquilize him.

The music dropped to a sweet, somber tune, announcing an end to that phase. While my magic bar replenished itself, I retrieved my lucky rock and relieved the nearest soldier of his gun. The building process got slowed by me burning magic to learn the proper use of the new weapon, but I'd learned long ago that such knowledge could save my skin later.

"What's the mission?" I wondered, as I flicked the switch to turn the weapon to stun.

Gold letters appeared at the bottom of my vision. They spelled out: ROYAL PALACE, CITY OF CARATRAN.

Sonia explained in her usual unhurried, melodious voice that makes me long for Nadia's efficiency with words. "You have followed rumors and whispers through many times and lands, and all lead you here to Caratran, current capital of Terabane. Within these walls, you will find many captives. Some wear chains and some do not realize they belong elsewhere. Chosen One, you must find and free the five captives, for their souls will charge the Sacred Stone."

"Sacred Stone," I repeated slowly. "Is that the rock I beamed the guy with?"

"The Sacred Stone is an ancient gift granted to the world, a symbol of unity among strength, power, love, hope, and wisdom. These five attributes must be balanced in the heart of the Chosen One, and indeed, in everyone granted the right to rule."

Though Sonia had dodged my question, I looked closer at the rock and reached the obvious conclusion. The smooth stone had five faint sections etched into its surface. Pocketing the Sacred Stone, I jogged over to another fallen soldier, found his weapon, and tucked it into my belt.

The music tempo picked up enough to encourage me to move on with the quest without being the sort where I knew something was gonna immediately jump me.

After a few minutes of fruitless searching, I got smart and asked Sonia to point me in the right direction. A series of three glowing arrows flowed out from my feet and veered left, so I followed 'em right into a mess of soldiers. Since I didn't have time to light matches and use 'em as tranquilizers, I shot one with a blue stun beam and turned the other two into toads. They both croaked and trilled their annoyance with me, but I didn't have time to sit there and comfort 'em.

Three parties of soldiers later—six of whom I turned into mice and two of whom I turned into bunnies—I found my first palace captive. She wore a lovely gray dress that declared her a lady-in-waiting, and she sorta looked like Cora, except her hair was much fancier. Her narrowed eyes told me she wouldn't go down easily.

The impression lied.

"How dare you invade this peaceful palace with—" She cut herself off with a long, loud scream good enough to attract every soldier in the entire palace wing. It's the sort of scream that cuts to your core and sends shivers everywhere. "Mouse!"

Whipping around, I saw one of my former assailants zipping along next to the wall. A thud behind me told me the lady had fainted dead away. I wasn't sure fainting could be considered "freeing," but I took out the stone and wished that it would do its thing. I usually try to be more specific with my instructions, but Sonia had been kinda stingy on details.

The Sacred Stone leapt out of my hand and hovered over the fallen woman. A stream of red light flowed from her body into the Sacred Stone, turning the whole thing a fiery color. As the light entered the stone it spun in crazy circles. Tendrils of red light whipped out of the rock, creating an eye-dazzling display that left me and the mouse mesmerized.

Once it finished charging, the stone shot straight back into my hand. Nodding farewell and thanks to the mouse, I went in search of the second captive.

Chapter 18
The Caratran Captives Part Two

ITEM 152: Jillian's seventy-sixth post-kidnapping journal entry
Item Source: Jillian Blairington

The more I blundered about the palace, the more unconscious soldiers and woodland creatures I left in my wake. While this did wonders for my confidence and stockpile of weapons, it didn't reveal any more of the captives until I literally bumped into an enemy soldier rounding a corner. The young man cried out and shoved a gun in my face.

He looked familiar, so I said, "Dustin?"

"I-I know not that name," stammered the soldier with Dustin's features, "b-but I demand a swift surrender from thee, else thy life be forfeit." His face belonged to my little brother, but his body had grown up a good decade.

Raising my hands in an *I-surrender* gesture, I willed the soldier to turn into a toad. Panic gripped me when nothing happened. "Well, now what?" I muttered, silently willing Sonia to answer me.

Thinking my words were meant for him, the soldier said, "My lord and king hath placed a high price upon thy brow, unfortunate miscreant. Aye, so high a price that I may settle fair the debts of family and friends alike."

The idea of being turned over for a price incensed me. "Oh yeah, well maybe my rock has something to say about that!" I assure you that sounded much cooler in my head, and anyways, it worked. I held the stone in front of my body like a protective talisman. It promptly leapt from my grasp and shot forward, stopping just shy of smacking the soldier in the nose.

His eyes widened with fear and awe as the Sacred Stone dipped and weaved and spun in a strange little dance. Green light charged out of the soldier and flowed into the stone, causing another section to glow with neon green light. The disturbing part was the green light connecting the soldier's eyes to the stone for three seconds. When the thing settled into its normal, non-flashy state, the soldier stared at me with a new intensity.

"Thou art the Chosen One." Dropping to one knee, he continued, "Forgive a wretch his wrongs when madness marked his way. Go in peace." Upon finishing his speech, the soldier rose, bowed, and vanished.

I blinked a few times to be sure he'd really disappeared. Shrugging, I moved on. A few more hallways passed without me meeting a soul, which I found creepier than meeting hordes of soldiers, especially because of the music change. Varick often chooses music that tugs one's heart in strange directions. This tune played reluctantly, like the one I sought wanted to remain hidden.

After a few pleas to Sonia for help, I found myself in front of a door. Haunting music reached through the door, lulling me into a peaceful state. I paused to listen to the soft chords filling the air.

"Judge not the young with eyes alone, but measure worth with heart and mind," instructed Sonia. "The power within can heal or harm. Choose wisely or suffer the consequences."

Inside the room, I found six identical children who claimed to be Michio. They made quite a racket trying to talk over each other, so I finally wished they'd all be quiet so I could think. The wish conjured six chairs, some rope, and sturdy, white cloths to use for gags. I hesitated for a second before willing the wish forward. Soon, all six tykes were strapped to chairs and mute. Nana would frown upon that method of child rearing, but I didn't have time to sort the answer out over cookies and tea. I knew instinctively that using the stone on the wrong Michio would reset the darn thing, making me track down the soldier and lady-in-waiting again.

Knowing Sonia could be quite literal sometimes, I took turns releasing the lads and questioning 'em. To aid my ears, I conjured an extra cloth to use as a blindfold for myself during the interrogations. They all did equally well on basic questions like age and current weather conditions, but only the real Michio could answer questions about TJ's favorite toys. Varick knew I had a dog, but Michio knew way more about him than Varick did. Problem solved, I applied the

Sacred Stone, filling up the power section with blue light.

The cook, who looked and talked an awful lot like Maisha, welcomed me like an old friend. We chatted as she filled the Sacred Stone with her purple light of wisdom. Before she faded away, she suggested I could find the last captive down in the dungeons. I'm not sure why it didn't occur to me to check for captives there first, but I'm glad I didn't 'cause it was the hardest one to fill.

The prison level was everything you'd expect from a futuristic palace obsessed with medieval times, except with less blood 'cause Varick's games keep to a Teen rating. I shoulda known who the prisoner would be, but surprise exploded within my avatar anyway.

Malia looked up and locked eyes with me as I approached. "I knew you would come," she said, smiling weakly. Her hair and features were different, older, and very beautiful. Long dark hair flowed downward in gentle waves, casting a shadow over her left eye. "I'm glad you did." Her voice hadn't started out strong, but her second statement was downright wispy.

I sprinted five steps closer then slammed to a halt when a wall of pure white energy produced a force field between us. Tentatively, I touched the field, receiving a medium-strength shock for my troubles.

"Ouch," I yelped. "That's gonna complicate things."

"Show me the Sacred Stone," Malia ordered.

As the stone cleared my pocket, it slipped from my fingers and slammed into the force field at waist height. Before I could stop her, Malia crossed the small prison cell and grasped the stone with her right hand.

We screamed at the same time, her from pain and me from helpless rage. My scream outlasted Malia's though 'cause she poured her concentration into filling the stone.

The whole force field filled with blinding yellow light.

I'm not sure how long it lasted, but I found myself kneeling an inch away from the buzzing field of light babbling, "Stop! Let go! Just let it go!" Tears blocked my vision. I dashed 'em away and squinted up at the Sacred Stone.

The light returned to normal levels, and that blasted stone had the nerve to hover near my head looking peaceful and cheerful.

Malia slumped to the ground dangerously near the force field.

"Why did you do it?" I whispered, as a dozen other "whys" bounced off each other in my head.

"Strength comes in many forms," Malia replied. "Some causes

are worth a little pain."

What I'd witnessed was much more than a little pain, but I didn't have the heart to argue with her. My fist closed around the Sacred Stone, and I woke up.

Chapter 19
Miracle Marbles

ITEM 153: Danielle's forty-third letter
Item Source: Danielle Matheson
Dear Dr. S.,

Christy and I called every family member, friend, and acquaintance who'd ever heard the word prayer and asked them to get busy. At Malia's suggestion, I even called Ann Duncan to request the names and numbers of some of her friends. Luckily, Ann was kind enough to offer to make those calls for me once she understood what I wanted.

As I finished my last call, Malia came up to me and quietly announced, "I am ready to explain more. May we speak in private?"

Avoiding Christy's curious glances, I led Malia into the restroom and shut the door. Since the only seat available was the lidless toilet, I leaned against the handrail lining the far wall.

"What's up?" I prompted, when Malia failed to start the conversation within two seconds.

"The plan is to perform many miracles," Malia explained.

"Isn't that counterproductive to the whole secrecy thing?"

"One miracle would be hard to hide, so we're going to perform many miracles," Malia replied.

I squinted at her, trying to unravel the tangled logic. "Wait a minute, let me get this straight. You're going to hide the healing of Christy's mother by healing other people?"

Malia shook her head. "No, we don't have the time or energy for that. Not all miracles are grand, unexplainable events. Nadia's made a list of things to do, small good deeds that when taken together must be seen as a miracle or a series of small miracles." Sensing my inability to immediately grasp her point, she continued, "Think of it this way. Imagine the healing of Christy's mother as a marble we need to keep safe. We could attempt hiding the marble in a pocket or a hiding place, but it may be safer in the company of a thousand other marbles."

The marble analogy helped slightly, but the idea of a thousand anything didn't sit well with me. Instead of dwelling on that, I asked, "How much can I tell Christy?"

"See if she and Dominique will join you in visiting some of the other patients. That is if you're willing to visit with other patients, of course. They could use the distraction, and Jillian, Michio, and I will need some time to prepare ourselves."

"Can we be here as you work?" I inquired, fearing her answer.

"Yes, you should all be present for the actual healing attempt," Malia said. "We will do that tonight, but it will be a very long afternoon if everybody stays here the whole time. I think Jillian, Michio, and I should stay in though because the people I sensed before are still here at the hospital."

"Do you know anything more about their intent?"

"No, but I feel it has something to do with Nadia being hard to contact right now," Malia noted.

"That's not good," I said, recalling the last time Nadia lost touch with her siblings.

"This isn't like before," Malia quickly assured me. "I can contact her, but she seems distracted. After giving me the list of people to help, she's left most of the planning to me. I have prioritized the list for you. It should be in your email now. Please click the link when you're finished with it."

"What will that do?" I asked, expecting a conspiracy theory answer.

Malia did not disappoint. "The link opens a program I designed that will delete all traces of the email ever being sent, received, or opened on your end and mine."

"Why would you need something like that?" I demanded, trying and failing at not sounding incredulous. My grip on the handrail tightened. *Who would care?* I silently added.

"Protection." Malia stared at me solemnly, and it struck me anew how unfairly life treated these children. No kid who'd barely made double digits should ever have to worry about erasing emails.

With a pink summer dress and some hair bows, Malia could fit right in with any of Katy's friends, except for those brooding dark eyes. There was absolutely nothing childlike about them. "The knowledge contained in some forms of communication could lead to very awkward questions if the wrong people found them."

"All right," I said, figuring too much caution better than none.

A knock on the door prevented further conversation, which is just as well. I don't think I had much more to say.

"Who is it?" I called.

"It's me," answered Jillian's voice. "Michio's gotta go twos."

I smiled and chuckled as Malia swung the door open to let Michio scamper in. We swiftly exited so the kid could handle his business in peace.

"Way too much information," I told Jillian.

She shrugged. "I didn't know how hard you'd be to convince."

"We were pretty much finished," I said, casting a look at Malia for confirmation.

Malia nodded agreement. "We may need to use some of the money Varick gave you, is that okay?"

"Sure, it's not my money."

"Yes, it is," Jillian argued. She glanced at Christy and Dominique who tried not to appear interested in the conversation. Lowering her voice, she added, "Varick gave it to ya to do some good. He's coming later to deliver more money and run a different errand. He wouldn't tell me what, but I guess it's important."

"Varick's coming here?" Christy asked.

For some reason, her excited, intrigued tone annoyed me. I'll have to do some soul-searching later on that one.

"Who's Varick?" Dominique's gaze bounced from Christy to me and back, trying to gauge who might answer her first.

Jillian beat us both to the explanation. "Varick's my brother."

"How many brothers do you have?" asked Dominique.

"It's complicated," Jillian and I answered together.

"Six," answered Malia a second later.

Dominique's eyes widened and she shook her head in awe. "That's a lot of brothers. Do you have a lot of sisters, too?"

"Varick's one of the brave men who rescued Danielle and me a few months ago," Christy gushed, before Jillian could answer Dominique's question with more than a nod.

"He helped," I acknowledged, eager to move on from the

101

current topic.

"He was wonderful," Christy insisted.

"Is he cute?" Dominique asked, eyeing Christy curiously.

"I'm cute!" declared Michio as he emerged from the restroom.

"Did you wash your hands?" Jillian asked.

Michio proved it by waving his hands above his head and showering us all with droplets of water, at least I hope it was water.

Catching his flailing arms, Jillian said, "We believe ya, thanks."

"I'm hungry. Feed me," said Michio.

"You had a sandwich an hour ago," Jillian pointed out.

"I know," Michio agreed. "Hungry again."

Rolling her eyes, Jillian shrugged and led Michio over to the food stockpile to forage.

"You didn't answer my question," Dominique said to her sister.

"He's very handsome," Christy admitted.

Her words sent a lot of strange emotions rushing through me. I tried to tamp them down, but I caught Malia looking at me with a cryptic expression.

"I'm going to visit a few of the other patients along this wing, you should come," I said, wincing at the poor transition. My voice sounded disturbingly unsteady.

"You've been here since last night, you should step out for a few minutes," Malia encouraged.

"We should stay with our mother," Christy argued.

"Jillian and I will stay and watch over your mother," Malia promised. "I have your cell number. I'll call you if you need to return unexpectedly."

I sensed Christy's resistance to the idea.

Brushing her hand along Christy's left arm, Malia said, "Please go. A walk will be good for you. Some of the people around here have no one to visit them."

"That's sad," Dominique commented.

"Very," Malia agreed. She maneuvered her skinny body between the sisters and picked up Dominique's right hand. "Your mother is blessed to have two daughters who care enough to spend long hours by her side."

I tried to catch Malia's eye to let her know she was overdoing it.

"You sound old," Dominique noted bluntly.

Malia smiled like it was the highest compliment. "Perhaps I have seen too much." She let her hands drop to her sides.

102

The Roman sisters nodded like her answer made sense, and before they could question Malia further, I swept them out of the room. As the door clicked shut behind me, I realized I had no idea where to go.

"Stay here," I ordered, reaching for the door handle. I whipped open the door and almost ran over Malia who stood there with my purse in hand.

"You will need this," she said, thrusting the purse at me.

I barely got my thanks out before she shut the door in my face. I would have been offended if I didn't understand her fear of letting Christy and Dominique slip back into the room.

"Where are we going?" Dominique wondered.

"I'll let you know soon," I answered, digging my phone out of my purse. Malia's email gave me a long list of names and brief descriptions of each situation. As promised, Malia had provided a suggested order for tackling them in. It took me a few minutes to decipher her system, but once it made sense, I realized she'd organized them by proximity to our current room. Taking a peek at the room number we were standing in front of and the one next door, I said, "Three rooms down on the left."

We practically ran down the hall like a band of teens released from school for the summer. I raised my hand to knock on the door.

"What are we going to do?" asked Dominique in a stage whisper.

"Visit with the woman inside," I replied, knocking three times.

"Are you ladies lost?" called a kind female voice from behind.

We jumped like kids with our hands pinched in a cookie jar. Dominique yelped, Christy gasped, and my hand flew to my chest to hold my heart in.

"Sorry," the nurse apologized. "I didn't mean to startle you, though I wish I had a camera."

"Hello, Nurse Keili," greeted Christy.

"We came to visit with Mrs. Carney," I explained.

"Oh, do you know her?" asked Nurse Keili.

"Not yet," I confessed uncomfortably. My mind raced for an explanation that didn't make me sound like a raving lunatic.

"I met her yesterday when she was walking the hall with her walker," Dominique piped up in her angelic voice. Maybe it just sounded that way because it saved me from saying something stupid.

"That's nice. She doesn't get many visitors," spoke the nurse. A shadow crossed her expression and her lips tightened like she wanted to hold back a negative comment. "Have a nice visit." This last part was spoken with extra cheer as she forced the emotions aside. With a tiny wave, she walked down the hallway to the room next door and entered.

Nadia's thoughts appeared in my mind. *Speak with her later. She will help you.*

We had a rather pleasant visit with Alice Carney. She seemed surprised at first, but it didn't take us long to get her talking. We heard about her two cats, Leo and Clyde, and her dog, Buster, who sometimes acted like a cat. She cried when I gave her the $92 to pay her electric bill, so she could keep the air conditioning on for her pets.

"How did you know?" Alice croaked the dreaded question as soon as she stopped sobbing.

Christy and Dominique's eyes echoed the question.

"A friend told me," I said vaguely. While technically true, I could tell the answer didn't satisfy any of them. "I can't reveal my source," I blundered on, feeling like a rookie reporter. Blood rushed to my cheeks, telling me my face would soon resemble sun ripened tomatoes. "My source heard of your need but wanted to remain anonymous, so they contacted me. We're just the messengers."

"Thank you," Alice whispered. "And please thank your source for me."

"I think my source already knows, but I will convey your thanks again," I promised. For the first time, I understood the appeal of speaking cryptically.

We talked for another half-hour or so before I managed to herd Christy and Dominique to the door so we could attend to our next errand.

I never considered how emotionally uplifting and draining doing good deeds could be. Throughout the afternoon, Christy, Dominique, and I delivered words of encouragement, smiles, and small sums of money to the desperately lonely souls populating the hospital. Mostly, we listened to their stories. Rich and poor stood on equal ground before the beast known as cancer. I could fill another hundred pages with their stories, but I'll sign off for now. The big night approaches and the children need to be fed again.

Yikes, that sounded entirely too parental.

The Good Will Distributor,

Danielle Matheson.

104

Chapter 20
A Second Council of War

ITEM 154: Jillian's seventy-seventh post-kidnapping journal entry
Item Source: Jillian Blairington

During one of my afternoon naps, I got summoned to a second council of war. It took place in the same conference room as the first one, but a lot more people showed up, even Naidine and Queen Elena. I wondered whether normal Nadia would show up as well, and she did in a way by asking me to bring Michio into the meeting. The task was super-easy to accomplish since he'd already fallen asleep again. That kid sure knows how to eat and sleep well. If I didn't know any better, I'd think he was training to be a Dream Shaper like me.

The only one not present who probably should have been was Danielle, but that couldn't be helped. She needed to keep Christy and Dominique Roman out of the room so they wouldn't be upset by the unusually deep sleep Malia, Michio, and I had to be in to attend the meeting. My Gift combined with Malia's help would allow me to wake everybody up instantly if necessary, but keeping the others out of the room seemed easier than having to explain.

Malia once again occupied the head position. Varick sat one chair down from her with Michio seated to his left and my right. To my left sat Naidine. Queen Elena had the end position directly opposite Malia. Even though the table sort of had two heads, Malia took control of the meeting.

"Thank you all for coming, and thank you Jillian and Nadia for making this possible," said Malia. "We are gathered to discuss the mission progress, some new information, and possible changes we need to make."

"What's wrong?" I demanded, pouncing on the serious tone. I managed to acknowledge her thanks without too much glaring.

When I bring people into a dream, they've got to be asleep, but since my work with Nadia, we've discovered that her Gift lets her use certain aspects of mine. I assumed Malia's thanks meant Nadia was allowing Varick to attend while maintaining consciousness.

Naidine answered, "The annual report did not go well."

I waited a few heartbeats for her to explain that statement, but when she didn't, I asked, "What's that mean?"

"There is a small chance government agents may interfere with your work in the hospital," Queen Elena explained.

"I may have felt two of them already," Malia said, referring to her shortened walk with Danielle this morning. "I just don't know what they wanted."

Everybody except Michio nodded. He sat in his booster seat and fiddled with some building blocks I'd given him.

"Right now, the men Malia saw are simply observing the visitors and waiting for more definitive orders," Naidine said.

"They have done nothing to cause concern, but their presence is disturbing," Queen Elena added.

"I'll avoid the government blokes to be safe, but I'm still going to the hospital," Varick declared. His dark green dress uniform with its shiny buttons lent his words more authority than blue jeans and a T-shirt would have.

On a whim, I imagined Malia, Michio, and I wore similar uniforms. Michio looked very cute exploring the buttons and shiny ribbons on the uniform jacket.

The task distracted me enough that I didn't get to ask Varick why he was coming before Malia said, "The main question is: do we move forward despite the government's interest in this hospital?"

"Yes," Varick and I answered simultaneously.

"No," answered Naidine with almost as much conviction as Varick and I had in our voices.

"No," breathed Queen Elena, looking like the word pained her.

"Yes. No. Yes. No," Michio chanted. "Maybe so!" He picked up a block in each hand and hurled 'em across the room where they bounced off the wall. I grabbed his hands to keep him from chucking more blocks. His vote didn't really count since he would fully support whatever decision we came to.

"Why do you want to stop now?" I asked, glancing back and forth between Queen Elena and Naidine. Casting a warning look at Michio, I let go of his hands.

He folded his tiny hands on the table and smiled at me in a way that made me wanna keep a dozen eyes on him.

"I am not comfortable with all of you being in the same place," Queen Elena admitted.

Naidine sighed before saying, "Malia has very good instincts. Like it or not, we have enemies who would take advantage of an opportunity like this."

"The risks versus the rewards are acceptable," Varick argued.

"If the government men represent a threat and act upon it, the projections are not favorable." Queen Elena's expression said she wanted to elaborate but didn't want to worry us by sharing those unfavorable projections. Slowly, she slid her gaze from person to person until she reached Malia. Her sad, knowing smile said she knew she was waging a losing battle. "You have the deciding vote, Malia."

"And as always, you have our full support in any action you choose to take," Naidine promised. Her words were like a comforting caress. It reminded me of a momma reaching out to lift up a discouraged child's chin.

Malia locked eyes with Naidine for a long moment. Finally, she said, "We move forward."

"Good," said Varick. "Now that that's settled, I should take my leave. Traffic's starting to pick up, and I'd like not to crash today." He disappeared before anybody could question his statement. Varick reappeared long enough to add, "You should let Michio go rest. He's going to have a long night."

Picking up on my concern for Varick, Queen Elena said, "Varick is operating a motorcycle. He will be fine, and you will see him soon."

"Too soon," commented Naidine. "There is much yet to discuss, but I agree with his point about Michio. If there are no objections, I believe we should release Michio to sleep. Would you mind arranging that, Jillian?"

I followed the instruction even as I wondered if talking to herself had ever bothered Nadia. Michio didn't really wanna leave the meeting, and he lodged his protest by tossing a block at my head. I turned it into a flower before it struck my face, but I decided the intent warranted a chat with Michio about appropriate behavior.

"Jillian, your role in the healing may have to be expanded." Queen Elena spoke gently, trying not to jar me too violently from my thoughts.

It didn't work, but I recovered quickly enough to object. "I'm not a healer."

"Perhaps not in the physical sense," Queen Elena granted.

"But you did teach Malia how to better control her nanomachines," Naidine continued.

"We need you to teach Michio," Malia finished.

"Teach him what?"

"You can teach Michio to harness the full power of his Gifts, like you taught me," Malia answered.

"Michio is very good at what he does, but he is still a distractible child," explained Queen Elena. "You must help him focus during the healing process. Malia can aid you, but she will also need to monitor the patient."

"This work must be accomplished much quicker than the work with Malia." Naidine spoke with speed to match her urgency.

"Why are you so worried?" I asked, not sure I wanted an honest answer. Glancing back and forth from one end of the table to the other bothered my neck, so I made the table smaller and round. This let me see Queen Elena, Naidine, and Malia at the same time. Queen Elena did a better job of hiding her worry than the other two. "What are you hiding from me?"

Queen Elena and Naidine shared a brief look and probably waged a lightning quick argument over whether to tell me or leave me hanging.

"We are moving soon," Naidine answered.

"Dr. Devya and Dr. Carnasis want to move everything to a secret lab," Queen Elena clarified.

"Ain't they all secret?"

"The government knows about most of the labs, but not all of them," Malia answered. "Nadia recently learned of at least a half-dozen labs that only Dr. Devya, Dr. Carnasis, and Cora know exist."

"The move to a secret lab could cause problems for our communication," said Queen Elena. Reading the confusion in my expression, she continued, "We are strong enough to maintain contact from anywhere in the world, but they will likely not leave Nadia conscious during such a complicated move."

I grunted and wanted to use one of my Old Daddy's

expressions of dismay, but Nana would disapprove of such unladylike words. Finding my way into unnaturally unconscious people's dreams ain't my favorite. It's very difficult to get into that kind of dream and like grabbing a greased snake trying to stay in one. Of course, a body's gotta be unconscious—or mostly so—for me to use my Gift, but trying to shift the sleep of a drugged person is like trying to lift bricks with my pinky. "Can't you just let Varick bust you out before the move?" I asked, only half-joking. Nadia had given her word to stay.

"This is not a concern for today," Queen Elena said. "We would not have mentioned it, but you asked why we are concerned with time."

"Concentrate on Michio's training," Naidine insisted.

"What will you be doing?"

"We will review the many projections and script several plans for exiting the hospital," Queen Elena informed. "With luck, we will not need them, but I have learned to never rely upon luck."

"And you?" I asked, looking to Malia.

"I have some patients and nurses to prepare for meeting Varick, Danielle, or the Roman sisters," Malia reported.

"We each have our tasks," Queen Elena noted, obviously meaning to conclude the council of war.

Everybody nodded, but nobody moved. I hardly dared to look at Queen Elena or Naidine, fearing the glimpse might be my last.

As the silence grew uncomfortable, I made the table and chairs disappear completely and threw myself at Queen Elena and Naidine. They vanished just as I reached 'em, and my hug encircled Nadia instead. "You stay in touch," I ordered hoarsely.

"You will be the first to know if anything happens," Nadia promised, returning my hug. "Be safe." With that simple farewell, Nadia stepped back and slowly faded from view.

Feeling Malia also withdraw from the dream, I figured I ought to get to work. Even so, I lingered in the deserted war room, letting the original table and chairs appear. The nameplates proudly declared each of our names, but the utter emptiness tugged at me.

Pushing the war room dream aside, I shifted my attention to finding Michio. He must have been waiting for me 'cause I sensed his invitation almost immediately.

I found myself in some tall grass, standing in front of a moat filled with evil looking, black water that bubbled. A colorful castle grew out of the ground on the opposite side of the moat.

"Nadia says you will train me," Michio said from atop the wall opposite my position. "Catch me first!" Flinging that challenge, Michio ran to his left into a wall of fog. A tall tower of more colorful bricks sprang to life.

"I do not have time to play games with you," I muttered, though it didn't surprise me that he was gonna be this way. At least he hadn't tried to set me on fire like Aiden would.

I imagined a big eagle that could fly me up to the tower top, but as I tried to climb onto its back, the ornery thing took off. I managed to grab its skinny left leg as it soared upward. Unhappy, the eagle tried to brush me off by barely skimming over the turret walls. I had to imagine the walls sinking a few feet to avoid injury. The eagle turned to try again. Figuring I'd be safer not fighting the stupid bird, I let go of its leg as soon as we reached the wall again. The eagle cawed in triumph and flew away.

"Good riddance," was all I had to say about the bird's getaway. I considered climbing the tower, but I honestly couldn't see the top from where I stood and didn't relish such a workout.

Next, I imagined a docile dragon to take me up to the tower top. The orange dragon that appeared beside me didn't look very docile, but it also didn't try to bite me as I climbed onto its back. Instead, it craned its neck around to look at me with big glassy, black eyes. To either side of me, stretching at least a car's length, the dragon's wings slowly beat at the air so it could hover in position.

Sighing, I said, "You ain't going anywhere, are ya?"

The dragon just looked at me with its scary looking teeth inches from my face.

I made it turn around and slid off its back. Then, I let it return to its normal nature, so long as it flew away from me.

The dragon shot upward so fast, I got flattened by the down draft. That's probably a good thing though 'cause the ear-splitting roar the dragon released woulda had the same effect.

Finally, I got smart and imagined that the top of the tower opened right next to me like one of the portals in *The Immortal Warrior* games. Nothing happened until I wished for the portal to release Michio. It spit him out like an unwanted guest.

"Cheater," Michio accused, landing on his knees at my feet.

"Efficient cheater," I corrected, reaching down to haul him up. "Quit fooling around. We've got work to do."

Chapter 21
Rooftop Rendezvous

ITEM 155: Danielle's forty-forth letter
Item Source: Danielle Matheson
Dear Dr. S.,

If breaking into a restricted area of a hospital was ever on my bucket list, I can now cross that off. Two minutes after finishing my fine cafeteria chef's salad, I leaned back against the wall and shut my eyes to rest.

Nadia's voice once again appeared in my mind like my own thoughts. *Varick is about to arrive at the hospital, but he would like a word with you on the roof before attending to his first order of business.*

I flinched, drawing strange looks from Christy and Dominique. Malia hid a knowing smile behind her bottle of apple juice and nodded encouragingly. Making a show of stretching, I pushed myself upright. My left knee cracked in protest, but I finished the arduous task of getting up. I had about a dozen questions for Nadia, but I couldn't sense her, which left only one way to get answers.

"I'm going to take a walk. I'll be right back," I informed the room at large. Striding out the door, I hoped Nadia would tell me which way to go very soon.

"Go left," Malia instructed softly, following me out the door. Once again, she held my purse out to me.

"I thought you didn't want to leave the room," I noted, trying to still my rattled nerves. I accepted my purse and slung the strap across my neck so I wouldn't have to carry the thing.

"I don't, but you won't get to the roof without me," Malia

replied, drawing even with me.

Conceding the point, I moved on, letting Malia lead the way. She set a pretty fast pace for a kid with such twig-like legs. As we reached the end of the hallway, we arrived at a door with a serious looking lock on it. An EMPLOYEES ONLY sign dominated the space at eye level, nearly obscuring a tiny sign by the handle that said: roof access. Without hesitation, Malia touched the lock. A dull, click-thud noise announced the deadbolt retreating. Twisting the handle, Malia swung the door outward and waved for me to enter.

"I'm going to lock the door behind you, but I'll return to let you out later," Malia said. "I need to get back now."

Before I could argue, the door swung shut and locked. Somehow, that lock-moving noise sounded more sinister the second time. Darkness closed around me, only slightly alleviated by dim lights lining the railing and stairs leading up. Not really having the option to go back at this point, I grasped my slippery courage and climbed up the stairs. The strangeness of the situation made my heartbeat sound unnaturally loud.

If something had jumped out at me right then, I would have had a heart attack or fainted. When I reached the top, it took me a few seconds to find the handle. Once my hand had found the cool piece of metal, I paused to breathe a sigh of relief, twisted the handle down, and gently pushed. When the door refused to budge, I pushed harder, eventually bringing my left shoulder to bear. Panic made me brace my legs on the top step and push even harder. Still, the door didn't budge.

Pull.

The single-word instruction burned through the panic. Breathing hard and feeling like an idiot, I followed the instruction. The door obediently swung inward. I wasted no time in stepping outside into the soupy air. Coming from the climate controlled interior to the great outdoors took some adjusting. The sticky air made me feel gross, like I'd come from an hour-long cardio workout.

The sun hadn't quite surrendered for the day, though it was on the way down. At least the view made up for the discomfort. From up here, I could see for miles in every direction. The forest stretching behind the hospital looked like a plush, green carpet running right to the ends of the earth. Even the sprawling parking lots and endless stretches of highway seemed quaint from this distance.

"I like to come to places like this," Varick commented.

I tried to suck in a sharp breath but the thick air refused to be hurried. My heart tripped over itself for the third time in about ten minutes, but I managed not to scream. Spotting Varick perched on the roof's edge, I made my way over to him, going slower as I neared the brink.

Clearing my throat and trying desperately not to look down as I inched forward, I asked, "You like to come to hospitals?" I forced my gaze to stay on those friendly forested mountains in the distance.

"Places with views like this," Varick clarified, turning toward me. He shifted to a sideways position on the wall, left leg dangling toward the inside and right knee bent. "The climb makes me feel free."

My attention veered back to Varick. "You climbed up here?" I asked, not bothering to tone down the disbelief.

"There are emergency stairs over there," Varick said, gesturing somewhere behind me.

"Did you use them?" I questioned, picking up on a strange note in his voice.

He grinned in answer, showing off a row of perfectly maintained pearly whites. I couldn't help smiling back and tried to hide the sad wave that hit me from nowhere. I hadn't spent much time around Jillian's brother, but that was the first time I noted him ever looking relaxed. The look suited him. I even forgave him for looking neat and collected while I felt like a waterlogged dog placed in a sauna.

Varick swung both legs in so that his back faced the spectacular forest view. "Come sit," he offered, gesturing to the empty space next to him.

"No thanks. I'm good here," I said, trying not to sound nervous.

Varick's blue eyes crinkled at the edges with amusement. "Are you afraid of heights?" That blasted British accent lent an exotic flavor to the innocent question. A warm breeze stirred the thick air enough to ruffle his short blond hair.

"Heights don't bother me, but the idea of falling does," I said, resisting the urge to back up a step. Needing to change the subject, I continued, "Anyway, Nadia said you wanted a word with me. What can I do for you?"

"I have an introduction to make," Varick announced. He dismounted and knelt by a blue backpack leaning innocuously against the wall.

I'd noticed the backpack, of course, but I'd ignored it to this point. It's not unusual to see Varick traveling with a backpack. He tends to have a lot of stuff to carry, and he's not exactly the fanny-pack type. I thought over his short statement and consistently drew a blank on what it could mean.

Varick spent an inordinate amount of time bent over the backpack, fiddling around in its guts. When he straightened and rose to a standing position, his arms cradled a small bundle of cloth. The bundle shifted and started making annoyed, fussy noises.

"This is our new sister, Anastasia." Varick turned the bundle so I could see the itty-bitty scrap of humanity. "Her name would have been Renee, but this one fit better."

Anastasia squinted up at me with beautiful dark peepers and ceased thrashing long enough to give me a measuring stare. Concluding I didn't have much to offer her, she scrunched her tiny face up and whined at Varick.

General niceties got stuck in my throat. I wanted to say she was adorable, because that much held truth, but my thoughts had trouble moving past the sight of the small bundle coming from that backpack. "You put a baby in a backpack," I murmured, trying to make what I'd just seen conform to logic. "*Why* would you put a baby in a backpack?"

"It's not an ordinary backpack," Varick said, sounding offended on the thing's behalf. "Come see."

I plodded over obediently and saw that the inside had been greatly modified. A cocoon or peapod would be a decent analogy for the inside of Varick's backpack. A small control panel blinked with green and orange lights.

"There's an envelope for you along with a set of clothes and a fresh nappy in the bottom compartment. Would you fetch them please?"

Hearing the term "nappy" coming from Varick drained much of my irritation with him. Eventually, I found the correct compartment and pulled out a letter-sized envelope bulging with cash, a white dishtowel, the tiniest outfit I'd ever seen, and a diaper that easily fit in the palm of my hand.

Naturally, I opened the envelope and thumbed through the money. It came out to two thousand dollars. "What's this for?" I asked, wishing my voice were stronger.

"Food, supplies, small gifts, and emergency travel expenses," Varick replied, keeping his attention on the baby. "You may not need it, but it's best to be prepared."

Agreeing with him, I stuffed the envelope into my purse along with the sad remains of the money left over from the glove compartment allotment. Turning my attention to the other items I'd removed from the backpack, I placed the dishtowel on the hard roof and laid the diaper and a light green baby onesie out on the towel. "These wouldn't even fit a chunky doll."

"They'll do for her." Varick sounded distracted. "She's a month early, but it couldn't be helped." He knelt down, gathered the clothes and diaper in one hand and folded the cloth over in half. Then, he eased the baby onto the cloth's center.

Anastasia gurgled and jammed a fist in her mouth to gnaw at her knuckles. I noticed a friendship bracelet wrapped about a dozen times around her tiny wrist and wondered where she'd gotten it.

"Would you like to change her or shall I?" asked Varick.

"You can do it," I said, feeling like a coward. "I feel like I'd break her. She's so tiny." My diaper changing experience is up to date, but even one-week-old Isaac Spencer Blairington was a giant compared to this kid.

"Babies are heartier than people think," Varick said. "And Anastasia's been given a treatment to keep her in good health until we can get her to a family." He proceeded to strip off the baby's clothes, change her diaper, and slip her into the new duds with the speed and efficiency of a soldier cleaning and reassembling a handgun.

The word "we" repeated on loop in my head, but I dared not say it out loud, lest he tell me his purpose here. All I wanted to do was watch him care for his baby sister. He handled the infant with practiced ease, occasionally making faces at her to hold her attention. Before I knew it, Varick placed the baby in my arms and began gathering up the supplies. He tucked the dirty diaper into a plastic bag before wrapping it in the towel along with the old clothes. Then, he stuffed everything into his backpack and strapped the thing onto his back. He looked ready to embark on a long hike.

Anastasia stared up at me with trust and curiosity in her gorgeous gray eyes. Her miniature nose twitched as her mouth gaped open for a huge yawn. She blinked at me, mewled, and nestled closer. If any moment could be described as perfect, that was it. Strange emotions welled up in me. I don't believe in love at first sight, but that baby girl had my heart wrapped around her delicate little fingers. I wanted to protect her from all life's dangers, but part of me knew I could do precious little for her. That terrified me.

"I'm sorry, Danielle, but I wanted you to understand." Varick came over and slipped a cap onto Anastasia's fuzzy head. Repossessing the baby, he wrapped her in a white blanket with a silky pink border.

My arms felt empty and cold, despite the warm air pressing close around me. My heart actually ached with the loss. It made no sense. "What do I need to understand?" I futilely wished my throat didn't hurt like I'd swallowed a cactus.

"Why we took her away," Varick replied.

"Why did you?" I asked, simply because I knew he wanted me to. I couldn't spare much emotion for the conversation. My eyes still locked on the baby resting quietly in Varick's arms. *And why must I understand?* I wanted to puzzle over the question but couldn't spare the energy for that task either.

"Anastasia means 'resurrection,' " Varick explained. "She was meant to have Gifts like Nadia, but one of the scientists sabotaged the project."

Anger shot through me, but I managed to keep my voice civil as I asked, "Is she all right?" She looked perfectly normal to me. "What went wrong? Why didn't Nadia stop it?" Outrage made each question sharper than the last.

"Nadia was in a coma," Varick reminded. He tucked the baby close with his left arm, reached for my clenched right fist with his free hand, and started leading me back toward the stairs.

"Oh." I mentally kicked myself for having forgotten that fact.

"And I don't know what Dr. Parris did to Anastasia. I think he was withholding treatments that would allow her easy access to her Gifts." Varick stopped his story long enough to release my hand and push through the door to the stairs. As he stood holding the door for me, he gazed down fondly at Anastasia. "She will certainly be intelligent. She may even be able to use some of her Gifts one day, but to them, she's broken because she will never have complete control over her Gifts."

Not eager to enter the dark stairwell, I halted in the threshold to take in the sight of Anastasia in the weakening evening light. "You mean she's healthy?" Hope brightened my tone.

"Perfectly healthy."

As we watched the baby sleep, the full meaning of Varick's errand struck me. "You're here to give her away!"

"Yes, and that is why you are here as well."

"I can't—"

"She will be safer with others." Varick's voice contained

sadness and strength.

"But she's your sister. You can't just give her away like—"

Varick caught one of my flailing arms. "We are not abandoning her, Danielle." He paused to let the words take effect, slowly releasing his hold on my wrist. "This is the best protection we can give her. Will you help me?"

Nodding stiffly, I trembled as Varick plopped Anastasia into my outstretched arms. In a daze, I slowly crept down the stairs, praying I wouldn't drop the baby. As I reached the bottom, the door swung open, revealing Malia. She reached out and steadied me, blasting away my anxiety and replacing it with purpose.

"They are waiting," said Malia. "Follow me."

"Her things are in here," Varick called from over my shoulder.

I turned in time to see him hand Malia the blue backpack before retreating up the stairs. "Why can't Varick make the delivery?"

Malia plucked the baby from my arms and held the backpack out to me. She said nothing while helping me climb into the backpack and adjust the straps, but as she handed me Anastasia, Malia answered, "We will all watch over her from afar, but the more layers between us the better for now." Malia briefly held one of Anastasia's tiny hands before adding, "You must make the delivery to Nurse Keili alone and insist on anonymity. She will do the rest."

The actual handoff was surprisingly easy but also heart-wrenching. Nurse Keili didn't want to take her at first, but after hearing the cover story Nadia provided, she accepted Anastasia and even called her an answer to prayer. Apparently a family about to adopt a newborn had just been devastated by news that the biological mother had reconsidered and was keeping her little girl. Nurse Keili had rushed off to catch the couple before they left.

Everything in me wanted to watch the exchange, but I returned to home base to write you instead because I was dying to tell somebody. Christy and Dominique must have gone out to visit more people, but I'll have to find them soon.

Jillian, Michio, and Malia are ready to start the healing.

The Emotionally Drained One,

Danielle Matheson.

Chapter 22
Conquer the Hordes

ITEM 156: Jillian's seventy-eighth post-kidnapping journal entry
Item Source: Jillian Blairington
Even with Nadia's hints and Malia's encouragement, training Michio turned out to be a great deal harder than training Malia. I don't understand how some people spend most of their waking hours with multiple children Michio's age. One four-year-old can be exhausting. I can only imagine the stress multiplied tenfold.

Michio's mind kept changing scenes like someone flipping TV channels at random. One minute we'd be in the Wild West shooting down cancer cells with target signs on their chests and the next minute we'd be in a pool the size of a parking lot trying to rescue healthy cells before they got drowned in bad cells. Next, we could be in outer space fighting off an endless stream of cancer cells coming out of a city-sized asteroid. Just as likely, we could be on a grassy meadow out under an intense sun trying to use mirrors to melt an ice giant. The scenes got weirder from there.

I guess it's partly my fault for giving Michio so many analogies about what we needed to do, but he could have helped by picking one. At least I got some good data from the exercises. Malia had written a program that let me track Michio's mood and the time spent on each scene. That helped me choose the simulations to run for Michio during the actual healing. Nadia had suggested making it like one of Varick's video games, and I agreed that turning the fight into a game would help Michio work. Even though we weren't really tricking him, I felt guilty for making him work so hard.

If we coulda done the healing without him, we certainly would have, but none of our Gifts directly involved physical healing. Only Aiden has a Gift like Michio, but he's still stuck in the lab they have Nadia in. Besides, Aiden's even younger than Michio. A year can make a big difference when it's a quarter or a third of a person's life.

I idly wondered if this sort of work would be harder or easier with Aiden present. On the one hand, having more help could be great. Then again, directing a second small child didn't sound like fun. As I wondered if Aiden would feel left out, Nadia told me she was working closely with him to better instruct me. Guess this makes it a whole family affair.

Only Benny Connelly, Dustin, and Anastasia aren't helping. Benny's not really been trained yet, but I can't fault him for that 'cause he's a Dream Shaper like me. My training started a little over a year ago. Dustin's always done his own thing. Even though Anastasia's only a few days old, she might have been able to help if she had all her Gifts, but we don't know if she'll ever learn how to access any of her Gifts, let alone all of 'em. My mind woulda fully wandered onto that problem, if Nadia hadn't refocused me. Can't blame Michio for all the distraction, I suppose.

Danielle woke us up for dinner. She'd run down to the cafeteria and selected a few salads. Since none of the salads appealed to Michio and we figured we owed him, Danielle let him choose what else we ordered. I thought he'd say pizza or chicken wings, but instead, he chose Chinese food. Dominique seconded his choice, so Danielle looked up a local place on her phone and let Dominique and Michio make our selections. Michio wanted sweet and sour chicken and lo mein, and Dominique wanted beef with broccoli. Danielle checked her cash supply then added some fried dumplings, three vegetable egg rolls, and a pack of crispy noodles.

Michio and I got through another three mini-training exercises before Danielle woke us up again. At Danielle's insistence, Christy swiped some crispy noodles and a few pieces of sweet and sour chicken and added it to her boring garden salad. Malia munched on a Greek salad. Despite a lack of hunger, I forced myself to eat two dumplings and an egg roll. Maisha woulda yelled if she knew I intended to work without eating well, so I also ate part of a Caesar salad too.

Dominique took it upon herself to help Michio with his dinner, which pleased me just fine. It worked out for everybody. Dominique got to dote, Michio got to make a mess, and Malia and I got to eat in peace. I had fun watching Michio slurp lo mein noodles from a distance outside the splash zone. He even made Dominique laugh by flinging crispy noodles at her with his plastic fork. Danielle had stepped out for her walk by this time, but I knew she wouldn't have approved. I thought Christy might stop the children, but I think she was simply relieved to see her sister laughing. Eventually, I stopped 'em, but only 'cause they were getting loud. I also didn't fancy getting into trouble with the nice nurses.

I helped Christy clean up the room while Dominique took Michio to the restroom to rinse off his face and get the worst of the sauce stains out. Then, Christy and Dominique went to visit some patients, while Michio and I did some last minute training. When Danielle returned, she seemed unusually quiet. She's not the sort to bounce off walls, but she came in very subdued, sat down, and buried her face in her iPad. That typically means she's writing Dr. S., so I didn't interrupt her. Even though nobody said anything, I felt the healing time fast approaching.

As I started thinking somebody ought to fetch Christy and Dominique, they returned to the room looking nervous.

"Is it time?" asked Dominique.

"How does this work?" Christy wanted to know. Her eyes sought answers from me.

In turn, I looked to Malia.

Waving Danielle over, Malia said, "I think this will work best if Michio lies on the bed over here." She patted the right side of the bed close to the patient's left side. "Jillian can pull up a chair next to Michio, and Danielle can sit at the end of the bed. She'll need to get up to explain to the nurses from time to time. I will be next to Danielle on that side." Malia pointed to the side where Christy and Dominique typically camped out. "Danielle, would you mind getting me a towel?"

"One towel coming up." Danielle went to the restroom to raid the towel rack.

Malia accepted the towel with a nod of thanks and finished her assignments by saying, "Christy and Dominique, you can both take your usual positions. Is that all right?"

"What can we do?" Christy's wavy tone said she worked awfully hard to keep a hold on her emotions.

"You're going to help me comfort your mother," Malia answered. "She has fought this disease for a long time. What we plan to do may frighten her. You can help me keep her calm, so Michio and

Jillian can attack the cancer directly."

"Can you do that?" Dominique asked, sounding awed and frightened. She addressed the question to Michio and me.

Michio smiled brightly and nodded with his whole body. Then, he clambered up onto the bed to take the position Malia had indicated for him. "Sleepy time!"

I worried that he'd fling himself down next to the sick lady, but Malia said, "Gently, Michio."

The simple reminder drew another eager nod from Michio, and he slowly eased down next to Christy and Dominique's momma. I admired his bravery. Most people act real strange around very sick people, but Michio nestled against the lady's side, taking her left hand in his right one and tenderly draping his left arm across her stomach.

"Before you begin, I wanted to thank you for everything. I-I know we may not remember and it might not even work, but thank you for trying." Christy couldn't manage more words, so she stumbled over to her assigned position and sat down beside her momma.

"Why wouldn't we remember?" Dominique wondered.

"I'll explain later," Danielle answered. She took Dominique by the shoulders and sat her in the chair next to Christy.

"Try to relax as best you can," Malia instructed. "Jillian will help you sleep now."

Taking my cue, I reached out with my Gift and locked on to Christy and Dominique. Slowly, so as not to scare 'em, I carefully let sleep overtake first Christy, then Dominique. I wasn't quite so gentle with Malia and Michio 'cause they had a lot more experience feeling my Gift. Finally, Danielle and I completed the circle of slumbering people around the patient. As agreed earlier, I kept Danielle at the lightest level of sleep so she could intercept nurses and visitors.

The dream we entered technically belonged to Susan Kilpatrick, the patient, but mostly, it was my creation. I believe that dream was the most complicated work I've ever done. It might have been simpler to leave Christy, Dominique, and even Danielle out of it, but Malia insisted they could help soothe the patient. Part of my attention stayed with the non-combatants, making sure they kept safe, but the lion's share went to helping Michio fight the cancer cells.

Since Michio responded best to the scene with hordes of aliens overrunning a small human settlement on a grassy planet, I went with that one first. Together, Michio and I let him live up to his name, which can mean "man with strength of three thousand." He ain't a

121

man yet, but I imagined him looking like he would at age twenty-three. Next, I stuck him in a suit of ancient armor and multiplied the image by three thousand. Finally, I loosed my new army on the cancer cells.

If it had been Varick's game, Michio probably woulda had a plasma gun to go blasting the cancerous aliens, but I wanted him to get real close to 'em at the start. Nadia supplied me with a lovely list of weapons from several eras, including swords (katana), throwing blades (shuriken), spears (yari), and sickles with attached blades (kama). Basically, anything that could chop, cut, or stab ended up being issued to the Michio army.

Most people don't know they have a lot of control over their dreams or the dreams of others they become guests in. Michio doesn't have this problem. He quickly learned that he could change the soldiers' weapons and armor to anything he liked. Soon enough, the army looked more like a Halloween costume party featuring armed Asian men. World War I German stormtroopers fought alongside modern US soldiers in desert camouflage, and French resistance fighters joined forces with Roman officers and Spartan troops.

At first, I tried to change 'em back, but I soon learned that I ain't an expert on killing things and accepted that maybe my little brother could teach me a thing or two about it. That is definitely something I'm leaving out of my account if I ever tell Nana.

For a while there, it was the strangest army ever assembled, but Michio is a quick learner. He and I studied each soldier and measured the ability for destruction, selecting for strength, speed, intelligence, and efficiency. Pretty soon, we took the attributes we wanted and formed a futuristic, lightly armored, well-armed soldier type and let each pick their own weapon from across the spectrum of weapons that existed in my memory banks. I brought that part with me courtesy of Nadia, seeing as the patient likely lacked that knowledge.

Of note, I observed that about half the soldiers opted for small firearms and the other half chose one-handed swords. When I asked a representative from each type, their answers were eerily similar.

The sword-wielding Michio soldier said, "There's something immensely satisfying about slashing the head off alien scum."

The gun-toting soldier likewise responded, "Who doesn't love to shoot aliens in the face?"

Slightly disturbed, I let both soldiers return to their work and concentrated on directing larger groups. One would think the soldiers would choose a faster firing weapon like an assault rifle, but both

Michio and I kept a tight hold over which cells got destroyed and which got spared. Fast-firing weapons aren't very helpful with making such decisions.

I can't tell ya how long we worked 'cause I didn't exactly keep track of the time. I can say I am mighty proud of Michio. The little guy fought with the heart of a warrior and the compassion of a papa guarding his only child. Though I gussied up the fight in flashy video game scenes, it came down to a strange sort of surgery. Michio and I worked our way through the patient cell by cell, evaluating whether or not it was cancerous, and executing the bad cells.

Danielle woke Michio from time to time so he could drink. I used those times to check on Malia and the others. Malia had the other difficult job. Under Nadia's direction, she drew the dead cells from the patient's body and directed 'em into the towel Danielle had removed from the restroom. Malia never once complained, but the task cost her much in terms of mental strain and physical energy. One of my latest Gift manifestations is the ability to track a sleeper's stress levels. I think it came about in response to working closely with Malia on Nadia's behalf.

In any case, I desperately wanted to help Malia, but Michio required most of my attention. His breaks were never long enough for me to do much for Malia. He got bored with the war on the grassy plain, so I moved him to a forest. When that got old, I sent him to a planet with exploding volcanoes and then to a place with icy snowdrifts everywhere. The final confrontation took place in the tight confines of narrow mountain passages.

Through every new place I imagined, I let music suggested by Varick rule the airwaves. It not only helped inspire the soldiers, it drowned out the terrifying sounds of war. Nothing likes to die, even a cancer cell. Cancer is an enemy that wants to consume, grow, spread, and consume some more. To stand in its way and say "No more!" takes weapons the world has never seen and soldiers it could never imagine, people like Michio, Malia, Nadia, and me.

Chapter 23
Quiet Morning for Moral Questions

ITEM 157: Danielle's forty-fifth letter
Item Source: Danielle Matheson
Dear Dr. S.,

Good morning. I see from the time stamp on your email that we were not the only ones having a late night yesterday. However, I must say that last night was the first excellent night's rest I've had in a long while. I'm not saying I got a lot of sleep, but the five or so hours that I did get were rejuvenating. I'm certain I have Jillian to thank for the unusually deep sleep, and I'm still battling mild guilt that she had to waste time and energy helping me get to sleep. It's a silly notion, I know, but it brings me back to your inquiries about my feelings on the issues of lying and morality.

First, allow me to apologize for dodging the issues thus far. The last few days I've been too tired to think about much of anything except preparing the children for their monumental task. Now that the healing is either well under way or complete, I can at last honestly say I've given your questions some thought. I can't know for sure if the healing is complete, as I'm currently the only conscious person in the room. I probably ought to still be slumbering, but I'm too wired to rest. It's like Christmas morning only forty times worse. I want to know if the healing worked. Since I won't know for a while, I may as well give you a thorough answer.

Before the fateful day Jillian and I wound up drugged and swept off to Devya's laboratory lair, my views on lying were Sunday-school simplistic. All lies are evil. While many lies stem from selfish desires and lead to destructive paths, my views have expanded to include the idea that sometimes lies are necessary evils. I acknowledge that even a well-intended lie can misfire, but between a rock and a hard place one must simply choose their flavor of pain, so to speak.

You may ask from whence this enlightened viewpoint springs, and I shall answer: Nadia. From a certain point of view, that girl is a chronic liar. She's very honest about being a chronic liar, and that's the confusing part. Take the cover story for Anastasia. Simply put, it's a lie. There is no desperately shy and ashamed young mother who abandoned her child on the hospital's threshold, eager to let the infant live but unable to raise her.

Truth can be troublesome. Most people don't deal well with the unknown, the unusual, the strange, or anything different from the confines of their own knowledge. I don't know much about Anastasia, but I'm told she's a "sabotaged" project from Devya's labs. If I'd told Nurse Keili the truth about Anastasia's origin and she in turn told the new parents, one or both parties would at best throw up their hands and back away slowly. At worst, they'd check me for a fever and show me to the psych ward, leaving that poor baby to the mercy of the foster system. I don't blame them for this reaction. I'm just trying to give you an example of troublesome truth.

From a kinder point of view, Nadia's a storyteller, a wordsmith who invents tales that make people want to do what's right. This doesn't mean she's going to strip a person's mind down to nothing and make them her mental slave. I doubt her Gift even covers something like that, even if one could rationalize such a feat.

In the last few months, I'm sure I've lied on Jillian's behalf. I know her parents failed to tell her school the real reason for her long absence. They wouldn't understand. That can be dangerous logic, but not in this case. On the one hand, my young friend and her beautiful siblings are symbols of scientific achievement. They're also people, children with wants, needs, and more to fear from the world than it has to fear from them.

In an ideal world, Jillian, Michio, Malia, and the rest of the children—Varick included—would be nurtured and accepted for who they are, not where they came from. Their Gifts would be celebrated and supported, and they could live happily ever after. The world we live in, however, quite obviously not an ideal one, would swallow them whole, suck out every last drop of talent and ingenuity, and then abandon them.

Protecting their secret has become paramount in the effort to safeguard the children. Since that involves telling lies or at least not always telling whole truths, I accept these as part of my new life.

In regards to your question about the difference between knowledge and wisdom, I'll admit you had me stumped for a long time. Without having a dictionary in front of me and being too lazy to pull up the app, I'll define them as best I can. I categorize knowledge as a body of facts, figures, and other pieces of information, mental tools if you will indulge the analogy. Wisdom is the skill of knowing when and how to wield such tools.

Jillian and her siblings collectively had the knowledge to heal Christy's mother from her cancer. Whether or not attempting to do so was wise has yet to be determined. You may think me a fool for continuing to worry over this point, especially now that it's too late to change, but I can't help it. I need to worry. We're purposefully keeping the Blairington and Davidson households in the dark here, so I inherited the parental right to worry.

Fending off the nurses was an incredibly easy job compared to the others. I merely convinced Nurse Keili of our intent, and she did the rest. I think Nadia prepared her ahead of time. Sometimes, I wonder how vast a network of contacts Nadia keeps. Soon thereafter, I tend to come to my senses and conclude that this is an *ignorance is bliss* situation.

The only question on your list I could answer immediately and emphatically was the one about being jealous of the children's Gifts. No. I'm probably one of the few people in history to never wish I had superpowers. If forced to choose one, I'd go with healing, but even my fondness for that one is quickly waning after witnessing Michio's battle last night. The kid soaked two fresh towels with sweat from the strain. Nurse Keili had wanted to put Michio on an IV drip, but I just woke him up long enough to pour some Gatorade down him.

I'm too much of a realist to stay in the dreamy state of enamorment with powers and Gifts I don't comprehend. I love knowing Nadia, but I think being her would melt something vital in my brain.

Having Varick's survival skills would be neat. It must be nice knowing that your body can handle crazy physical demands, but fear and paranoia travel with such knowledge. How can you trust people if you possess foreknowledge of their evil intent? I'm not even sure how he can hold a conversation with an annoying person and not obsess over knowing a hundred and one ways to kill the twit. That level of power must be terrifying.

Jillian once told me that she and Nadia destroyed a mental code that taught Nadia how to kill a person with a thought. That sounds like a disastrous recipe to me. The world's lucky these kids come with a decent set of morals. I find that ironic, since their creation can be seen as highly unethical.

I should cease rambling about morality and make my morning cafeteria run now. The natives are stirring. That's a relief. I was getting lonely here. I've been washed, dressed, and wide awake for at least an hour. My stomach's queasy with raw nerves.

Jillian and the others make for a very eerie sight. They're still arrayed around Christy's mother like exhausted refugees. The formerly white towel I gave to Malia last night is now yellow with a crust of dead cells, the only evidence of their work. Christy's mother sleeps on, though her breathing seems to be less labored. Christy and Dominique are curled up together in Christy's chair. Malia and Jillian maintain almost identical poses at the bottom of the bed. Their arms cross to form a pillow and their heads rest on their arms, facing toward the patient. They're both awake and waiting, but I'm not sure why they're waiting.

The Watcher,
Danielle Matheson.

Chapter 24
Complications

ITEM 158: Jillian's seventy-ninth post-kidnapping journal entry
Item Source: Jillian Blairington
Upon waking up from the long night, I let myself rest on the bed and think. Michio didn't want to wake up just yet, and Malia lay across from me also awake but saying nothing. My connection to Malia let me feel Danielle's anxiety, but she slipped out of the room before I could assure her we had succeeded. I hesitated to make any such announcement 'cause even though I thought we'd gotten rid of every cancer cell, the patient remained unconscious.

"Jillian, a word," said Malia, drawing my head up with her soft words.

Forcing myself up with a groan, I looked hard at my sister, trying to get information from her expression. She merely rose gracefully, grabbed a brush from her suitcase, and padded over to the restroom. Curious, I followed her into the tiny room and sat down on the only seat available, the toilet. It's a little strange to use a toilet for a seat, but we'd been living close enough these last few days to make the awkwardness familiar.

Malia spent a few minutes setting her long, dark hair in order before turning her attention to my messy bed head. I chuckled but let her fuss over my stubborn hair. She continued slowly running the brush through my hair long after the last knot called it quits. The old me woulda demanded she speak her mind, but I'm starting to recognize Malia as someone with a sensitive soul. Nana says the best way to handle a sensitive soul is to wait 'em out.

"My fears are coming true."

I winced as much from Malia's gloomy opening statement as from the surprise twinge from a few angry hairs yanked the wrong direction. Much as I wanted an explanation, I knew frustration and firmness wouldn't help Malia share her burdens. "What fears?" I asked, going for a gentle tone.

Instead of explaining, Malia put down the brush and inquired, "May I cry? It will level my emotions."

Shooting her a look that said it was the oddest request I'd heard this week, I said, "It's all right with me." Sensing she wanted more than mere approval, I added, "What should I do?"

Malia double checked that the door was closed and motioned for me to sit on the floor. "If you're willing, sit there and hold my hands. Do not be afraid."

I sat where she wanted me to sit and held my hands out, palms facing up. Folding herself to a kneeling position, Malia grasped my hands and started weeping. I'm not talking one or two tears slipped out sort of crying. This was the muscles-locking, shoulders-shaking, quiet sobbing that usually speaks of disaster, devastation, or death. She crushed my hands with the force of her grip. I wanted to shush her, but I knew she needed this cry. Momma has spells like this from time to time, but I found it disturbing coming from Malia. She's one of the most emotionally stable people I know.

When I felt my fingers losing feeling, I worked my knees under me and tugged Malia into a hug. She threw her arms around me and held on like I was a fireman come to haul her out of a burning building. We stayed that way until my knees felt as if they'd stay locked forever. I pulled Malia to a standing position and let her finish her cry in my arms, soaking my poor shirt. When she finally stilled for a full minute, I said, "You ready to talk about these fears?"

Loosening her fierce grip on me, Malia stepped back and smiled. "I am, but let me clean up first." She turned to the sink and rinsed her face off, laughing when she realized there was no towel.

"I'd offer you my shirt, but I don't think it'd help ya much," I noted, smiling to let her know I was teasing.

"Thank you," Malia said with sincerity that went much deeper than acknowledgement of my silly shirt offer. She swiped her damp hands over her face to get the worst of the water off. "I needed that."

"We all need that sometimes," I said with a half-shrug.

"Today is certainly such a day."

"Which of your fears are coming true?" I prompted, worried by her weary tone.

"A lot of them," Malia admitted, attempting a smile. "The healing worked in so far as the cancerous cells are gone, but the patient's immune system is fighting back harder than expected. Michio will need more time to complete the healing." She stopped talking and got a distant look in her eyes.

"How much more time does he need?" I asked, not liking that news at all. Each moment we spent here was another moment we could be discovered.

Malia shrugged. "An hour, maybe two or three, but that isn't our only problem. The Pendletons will likely return soon, and I think they mean to cause trouble."

It took me a second to make the mental connections. "Christy's kin? What problems could they cause? They didn't strike me as particularly dangerous folks."

"Their presence alone could cause problems," Malia pointed out. "Even if the patient awakens fully healed, she will need time to recover her strength."

"We'll keep 'em out of the room then," I said. "Danielle can do that if the nurses help."

"We might not be here. That is our third and greatest problem." Malia spoke with such quiet conviction that I could only blink at her. "My mother is coming."

"Your mother. Dr. Robinson. She's coming here?"

"Yes and no and yes," Malia answered.

I gave her a disapproving, *make some sense* frown.

"Yes, my mother is coming, but she is not currently using the name you know her by," Malia clarified.

"What name is she using?" The question came out sharper than I'd intended.

"I left a letter for you in your bag that should explain much. Danielle will return soon. We should eat, and then, I must help Michio with the patient's immune system. Read the letter after breakfast."

"I should help you and Michio," I argued.

Shaking her head, Malia said, "Your time would be better spent reading my letter and coordinating with Nadia, Varick, and Danielle. They will know what to do." Forcing a smile, she added, "I have a plan, but I'd rather not rely upon it. That is Nadia's area of expertise. Mine is emotions, and I have work aplenty."

Instinctively, I snatched up Malia's left hand. "What plan?"

She squeezed my hand and sent me calming feelings of reassurance. My grip slackened, and Malia slipped away. She exited the restroom to greet Danielle and help her with the breakfast packages.

Shaking my head, I followed Malia into the common room, got some fresh clothes from my suitcase, and returned to the restroom to change. By the time I finished with the rest of my morning activities, everybody was awake and digging into the containers of scrambled eggs, sausages, and pancakes Danielle had bought. We steered breakfast chatter away from the patient, but the unspoken question burned behind Christy, Danielle, and Dominique's eyes.

Dominique's patience cracked first. "Did it work?"

I looked to Danielle and nodded toward Michio, flicking my gaze to the restroom. She got the hint.

"Hey, big guy, let's go get you some fresh clothes," said Danielle.

"Eat more," Michio responded, pointing to the pile of eggs.

"Later," Danielle promised. She scooped him up, grabbed some clothes for him, and fled to the restroom.

I let Malia break the news of our partial success. She was much better suited for bolstering their hopes anyway.

Quickly finishing my soggy pancakes, I chugged the rest of my milk carton and did what I could to clean up. It took a lot of will power to not tackle my suitcase and dive in looking for Malia's letter. I found the missive tucked up neat-like in one of my clean socks. Heart beating harder than it ought to, I unfolded the hand-written letter.

Chapter 25
The Director

ITEM 159: Malia's handwritten letter to Jillian
Item Source: Jillian Blairington

Dear Jillian,

My courage fails me. I find it much easier to confess to paper than a person. You will no doubt remember my mother, Dr. Karita Robinson. She poisoned you and Nadia upon your last face-to-face meeting. Her need to recover Michio and me makes her a formidable foe. Complicated does not begin to explain our relationship.

You may soon meet her as Dr. Kathleen Lynchberg, the name she chose upon leaving Dr. Devya's labs. She has many names and titles, but in this role, she is the Director of Scientific Studies for a branch the United States government has never publicly acknowledged. Their informal name is one you have heard before. They are known as the Guardians.

I haven't time to explain everything, but I will do my best. My mother is under orders to claim not only Michio and me, but also you and Varick. If a complete break has not already happened between Dr. Devya and his original supporters, it will occur very soon. I fear for their safety. If a confrontation turns violent, Nadia may be the only survivor, for they will not risk harming her. Cora, Dr. Carnasis, and Dr. Devya may have much to answer for, but they do not deserve to die.

The government sent my mother because they believe she can use our connection to her advantage. They do not realize I intend the same.

This woman ought to be a stranger to me, but she is still my mother, perhaps she will listen to me. Nadia does not agree, but I have to try.

Yours respectfully,
Malia

***

ITEM 160: Danielle's forty-sixth letter
Item Source: Danielle Matheson
Dear Dr. S.,

One can hardly forget a lady like Dr. Karita Robinson. When I first met her, she still clutched a recently used handgun in one neatly gloved hand. That leaves an impression on a person. The fact that she's also tall, beautiful, and brilliant also leaves an impression, but the handgun memory definitely dominates. My second sighting of her, just a few moments ago, made me fight hard not to revisit my high school sprinter days.

I don't think she saw me, which is the only reason my heart stopped doing triple time. I'd gone down to the cafeteria to buy some coffee for Christy and me, since I sensed the morning could be a long one. The sight of Dr. Robinson flanked by two dark-suited, grim-faced men made me jumpy enough to spill some scalding coffee onto my right hand. Biting back a curse, I hurried to a napkin dispenser and sopped up the mess, dabbing gingerly around the wounded skin. I'd been considering the pastries in the display case at the time, but all thoughts of that fled as I concentrated on not being conspicuous.

Soon as I stepped into the safety of the room, I thrust Christy's coffee into her hand, gave what remained of my decaf light and sweet to Dominique, and made eye contact with both Jillian and Malia.

"She doesn't drink coffee," Christy protested half-heartedly.

"Yes, I do," Dominique countered.

"It's mostly milk and sugar anyway," I assured my friend. "Will you two watch Michio for a minute? I need to speak with Jillian and Malia."

Picking up on my serious tone, Christy clamped down on her obvious urge to demand what had upset me.

Once safely ensconced in our glamorous conference room, I studied my young friends. "Do you know who I just saw downstairs?" Not having anything better to do with my arms, I crossed them across my stomach.

Jillian exchanged a knowing glance with Malia before answering, "Dr. Robinson."

"She's earlier than expected," Malia added.

"When were you two going to tell me she might come to call?" I demanded.

"I heard of the possibility this morning," Jillian said, holding

133

hands up defensively.

"Why is she here?" I speared first Jillian, then Malia with a glare. "There's no way her presence is a coincidence."

"She is supposed to take us into custody," Malia explained with an inordinate amount of calm. Someone listening only to the cadence of her speech would think she'd just ordered a donut. "We—that is, Nadia and I—learned of the possibility yesterday, but we didn't want to burden you and Jillian until today."

Fighting a losing battle with my irritation, I uncrossed my arms and placed a hand on each of Malia's bony shoulders, counted down from ten to one, and said, "Tell me everything."

"There's not much to tell," Jillian warned, waving for Malia to continue.

Unfortunately, she was right. It took Malia about thirty seconds to summarize Dr. Robinson's alias, orders, and resources. She ended by saying, "Varick does not think she poses a serious threat to us yet, but more government people are arriving each moment."

"He's still here?" Despite my tone, it didn't surprise me that Varick would stick around and monitor a situation involving three of his siblings.

"He wanted to see this through," Malia said. She reached up and patted my hands, which were still on her shoulders. "We all do. It would be safer to leave, but our work is not yet finished. Michio will need more time this afternoon. May I go help him?"

Feeling embarrassed, I released Malia's shoulders and nodded. As she reached for the handle, I asked, "What should I do?"

Malia's expression measured the sincerity of my request. "Keep Christy and Dominique distracted and away from the room as long as possible, but do not let my mother see you." Leaving those instructions, she breezed out of the room.

I'd completely forgotten about that part. When Malia had described the Dr. Robinson situation, she'd consistently referred to the woman as "The Director." The reminder landed hard in my gut. I looked to Jillian for an explanation to a question I couldn't even word for several seconds. "How bad is it?" I whispered after opening and closing my mouth a dozen times.

"The cancer's gone, but she could still die," Jillian replied in her soft, Southern drawl. The accent was more pronounced thanks to the slow rate at which she spoke. "Malia and Michio still gotta battle her immune system 'cause it doesn't know how to quit fighting."

The horrible possibility stole any response I might have considered.

"Don't let 'em know yet, Danielle."

I blinked glassy eyes at Jillian, as her meaning slowly sank in.

"Let 'em keep their hope at least one afternoon."

Her statement reminded me of my recent defensive essay on the merits of certain lies. The possibility that Christy and Dominique's mother still faced mortal danger was one truth I would gladly bury. Gathering the scraps of courage not scattered by my encounter with Dr. Robinson, I returned to the room and suggested an outing to Christy and Dominique. They agreed but needed to change and primp for the day, so I decided to dump my woes on you.

I've got to cut this letter short though because Christy's finally out of the little princess's room. That means it's time for me to take up my Roman sister distraction duties. I feel like a rodeo clown hired to keep the raging bull-like emotions from trampling these girls.

The Rookie Rodeo Clown (Epic Fighter of Frowns),

Danielle Matheson.

Chapter 26
Unexpected Move

ITEM 161: Jillian's eightieth post-kidnapping journal entry
Item Source: Jillian Blairington

Since I'd spent most of the night in a working sleep helping Michio, I let myself take a nap. I wanted to help Malia and Michio with their current work, but there wasn't much I could do. Someday, perhaps Malia will teach me how to use some of her Gifts so I can help her, but she kept busy enough teaching Michio right then. I probably should have put myself into a restful, relatively dreamless sleep, but I let my mind wander the hospital hallway sampling dreams.

Not everybody was sleeping of course, but I found a few dreams to watch. One lady pictured herself shopping for shoes. I had a little fun helping her by switching the colors, patterns, and types of shoes. As she marveled at the wide range of choices, I moved on to another dream.

The next dream I found felt very sad, so I paused to see why. The mental pictures formed a slideshow featuring one lady and covered about two decades. I could tell that much from the change in clothes and hairstyle. Enough of the images featured doctors' offices and hospital rooms to tell me the lady must be the cancer patient. A few pictures also featured a handsome, sad-eyed man. He didn't react to the pictures, so I knew he must be my dreamer. I spent a few minutes helping the man sort through his pictures. Then, I searched his mind for a few of his favorite songs and played 'em while he watched the happy picture show we'd arranged. I left him to experience the memories in peace.

I never got to enter a third dream. Some time ago, Nadia had taught me how to mark certain people so I'd be more attuned to their thoughts. I can't see their thoughts like she can or have any influence on a person, but if the right circumstances exist, the marked person can enter my dreams. Danielle had one of those marks 'cause she volunteered to let me practice new aspects of my Gift on her. I'd forgotten about it since I'm usually not asleep mid-day and don't have much cause to see what Danielle's up to when I'm not with her. It feels too much like spying.

Once upon a time, I used to fear these dreams that let me see and hear things happening nearby. I still can't control 'em very well, but I have gotten better with blocking 'em. Making the decision to block or not block a dream can be tricky sometimes 'cause general curiosity always sits on the side of letting the dream play.

Not quite sure what made me stay and watch this particular dream. Instinct, I guess. At first, I didn't realize it featured Danielle since I saw only a middle-aged woman tucked up tight in a hospital bed. She wore a pink polka dotted hospital gown and a matching kerchief on her head. Her lined face looked weary but she smiled like she'd received some good news. She said something and reached out her right hand toward something I couldn't see.

Dream surfing with sound can be disorienting, so I usually do it without sound. It took me an extra second to remember how to turn sound back on 'cause I don't usually shape much about my own dreams, especially these ones. Switching the sound on, I adjusted the view so I could see more of the room. That's when I saw Christy, Dominique, and Danielle. Their faces and postures displayed a mixture of rapturous joy, eagerness, and stunned disbelief.

"I'll be back soon, Miss Alice!" Dominique exclaimed. She clutched the lady's hand and squeezed affectionately. "I promise."

"Don't worry about me, honey," Miss Alice said, smiling bravely. "Have a nice visit with your mother. I want to meet her very soon."

The mention of Dominique's momma sent a jolt through me. I almost abandoned the dream right then and there. Malia gave me the impression the work with the patient would stretch well into the afternoon if not the evening. Although dream time can deceive me, I didn't believe half a day had gone by. I wanted to wake myself and see if it was true.

"I'll tell her about you." Dominique released the lady's hand

and waved as she bounced toward the door. "Goodbye!"

Danielle and Christy murmured their farewells, both looking more stunned than excited, but they followed Dominique out of Miss Alice's room. The dream might have glided away then, but something didn't sit well with me. I locked on to Danielle's presence, so I could follow the girls out into the hallway where my icky feeling bloomed into outright dread.

Christy and Dominique's aunt and uncle stood right outside the room. Aunt Sophie's face strained against her scary-happy smile. Uncle Phillip's expression defied reading, but he didn't seem nearly as happy as his wife. I was so busy trying to decipher Uncle Phillip's expression that I didn't realize Danielle and Christy had stopped moving.

"What are you doing?" squeaked Christy.

"We're going to take a short walk to a place where we can have a private conversation," said Aunt Sophie. Her smile stayed steady, but her brown eyes glared at Christy before moving to Danielle. "If either of you scream, she dies."

Only then did I notice the firm grip Aunt Sophie had on Dominique's left arm and the wicked-looking knife she tapped impatiently against her right thigh. Dominique's lower lip trembled and her shiny green eyes looked to her sister for help. She sniffled.

"Don't you dare cry," snarled Aunt Sophie.

"How the heck did you get that in here?" Danielle asked, referring to the knife.

"Come with me," demanded Uncle Phillip. He draped an arm around Christy's shoulder and started leading her down the hallway.

"Follow them," Aunt Sophie ordered Danielle. She nodded at Uncle Phillip and Christy who were rapidly moving down the hall.

"And if I refuse?" Danielle looked downright rebellious.

"Don't," said Aunt Sophie, moving the knife so that the bright light glinted off its shiny surface.

Sighing, Danielle let herself be herded along in the path forged by Uncle Phillip and Christy. They didn't go far before ducking into a hallway that led to a few storage rooms. Uncle Phillip took a key from his pocket and unlocked the second door down on the right. He and Christy disappeared inside. Danielle dragged her feet, taking tiny steps to gain thinking time. A shove from Aunt Sophie kept Danielle moving.

"Please don't do this," Christy begged.

My presence arrived in the storage closet with Danielle in time to see Uncle Phillip binding Christy's wrists together with duct tape. She sat on a box of medical supplies with her ankles already bound. Danielle's eyes darted about the room, looking for a weapon, but she only saw more boxes. She instinctively moved toward the left wall, away from the other people in the room.

"Sit down next to Christy," Aunt Sophie instructed.

"No thank you," said Danielle.

"It was not a request."

"Is my mom okay?" Dominique's question sliced through the mounting tension. "Did she really wake up?"

"They lied, Domi," Christy whispered.

"Why would they lie?" The child addressed the question to everybody.

"Yes, why lie?" Danielle repeated, seeming more annoyed than scared. "I'm pretty sure you're breaking a few dozen laws here."

"They're after Dominique," Christy explained in a shaky voice. Her head hung in defeat.

"What could they—"

"Shut up and listen unless you want to get hurt," interrupted Uncle Phillip.

Danielle stopped speaking and silently dared Uncle Phillip to start explaining.

"Sit down next to Christy." Aunt Sophie coldly repeated her earlier order. She must have squeezed Dominique's arm because the girl whimpered.

I hoped Danielle would stand her ground, but she took a long look at Aunt Sophie's fierce expression and inched her way over to Christy. When she got close, Uncle Phillip seized her arm and shoved her into Christy who grunted with the impact but used her bound hands to steady Danielle. Once seated, Danielle wrenched her arm free from Uncle Phillip's grasp. A red mark told me the move probably hurt her, but Danielle was too fired up to care.

"Behave," advised Aunt Sophie.

Danielle tried to stand up but got shoved down again.

"Give me your hands and keep your feet still," instructed Uncle Phillip.

Danielle's stubborn expression said she would much rather kick him.

"Don't fight him, Danielle." The plea in Christy's tone stole most of Danielle's defiance.

She looked first to her friend then followed Christy's gaze toward Aunt Sophie and Dominique. The girl had her body pressed up against Aunt Sophie, trying to keep away from the knife tucked against her right ribs.

Noticing she had Danielle's attention, Aunt Sophie said, "I don't want to kill her here. I have a plan. If you force me to alter that plan I will kill you next."

"What is wrong with you people?" shouted Danielle. "You're in a hospital threatening a child with a knife." Each phrase in her last statement came out in short bursts. Despite obvious outrage, Danielle sat relatively still as Uncle Phillip expertly wound tape around her wrists and ankles.

"We're not here to hurt you girls," Aunt Sophie claimed. Her words didn't carry much weight when compared to the knife still poking Dominique in the side.

"We need to keep you from interfering," explained Uncle Phillip. He sounded almost apologetic.

"Why do you want to hurt my sister?" Christy's quiet question carried the full weight of her confusion, pain, and betrayal.

"You don't have to understand, my dear," replied Aunt Sophie, sounding oddly pleasant.

"Please let her go," Christy whispered. "I'll go with you. I won't even fight you."

Danielle's dark expression said: *You won't get a similar promise from me. I'll definitely fight you.*

"Neither will our dear Dominique," purred Aunt Sophie. She gave Dominique's left shoulder a friendly pat as she moved the knife away from the child's side. "You'll be a good girl, won't you, Dominique?" crooned Aunt Sophie. One could practically hear the sugar falling from her words in wet clumps.

Dominique appeared too stricken to speak. Her eyes sought comfort from Christy.

Uncle Phillip punched one of the nearby cardboard boxes, and said, "Answer when spoken to or I'll beat some manners into you!"

The girls collectively tensed at the abrupt noise and harsh tone, but Dominique managed to nod.

"Speak!"

"Patience, Phillip," spoke Aunt Sophie, still using her sweet tone. "Give the child time to think." Kneeling next to Dominique, Aunt Sophie turned the girl so she couldn't see Danielle and Christy.

"You have very few options, my dear. So let me tell you what you're going to do. You're going to take my hand and walk out of here without a fuss. When we're safely away, we'll send someone to free your sister and her friend."

Up to this point, Christy's comments and questions sounded unsure, but there was no hesitation when she said, "Don't do it, Domi. Soon as you can get away, you run. You hear me? Run."

"You're not helping, Christy," scolded Aunt Sophie, sounding deeply disappointed. She waved to her husband, and he slapped a piece of duct tape over Christy's mouth. "That's much better."

Dominique twisted around, and her eyes moved to Danielle for her opinion.

"I'm with Christy on this one, kid. Kick, scream, bite, and claw as soon as you get near a crowd." Danielle's advice earned her a thick strip of duct tape, but she smiled defiantly as Uncle Phillip applied it, letting him know she'd finished her say.

Christy tried to speak through the tape but managed only an angry buzzing noise. Dominique breathed hard and watched as Uncle Phillip placed a meaty hand on Christy's shoulder to make sure she stayed seated. Dominique opened her mouth to speak but settled for a shaky breath.

"We don't have a lot of time, Dominique," said Aunt Sophie. "Make your decision. Will you come with us?"

"Are you going to kill me?"

"That is not the question right now. If you love your sister, you'll come with us. That's all there is to it." Aunt Sophie ran her fingers down Dominique's wet cheek.

Christy and Danielle both shook their heads emphatically, but I don't think Dominique could see 'em very well. Frustrated, Christy slammed her bound hands into Uncle Phillip's gut, shrugged off his hand, and lunged, aiming her bound hands at Aunt Sophie's face. Recovering quickly, Uncle Phillip caught Christy and flung her none-too-gently back into her seat. He gripped her throat hard with his left hand and raised his right fist to punch Christy.

"Stop it!" Dominique's cry made him hesitate. "I'll go!" She swallowed hard, and then repeated the decision quietly, "I'll go."

"There's a good girl," praised Aunt Sophie. She put the knife in her purse and held a hand out toward Dominique.

The girl eyed the hand like it was a rat but took hold of it anyway.

Uncle Phillip taped Christy's hands to a metal shelf to her right and Danielle's hands to a shelf to her left. "Someone should be by in a few hours to set you free. I'll leave the light on for your comfort."

Christy and Danielle did not look comforted. Christy looked like she couldn't decide whether to cry uncontrollably or try her luck with kicking Uncle Phillip. Danielle's steady gaze promised she wouldn't let the situation stand as is for very long.

Every part of me screamed to do something, but I forced myself to pay attention to as many details as I could. I might have been able to make Aunt Sophie and Uncle Phillip sleep if I could actually find 'em, but I didn't even know what part of the hospital they were in. Besides, I didn't want to risk making a mistake that would get Dominique killed. Aunt Sophie looked mighty ready to stick somebody with that knife.

I waited until the door clicked shut behind the villains to be sure they didn't return to hurt Danielle and Christy. Then, I woke up to call Nadia. If she could find Varick, maybe he could save Dominique. A sinking feeling said that if the Pendletons got Dominique away from the hospital, we might never see her again.

Chapter 27
The Other Crisis

ITEM 162: Jillian's eighty-first post-kidnapping journal entry
Item Source: Jillian Blairington
My query barely got out of my head before I heard Nadia's response. *Varick is on his way. Tell Malia.* Nadia's usually pretty decent about timely responses, but the instant nature of this one stressed my strained nerves. She sounded rushed, which is never a good sign.

Knowing I wouldn't get a full explanation until I complied, I got up to notify Malia. She wasn't exactly asleep, though her meditative working state comes awfully close to a nap. I coulda tried to use my Gift to wake Malia, but I needed to get up and move anyway.

Shaking my sister's shoulders, I said, "Malia, something's wrong. Dominique just got kidnapped. Come on, snap out of it. I need your attention."

"I am here," Malia said, turning her head to look at me, "but we have more work to do."

I quickly told her everything I'd seen in the dream, including the fact that I didn't know where to find Danielle and Christy.

"They are close," Malia said.

"Where?" I demanded, ready to charge off wherever to free my friends.

"Somewhere on this floor," Malia replied. "Nadia will show you the place when the time is right."

"What's wrong with now?"

Malia frowned, like she didn't know whether or not to speak. Eventually, she said, "There is another crisis occurring. We will need to speak with Varick before doing anything."

Michio stirred and looked at me curiously. "Can I play now?"

"Go bring me that orange Danielle got," Malia suggested. "I'll peel it for you. It's time we took a break anyway."

Michio leapt off the bed and ran to get the orange.

Sensing my impatience, Malia said, "There's no use in worrying him. We don't know much, and we can't plan until Varick arrives."

"What other crisis?" I tried to whisper so Michio wouldn't hear. It didn't work 'cause the kid's got big ears.

"What other crisis?" he mimicked, blinking his big black, innocent eyes at Malia and me.

"Nothing you need concern yourself with," Malia told Michio.

For once, I wished Malia wasn't always so darn calm. The fact that she spoke truth definitely didn't help. I'm not sure if she used her Gift on me or not, but I calmed down some as I watched her methodically peel the orange and pull off pieces for Michio. Malia offered me a piece, and I took it, automatically nodding thanks. The pleasant taste soured in my mouth when I thought about the danger facing Dominique, Danielle, and Christy.

"Don't think about it." Malia knew exactly where my thoughts were wandering.

"I can't help it. I want to help 'em now."

"Help who?" piped up Michio.

"Finish eating so we can get you rinsed off," Malia instructed, handing Michio the last orange slice.

Michio still had half a slice in the other hand, so he alternated biting at each until they were gone. Malia gathered the scraps and orange peels and walked 'em over to the garbage before shooing Michio into the restroom to wash up. A heavy, citrus scent lingered.

The lady on the hospital bed moaned and opened her eyes.

"Uh, Malia," I said. "She's awake."

Malia tore out of the restroom like someone had set it on fire. She hadn't bothered drying her hands, so she wiped 'em on her shirt as she rushed to the bed. Barreling past the chair she'd been sitting in, Malia picked up the lady's hand and leaned close. "How do you feel?"

"Tired," answered the lady. "Who are you? Where are my girls?"

A steady thud-thud-thud noise came from the restroom drawing my attention, so I'm not sure what Malia told the lady. I found Michio jumping up and down.

"Turning off lights," Michio explained before I could question him on the jumping.

Flicking the light switch off, I took him by the hand and led him back into the main room. As we reached the foot of the bed, Michio climbed up and crawled to the lady.

"This is our brother, Michio. He's the one who healed you," Malia announced. "I will—"

A gentle knock interrupted Malia.

"Come in," I called.

Varick entered carrying a large glass vase bursting with pink and white flowers. Malia sucked in sharply. The lady started breathing rapidly, and tears welled up in her eyes. Malia drew the lady's arm up near her chest and bowed her head over the hand, struggling to keep the woman calm.

"I gather these are not expected or welcomed," Varick noted. He placed the vase on the ground and plucked out the card. He passed the card to Malia who placed it in the lady's trembling left hand.

The lady didn't bother reading the card, but I think she knew who had sent the flowers. Tears flowed down her face, but I couldn't tell if they were happy or sad tears. When the lady's breathing evened out, introductions went round. I still had a hard time thinking of Susan Kilpatrick as anything other than "Christy's momma," "the patient," or simply "the lady."

"Jillian and Varick will bring Christy back very soon," Malia promised.

"What about Domi? Where's my baby? Is she safe?"

"Christy will explain when she gets here," Malia soothed. She looked hard at Varick and me and nodded toward the door.

Taking the hint, Varick and I bolted from the room.

"Where are we going?" I asked as the door shut behind me.

Varick held up a finger for patience. "Nadia is analyzing the dream you witnessed. She will let us know their location shortly." Even as he finished his sentence, Varick picked a direction and started down the hallway.

I had to jog to keep up with his long strides, but I didn't mind the haste. Poor Danielle and Christy deserved to be found as soon as possible. To my surprise, Varick turned right and found the door from my dream almost immediately.

"That's the door I saw," I said in case he had any doubts.

Varick tried the handle but found it locked. He jiggled the

145

handle three times, closed his eyes, and concentrated. The lock sprang open. Motioning for me to wait, Varick rammed his right shoulder into the door and burst through, ready for an ambush. I peeked around the corner in time to see Christy and Danielle's stunned, grateful expressions. They both started talking at once, but the tape across their mouths turned their words into gibberish.

Drawing a knife from each boot, Varick held one out toward me. "Do you know how to use this?"

I nodded and accepted the knife. Much to Momma's dismay, my Old Daddy had taught me how to handle knives.

"Start with the feet," Varick suggested.

Both girls buzzed their disapproval through the tape, but I followed the order by sawing through the tape holding Danielle's ankles together. The duct tape didn't want to be cut, but Varick's knife was in top-notch shape. As soon as Danielle's hands were free, she ripped the tape from her mouth, chucked the sticky wad aside, and tackled me with a deep hug. I had to quickly move the knife to avoid stabbing her. Varick had the same reaction from Christy.

The story poured forth from both girls like water out of a fire hose. Finally, they quit chattering long enough for us to tell 'em that Christy's momma had awakened. We didn't even get to the part about the flowers 'cause Christy tore out of the room, nearly bowling Varick over in the process. Danielle limped after her friend, pausing in the doorway long enough to massage her right calf. I returned Varick's knife, and he slipped both weapons into his boots.

"Better hurry back," I said to Varick. "Malia's gonna need ya to calm Christy. I'll help Danielle."

Varick accepted the plan and jogged to catch up with Christy. Danielle and I were only about a half-minute behind 'em getting back to the room, but it was long enough for some of the hysterics to die down.

Malia had surrendered her spot to Christy and now stood behind Michio who sat in his usual spot on the lady's left side. Christy held her momma's right hand, though she looked like she'd rather be in her arms.

Christy and Danielle took turns recounting their scary encounter with Aunt Sophie and Uncle Phillip. They were fairly accurate with the account, but I noticed they downplayed the knife involvement. That's probably for the best.

The lady listened without comment, but when they finished,

she tightened her grip on Christy's hands. "You have to get her back!"

"What is their intent?" asked Varick.

Tears spilled down the lady's cheeks yet again.

Malia reached past Michio to place a hand on her left arm. "Tell us everything, quickly now. We haven't much time. Dominique's in grave danger."

I didn't think mentioning the danger was a good idea, but strangely, it helped the lady focus. Her pale green eyes sharpened and her tears slowed. "The flowers," she rasped.

Christy glanced at the flowers and groaned.

"It is clear they have a special meaning," Varick commented. "What is it?"

"That was the arrangement we brought to Noah's funeral," Christy explained. "Noah was my cousin. He drowned the day Dominique was born." The meaning slammed into Christy with breath-stealing force. "Oh, no. No. No." Leaping out of the seat, she said, "We have to go after them right now!"

"Not everybody," Malia countered. "I need you and Michio to stay here. Varick and Danielle can go after them. Do you have their address?"

Danielle had a *why choose me* look on her face, but she merely nodded, and said, "Christy can text me the address."

"No way, I'm going with you!" cried Christy.

"No!" The protest came simultaneously, though with varying degrees of force, from Christy's momma, Varick, and Malia.

Christy choked back tears. "She's my sister. I have to go." She looked to her momma, Varick, and Malia for their objections.

"Stay with me," pleaded Christy's momma.

"It's too dangerous," Varick explained.

"But—"

Malia cut in smoothly. "Dominique knows Danielle and will trust Varick for her sake, but having you along will only give your aunt and uncle more opportunities to hurt your family. Please trust me. Your mother needs you here more. The less she has to worry about, the faster she will recover her strength."

The argument deflated the rest of Christy's would-be protests.

"What about me?" I asked, once the dust had settled.

"Stay here and see if you can monitor the situation," Malia said. "Michio and I will continue our work with Christy for support. Danielle can drive, and Varick will make sure Dominique is safe."

"I want to go, too," Christy's momma said. Her faint tone indicated she knew that would be impossible, but needed to say it anyway.

"I know," Malia whispered, "but you can do the most good by resting. Dominique will want to see you strong again."

Before everybody went their separate ways, I pulled Malia aside. "You never told me about that other crisis."

"Let me get Michio and Christy settled with Susan and I'll be over to discuss it with you."

Not exactly happy with Malia's answer but also lacking a choice in the matter, I bid farewell to Varick and Danielle and walked 'em to the door. "Be careful."

I stepped into the restroom to wait for Malia. The delay was probably only a minute or two, but it stretched on and on until I must have paced that tiny restroom twenty times.

Finally, Malia came in, closed the door, and began. "The other crisis is a plan set in motion by my mother. Danielle and Varick may have a tough time leaving."

"Why do you say that?"

"The government is amassing a small army," Malia replied. "They planted a man to take hostages on the first floor."

"That ain't right."

"I don't think he'll hurt anybody," said Malia. "It's simply a good excuse for them to station a lot of police officers and agents here. I think most of the hostages are also agents."

"Guess that makes sense," I grudgingly admitted. "Seems like an awful lot of effort."

"We're playing a strategy game against my mother." Malia frowned. "She always was good at strategy games. I'm told she even bested Nadia a time or two early in her training."

"Can we win?" I wondered, not liking Malia's frown or the news that Dr. Robinson had ever beaten Nadia at anything.

"We must," Malia responded, giving me a small, encouraging smile. With nothing else to say, Malia returned to her work helping Michio battle the lady's immune system.

We will. The thought came from Nadia, but I wholeheartedly wanted to believe it.

Chapter 28
The Tragic Past

ITEM 163: Danielle's forty-seventh letter
Item Source: Danielle Matheson
Dear Dr. S.,

This is my first attempt using the thoughts-to-words writing program Malia made for Jillian. They wanted to test it on various electronic devices and my iPad and cell phone made convenient targets. Since I'm not driving and a GPS is doing the navigating, I need to concentrate on something besides the fact that I could die this afternoon.

That's not melodrama speaking. I just spent a half-hour bound with duct tape and stuck in a storage closet with my good friend Christy Roman. I'm sorry I can't recount the conversation word for word. Maybe I'll try later. Jillian could probably tell you if you're really interested in knowing what was said. Mostly, I think my brain got stuck somewhere in *I'm surrounded by crazy people* mode.

Varick and Jillian swept in and rescued us in true heroic, knife wielding style. That should be the end of it, right? It's an exciting tale to keep to myself until I'm old, gray, and bouncing grandbabies on arthritic knees.

By the way, should I be disturbed by how skillfully Jillian handled that knife?

Unfortunately, the dramatic rescue came too late to save Dominique Roman. I almost wish Christy's little sister had spent the whole, miserable time trussed up beside us, but the "nutters"—Varick's term for Aunt Sophie and Uncle Phillip—took her. It's probably a good thing I'm not driving right now, since I get furious every time I picture that innocent child's pale, frightened face.

Our exit from the hospital took far more time and effort than we'd planned on or wished for. It took a little time to convince Christy to stay with her mother.

Wow. I forgot to tell you Christy's mother woke up. The healing thing Michio, Jillian, and Malia spent all last night and most of this morning doing must have worked. Christy's mother isn't quite out of the woods so to speak, but she's definitely much improved. I think the mother-daughter pair would have hijacked an ambulance to come with us, but Malia convinced them Varick and I could handle getting Dominique back. That kid's about the only person I know who can give Jillian a run for her money in the persuasion department.

I expected to simply waltz out of the hospital, get in my car, and take off. As usual, plan and reality quickly parted ways. Varick and I were about to step off the elevator on the first floor when he caught my arm and held the door-close button. I had a flashback to Malia doing almost the exact same maneuver.

Varick poked the button for the third floor and fired off a random question. "How are your acting skills?"

"They're fair to nonexistent," I admitted, simply not having time to make something up. "Why?" I dragged the word out an extra beat.

"Allow me to speak for us," Varick insisted. "Keep your chin down and look stunned and irritated."

The elevator chimed triumphantly to let us know we'd arrived at our selected floor.

"You're my pregnant wife and we're here for some tests." Varick tossed that bombshell at me as the doors swung open.

Now that I think about it, he probably timed it to make acting skills irrelevant. My stunned look came very naturally along with a sweeping wave of irritation.

"We are not lost," Varick declared, stepping out of the elevator with me in tow. "We are simply taking the long way." He strolled up to the nurses' station and chatted a moment with the nurses.

I peeked up and nearly stumbled backward as I recognized Nurse Keili.

Varick caught my arm and hurried me away, whispering, "Head down, keep walking, avoid eye contact. Nadia's illusion won't fool them if they look closely."

150

We fled to the stairs and slipped inside. I was eager to plunge down the stairs and escape the madness, but Varick hesitated.

"What now?" I asked, dreading the answer.

A spark of amusement lit Varick's eyes, which were currently bright blue. "New plan. Chin up, walk with confidence, and follow my lead. We just joined the United States government."

Though I was pretty sure Varick had burned up his logic quotient for the day, I nevertheless attempted to follow the instructions. He started down the stairs with a business-like gait that exuded confidence with a hint of arrogance.

As we neared the bottom landing, a man's voice called out, "What are you doing here? This hall's restricted."

"We're not headed for the hall," Varick snapped with enough bite to say *we have as much right to be here as you do.* I noticed his voice was lower than normal and had lost the British accent.

"Where are you going?" queried a second man. This one seemed less hostile but equally suspicious. "I don't recognize you."

"Get used to it, Adams," said Varick, leaning on the door to push it open. He held it like a gentleman. "It looks like they're rolling out the works for these folks."

I stepped outside and blinked in the sudden sunlight.

"Yeah, the Director's on her broomstick today," groused Agent Adams without a trace of suspicion. "Steer clear of her if you can."

"We plan to," replied Varick.

I doubt the agents picked up on the irony in Varick's tone, but it put a smile on my face. I let Varick lead since he seemed to know where to go. We rapidly put some distance between us and the side door we had exited.

Reaching the parking garage, we turned right and studied the long line of cars.

"My car's on the top deck," I said.

"We're not going to your car," Varick informed. "There are agents watching it."

"Well, that's terrible news," I mumbled, fighting off a panic attack. *What will we do?*

"We're going to nick a car," Varick said, as if he'd read my silent question. Given Nadia's abilities and Varick's close connection to her, reading my mind was entirely possible.

It took my brain a few seconds to translate the term into American English. Varick aided the translation by stopping in front of a black SUV with government plates and grinning impishly.

"We can't steal a car," I argued, honesty genes kicking into overdrive. "We especially can't steal a government car!" There's got to be some sort of extra punishment for making off with government property.

"Call it vehicle relocation if you like. Just get in." The locks sprang open at Varick's touch, almost like an invitation.

"Malia said I was supposed to drive," I said half-heartedly, as I climbed into the front passenger seat.

"Malia thought we were taking your car," Varick returned. He concentrated a moment and placed his right pointer finger over the ignition slot. The vehicle roared to life. Grin turning manic, Varick clicked on his seat belt and adjusted the seat controls.

My mind fixed on the only other experience with Varick's driving, and my heart responded by missing three beats. "Why take this particular truck?" I wondered. I wasn't really arguing at this point, but I needed to fill the air and forget that other drive with Varick. Putting on the seat belt took about two seconds, and Varick was already pulling the truck out of the slot by this time. My left hand clutched my purse and my right latched onto the balance bar.

"They won't stop us, and government people are very reliable about topping off the gas tank," Varick explained. "Did Christy send you the nutters' address yet?"

"What makes you think they'll take Dominique to their home?" While waiting for an answer, I dug around in my purse until I came up with my phone. Still waiting, I fired off a quick text to Christy reminding her that I needed her aunt and uncle's address.

When Varick's response finally came, he spoke with unusual gentleness. "Get me the address and then call Christy. She'll fill you in on her cousin's death."

His answer left my stomach in knots, but my phone chimed as Christy's response came in, giving me something to do. Varick tapped a few buttons on the console, and a navigation system came online and politely requested the desired destination. I held the phone between us and read the Myerstown address aloud as Varick typed it into the keypad. The ETA—estimated time of arrival—read 1:37. A glance at my watch said that was about an hour away.

Picking up on my concern, Varick said, "They're not that far ahead of us. We'll make it." He stopped talking as we rolled past a checkpoint.

I stopped breathing, but the government people simply scurried about removing the road blocks and waved us on.

"You should call Christy now," Varick reminded, once we pulled out onto the highway.

Too curious to be annoyed, I called Christy. Her panicked greeting made me instantly contrite. After a few minutes of soothing, assuring, reassuring, and re-reassuring, I settled down to business. "Christy, I need to know about your cousin's death."

Silence answered me.

"Christy? Can you hear me?"

"What do you need to know?" My friend sounded like she hadn't had a drink of water in a month.

The haunted quality of her voice kicked an alarm bell in my head. Little pieces of long past puzzles snapped together for me. "What did you see?" I turned the phone to speaker so Varick could hear what Christy had to say.

Christy's voice came through the phone, flat and emotionless, like she'd told the story a hundred times and didn't relish the hundred and first telling. "Noah was playing on the edge of the pool. I told him to stop it. I told him his mom would yell, but he wouldn't listen. He ran at me and knocked me down then dared me to catch him. I turned and ran for the house to tell on him. Aunt Sophie was on the phone up in her room and didn't want to hear my complaints. I went to the room I stayed in when visiting and looked out the back window toward the pool. Noah was floating, just floating."

"Did you tell your aunt?" I asked, trying not to sound condemning.

"Not right away," Christy admitted. She drew a noisy breath and slowly released it. "Noah liked to play dead sometimes. He'd hold his breath and float then laugh at the panic it caused me. So I watched, waiting for him to pop up and laugh like always. Then, I saw the blood and watched some more because I couldn't move or think or breathe. I could only watch." Her voice faded to a dim whisper. "He was so still."

I adjusted the volume controls in case she had more to say.

"Christy, what did you tell your aunt?" Varick asked. His firm voice drew a curious look from me.

"I don't remember," Christy said.

"This is important. What did you do when you realized something was wrong with your cousin?" Varick's fierce gaze settled on my phone like he could reach through it and mentally shake Christy.

"I'm sorry. I can't remember." Christy's tone flipped from apologetic to defensive. "I-I think I screamed. What does it matter?"

Varick snatched my phone out of my hands, brought it closer to his mouth, and said, "Give the phone to Jillian."

Christy must have been eager to hand her phone to Jillian, for within ten seconds, a tentative, "Hello?" came over the line.

Skipping pleasantries, Varick asked, "Jillian, is Christy still there?"

"Yes."

"See if she'll let you pull a specific dream from her," Varick instructed.

There was a pause long enough for Jillian to convey the request to Christy and get an answer. "She agrees. What am I looking for?"

"Find the afternoon of her cousin's accident," commanded Varick. "It should be prominent in her memories both for the trauma and because her sister was born that day. We need to know what she told her aunt about the accident and how her aunt reacted. If I'm right, it's important for explaining why they took Dominique and what they hope to accomplish. Can you do that?"

"I'll call you when I have your answers," Jillian promised. She ended the call, though I'm sure she only narrowly beat Varick to it.

"Now we wait," Varick said grimly, returning my phone. "It shouldn't be long. Jillian knows we're in a hurry."

The wait turned out to be seven excruciatingly long minutes, but his prediction was thankfully correct. I have no idea how Jillian managed to work so fast, but I was grateful for the speed. She keeps saying dream time and real time differ, but I never really believed her until today.

I nearly dropped my phone when it started blasting Christy's ringtone. Since we were miles beyond pleasantries, I accepted the call, made sure it was on speaker, and asked, "What did you learn?"

Jillian's answer stabbed my heart. "They're gonna drown Dominique." From her soft tone and the white noise of a fan, I gathered Jillian had fled to the restroom to make this call. "You don't need to know everything said. It was mostly cursing and screaming, but the lady clearly blames Christy for the accident that killed her son."

"Was it Christy's fault?" I didn't want to ask that question, but I needed to know.

"I doubt it," Jillian drawled. "She didn't push him in, if that's what you wanna know. Once the adults stepped in, they kept her away

154

from the scene, but she has memories of blood on the side of the pool where the boy hit his head."

"Why does her aunt blame her?" asked Varick.

"Her only fault was not telling someone sooner," Jillian answered. "She watched for almost a minute before calling for help."

"Would it have mattered?" I wondered, breathless.

Jillian didn't respond right away, but eventually, she said, "I don't think the question has an answer. The only one that counts is that Mrs. Pendleton believes it would've mattered, so she blames Christy."

My heart went out to my friend. I'd known there was tragedy in Christy's past, but my parents had sheltered me from the true depths of those wounds. One thing didn't make sense to me. "If she blames Christy then why take Dominique?"

Varick answered for Jillian. "To make her watch." He recklessly passed three cars from the right side, but I said nothing and silently willed him to go faster still.

"That's what Nadia, Malia, and I think," Jillian agreed. "I'm trying not to tell Christy or her momma. Get Dominique back quickly."

"That's the plan," Varick declared.

We thanked Jillian for the information and continued our mad pursuit.

The navigation system says we're about three minutes away from our destination. I don't know what awaits us, but I have a bad feeling. I've tried to pray, but nothing profound is coming to mind.

I'm aware that if we fail, Dominique Roman will die.

I will not sign this letter in the hopes I can continue these thoughts later.

Chapter 29
Poolside Showdown

ITEM 164: Jillian's eighty-second post-kidnapping journal entry
Item Source: Jillian Blairington

Watching Danielle and Varick escape the hospital was like seeing a spy movie with lots of comedy parts. I couldn't maintain a steady sleep 'cause I was too wound up and didn't feel like putting myself back to sleep. I had a feeling I'd need to use my full Gifts later. Nadia and I settled on a compromise. I dozed and she sent me some of the images from their exciting exit.

Danielle was one grumpy looking pregnant lady and one serious looking government agent. Someday, I'll have to show her the pictures in a dream. The black suit jacket, white blouse, and dark sunglasses made quite the impression on me, even if the agent men were too polite to stare. I'm not sure Danielle realized Nadia was switching the illusions as Varick changed each scenario.

The successful escape kept me happy until Varick made his request for me to look into Christy's dreams. The assignment bothered me 'cause I knew it would hurt Christy. She went through with it for Dominique's sake, but the memories were buried deep for a reason.

I don't like hurting people. The notion's probably as dull as saying I like breathing, but I feel like a dentist. I ain't saying dentists are bad people. I'm saying they've got a job that makes 'em cause pain to dig out rot.

In hindsight, I shoulda been slower and gentler in my search. Following Varick's advice, I looked for the most painful memory I could find. Christy's mental defenses have had plenty of years to prepare, but with a little help from Nadia and Malia, I got past her defenses. Behind the locked doors, traps, and bluffs, I found a child very much like Nadie, the emotionally fragile figure that dwells within Nadia. When pressed for her name, the child asked to be called Christina. I'm guessing that's Christy's given name, but after hearing the way Christy's aunt rendered her name on that day, I don't blame her for abandoning it.

I spent much dream time earning Christina's trust, but eventually, she shared the memory with me. I won't describe it in detail 'cause the story's not mine to tell, but I told Varick and Danielle the important parts.

Christy's aunt changed the day Noah Pendleton died. I ain't a grief counselor, but I think it's safe to say Aunt Sophie never let herself heal properly. Nadia says she buried the pain, watered it with bitterness, and reaped a crop of weeds that choked a lot of her capacity to love. Aunt Sophie believes that if her sister and niece can experience the same level of loss, they'll understand her. I don't know if her husband feels the same way, but he's supported her on this quest for vengeance thus far.

Nadia will let me know when Varick and Danielle arrive at their destination. When that happens, I'm gonna put myself into a working sleep so I can watch. I'm not sure if Danielle's mark is strong enough to let me find her and pull the image into my dream, but I have to try. I'll leave the thoughts-to-words program on so the recording can be fresh, but if it doesn't work, I'll write about it later.

***

Catching hold of Danielle didn't work very well while the SUV they borrowed was moving along US Highway 78 West. I guess I'll have to practice to manage that in the future, but I should be all right now that they've slowed down. Danielle is in the front passenger seat and she looks nervous. I don't know if they have a plan, but they don't seem to be talking much one way or the other.

Varick parked the car, leapt out, and ran toward the side of the house. Part of me wanted to follow him, but I decided to stay with Danielle 'cause I haven't left a mark with Varick and may find it hard to draw him into my dreams.

Danielle climbed out slowly and carefully approached the front door. She knocked and rang the doorbell several times. When nobody answered, Danielle glanced about before jogging around the house, going opposite where Varick went. Tuning my senses to experience

Danielle's feelings, I felt her fear, anger, irritation, and determination. Strangely, I heard her rapid heartbeats pounding between my ears and felt the bright afternoon sun beating down on her. For a moment, I let myself see what she saw, but I quit that 'cause the running gave her wobbly vision like shaky cam. She also had to squint against the sunlight, narrowing her field of vision.

Danielle moved around the side to the back of the house without a hitch. The first real obstacle to stand in her way came in the form of an eight-foot high wooden privacy fence. A quick glance told her the entire backyard was surrounded, and a sturdy looking padlock said visitors weren't welcome.

Uncertainty dominated Danielle's thoughts, but fear for Dominique helped her conquer the feeling. Taking a running start, Danielle jumped as high as she could and grabbed the top of the fence. I winced as her knees and legs banged off the fence. She didn't have the upper body strength necessary to pull herself over the fence. Dropping into a crouch, Danielle breathed hard and looked around for help. She found it in the form of a neighbor's oak tree.

Hope renewed, Danielle raced to the tree and leapt for the lowest branch. Once she had a good grip, she simply swung her legs up and wrapped 'em around the branch. A little more maneuvering had Danielle upright. From there, she had no trouble climbing high enough to see over the privacy fence.

The sight that met Danielle's eyes is the sort that sticks with ya forever. Her tree hung over a small storage shed. A small patch of lush grass grew in front of the shed and beyond the grass sat a perfectly maintained in-ground pool. The pale blue waters sparkled invitingly, begging to be put to good use on this flawless summer day. A pair of lounge chairs occupied the wooden deck area that ran out from the house, stopping only where it met the cement area surrounding the pool. Dominique Roman sat next to the pool near the deep end, Danielle could tell 'cause the other side had stairs.

The main thing marring the scene was the thick strips of duct tape keeping Dominique's arms behind her back. Danielle couldn't see her feet from this angle, but she assumed they too were bound. The fact that Dominique remained so quiet told Danielle more tape probably covered the girl's mouth. Danielle's lips twitched in sympathy, remembering the itchy feeling of duct tape. Dominique's light brown hair draped over her shoulders and blew in the slight breeze.

Impulse bid Danielle to hop down and free Dominique, but a

keen sense of danger kept her still. She hardly dared to breathe as she methodically searched for signs of Dominique's captors. She didn't have to wait long.

Uncle Phillip emerged from the storage shed carrying a shovel. He marched purposefully toward Dominique.

A ringing phone woke me up, shattering the dream. Not waiting for Christy to answer the phone, I fiddled with the oxygen levels in my brain until I passed out, frantically trying to reestablish my connection to Danielle.

I think I only missed a few seconds, but Danielle's next view showed Uncle Phillip winding up like a major league baseball player ready to smack a ball out of the park. Only there was no ball. His ninety-pound target teetered on the pool's edge, bound hand and foot awaiting the blow.

A sharp cry from Christy nearly broke my concentration, but I forced myself deeper into the dream and continued watching. The shovel started its forward trajectory. Danielle would never get there in time. I didn't know if I could put somebody to sleep from this distance. I'd never done it alone before, but I didn't have a choice.

As a scream erupted from Danielle, I used her as a focal point to locate Dominique. When I found my target, I grabbed hold of her consciousness and buried it, making her pass out. She fell in slow motion, but the combination of Danielle's scream and Dominique's sudden collapse threw Uncle Phillip's aim off. Instead of knocking Dominique senseless, the shovel opened a deep cut along her upper right arm. She crashed into the water and started sinking. I let the water carry her back to consciousness.

Danielle froze, mesmerized by the strange scene.

Uncle Phillip looked down at the shovel in his hands like he'd never seen such an object before.

I gave Danielle the mental version of a sharp pinch, and she snapped into action. Dropping onto the roof, Danielle rolled to a crouch and jumped off the shed. A bullet thudded into the shed, motivating her to move faster. Ripping off her shoes, she dove into the water.

A splitting headache told me I'd done too much too fast, but I struggled to maintain the connection to Danielle. The fact that she was currently cold and wet didn't do anything nice for my head, so I switched to Varick's presence.

I found my brother on the roof of the Pendletons' house.

Changing my perspective allowed me to watch as Varick scampered down the roof, pausing at the edge to check his position. Apparently satisfied, he swung his legs down and dropped onto a narrow windowsill.

A woman's bloodcurdling scream narrowly preceded three gunshots from the room. I expected to see Varick's body tumbling down, but he managed to press his body close to the right side of the windowsill. He hung awkwardly with one hand gripping something inside the room and one leg braced against the sill. Another shot clipped the window frame near Varick's head. Grunting, he moved his foot and let his body swing down, arriving at the window directly below the one he hung from. He wasted no time kicking the window in and entering the house.

More gunshots sounded from the room above. Varick sprinted through the house, up a set of stairs, and charged into the room with Aunt Sophie. She whirled and aimed at Varick, but he was already too close. I thought he'd punch her, but instead, he put her in a headlock and applied pressure until she passed out. He took thirty seconds to empty her gun and bind her hands with shirt strips. I'm not sure where he got the shirt, but since his shirt looked perfectly whole, I assumed it came from the room.

Rushing to the window, Varick checked outside and saw Uncle Phillip running toward the pool with another handgun. Danielle and Dominique were at the shallow end coughing up water. Danielle had freed Dominique's mouth from the tape and now held the girl's head above water. Even though the steps were very close, I could tell Danielle didn't have the strength to climb 'em, especially while holding Dominique. Uncle Phillip was shouting, but Varick couldn't understand his words. When he reached Danielle, Uncle Phillip seized her left arm and dragged her to the side of the pool.

Scooping up the handgun he'd emptied, Varick scrambled out the window, braced himself, and jumped to the ground, somehow landing beyond the back deck. Rolling with the momentum, Varick came up on his feet and sprinted toward Danielle, Dominique, and Uncle Phillip.

"Stop!" Varick and Uncle Phillip shouted together.

Varick froze. He was only halfway around the pool. His empty handgun pointed directly at Uncle Phillip's face.

Uncle Phillip also froze, but he had a loaded handgun pressed against the back of Danielle's head. His other hand had fastened onto

Danielle's shirt, pinning her against the side of the pool.

Only cheerful bird chirping could be heard for several seconds.

Uncle Phillip spoke first, "You know how this works. Drop the gun."

"This isn't what you want, Phil," said Varick, carefully enunciating each word. He kept his gun hand steady. "This isn't even what your wife wants."

"You know nothing about what we want!" Uncle Phillip spat. His anger made him press the gun harder against Danielle's skull.

She closed her eyes, still holding Dominique afloat.

The sound of police sirens sent a shiver of fear through Varick. "You want your son back." Straightening out of his shooting crouch, Varick let the gun drop harmlessly onto his trigger finger and held the weapon away from his body. "Destroying the rest of your family won't bring Noah back. Let them go."

"They deserve to die," mumbled Uncle Phillip. "Christy must be punished. She could have saved my boy, but she failed!"

"Noah's death was an accident. He was an innocent child who unfairly had his life cut short, but this is not an accident." Varick waved down toward Danielle and Dominique. "Look at them. They are both innocents. Destroying their lives will tear apart their families, but it cannot undo the past."

Uncle Phillip held his gun steady for another eternally long second then turned it on himself. He only got the weapon halfway across his chest before Varick's tackle caught him by the shoulders and slammed him against the ground. He broke down weeping, letting the gun drop away. "Let me end it!"

"You're all right," Varick murmured. "You're all right." Recovering Uncle Phillip's gun, Varick emptied the weapon and threw it in the deep end of the pool. Then, he fished Danielle and Dominique out of the water.

"Cut her loose," Danielle pleaded.

"We'll do that later. Cops are coming. Can you walk?"

"I'll manage."

Varick scooped up a sobbing, sopping wet Dominique and ran for the house. "Grab your shoes."

With the danger over, I let the dream come to an end.

Chapter 30
If I Die Today

ITEM 165: Danielle's forty-eighth letter
Item Source: Danielle Matheson
Dear Dr. S.,

I'm alive, actually a little shocked at that fact, but not ungrateful. If I die today, give my family my love. When I finish this letter, you'll understand why those fatalistic impulses keep popping up. I'm typing this nice and slowly for two reasons: one, my fingers need the task and two, it slows my brain down enough to process the last few minutes.

When we arrived at the correct address, Varick told me I should knock on the front door then try around back if that didn't work. Nobody answered my knocks or the doorbell, so I found my way to the back only to have a rude encounter with the grandfather of all anti-neighbor fences. Ironically, the neighbor's tree helped me conquer the fence.

I remember feeling quite pleased with myself for having climbed the tree, but the sight of Christy's little sister wrapped in duct tape and tossed poolside played tricks with my head. Even if it had been my own sister, Katy, I couldn't have been more outraged. I was literally trembling with the need to get down there and rip off that tape. Call it cowardice or foresight, something kept me waiting and watching.

As I prepared to drop onto the shed roof, Uncle Phillip emerged carrying a shovel. The oddness factor made me freeze. He walked calmly over to Dominique. I'm not sure if he said anything as he yanked Dominique to a standing position. He could probably have shouted at the top of his lungs, and I still wouldn't have heard him. My ears clouded with the buzzing white noise that heralds passing out.

A scream died in my throat, strangled to death by horror. The shovel finally made weird sense. My mind went helplessly blank as I watched the shovel swing back then forward. I got a strong sense of Jillian's presence looming large in my mind. A strange sensation hit me like a beach ball bouncing off my skull followed by what felt like swift wind rushing out of me. I recovered my ability to scream.

Dominique collapsed before the shovel could finish its deadly arc. She landed in the deep end with a huge splash that tossed water everywhere. A short, sharp pain like something had bitten me in the neck prompted me to move. I fell onto the shed roof, landing awkwardly enough to know I was going to fall, so I rolled with it.

I don't remember getting up, but I must have. The next thing I remember is diving into the pool and swimming for all I'm worth toward the bottom. The painful chill caught up with me about the time I reached Dominique's writhing form. I tried to pull her close so I could bring her to the surface but she knocked her head into mine. The little air I had left rushed out in a cloud of bubbles, and I swallowed some water.

Fighting my wet clothes, I surfaced, coughed a few times, and sucked in air greedily. Something splashed a few feet away from me. I didn't know what had caused the splash, but I instinctively knew it couldn't be good. Taking a deep breath, I dove down deep, praying Dominique wouldn't fight me this time. I opened my eyes and saw her still struggling, but her movements were sluggish. A few kicks and arm strokes brought me even with Dominique. I grabbed her face and held it between my palms, willing her to open her eyes and see me.

Dominique's eyes flew open, but it took two seconds for the panic to clear enough for her to see that it was me. She went limp with relief. My lungs ached with a need for air. I could only imagine what Dominique must be feeling. Frantically, I gathered her to my chest with one arm, kicking hard and using my free arm to fight toward the surface.

A white streak made me detour to the side of the pool. I burst above the water and heard the echoing crack of a gunshot. The panic caused a surge of adrenaline. I ducked and turned Dominique so she faced me again. Ripping off the tape, I flipped her onto her back and pushed her head above the water, making sure her body lay flush against the side of the pool. Her whole body shook as she coughed and sputtered and gasped.

My fingers ached from holding the side of the pool, but I didn't dare release my grip. I couldn't risk us floating in the middle of the pool, not with that maniac shooting at us. I made a cocoon-like structure with my body by wrapping my legs around Dominique's legs and pinning them to the side of the pool. When the gunfire stopped and my left hand wouldn't keep its hold any longer, I turned my thoughts to the problem of getting out.

"We need to get out of here," I told Dominique in an urgent whisper. "Stay relaxed and let me pull you along. Take a deep breath in case we need to go under. Got that?"

A wet sniffle told me she was crying, but she nodded stiffly.

Staying close to the side nearest the house, which presented a more difficult shooting angle, I awkwardly paddled to the shallow end. Strength reserves waning, my last few kicks were little more than weak flutters. I nearly cried with relief when my left hand met the glorious, smooth surface of the steps leading out of the pool.

My relief shattered into a new round of panic when a strong hand grabbed my left arm and dragged me toward the side nearest the shed. I tried to pull away and fight, but with Dominique filling one arm and my legs trapped in the water, it wasn't much of a fight. About the only thing I managed to do right was curl my neck forward so my back hit the pool's edge first instead of my head.

The impact knocked my wind out. Dominique sputtered and coughed up water, having spent the last part of our wild ride with her head being dragged through the water. The harsh grip on my left wrist released, letting my arm flop back into the water. I tucked the arm around Dominique and drew her closer. A hand landed on my left shoulder and pulled me to a standing position.

Before I could even ponder my next move, all options disintegrated. Something hard pressed painfully against my head, and it didn't take a genius to draw the conclusion: gun. Varick had a conversation with the gunman, but not much of it sank in for me. I couldn't stop thinking, *I don't want to die* and wondering if the anticipation of death would kill me first.

Since Dominique's ear was next to my mouth anyway, I whispered a stream of sentences I could only wish wouldn't turn into lies. "We're okay. We're okay. Don't be scared. Just close your eyes. Varick will save us. You'll be all right."

Somehow, Varick did save us. I didn't get a chance to thank him right away though because we had to flee almost as soon as he pulled us out of the pool. It's a good thing he mentioned grabbing my shoes. My rattled state of mind wasn't exactly conducive to thinking of such details.

I'm not sure what Devya did to Varick's genes that allows him to be so cool under pressure, but I'm officially jealous. Varick even thought to grab a few towels to throw over the leather seats so we wouldn't ruin our borrowed vehicle.

I climbed into the back where Varick had plopped Dominique on a pilfered towel, holding her in place as Varick started the SUV and calmly executed a U-turn. If it had been up to me, we would have peeled out of there like zombie hitchhikers were trying to hop aboard.

"You can cut her loose now," Varick said, holding a knife toward me, handle first.

Dominique looked at me hopefully. She didn't seem up to a conversation, and I didn't feel like chatting either. Accepting the knife from Varick, I slowly freed Dominique's hands and feet. You know, cutting through six layers of duct tape without stabbing the one you're trying to release is a lot harder than it sounds. Thankfully, Dominique was patient with me and very brave throughout the process. Once free, however, she let her guard down and started crying.

Wordlessly, I returned Varick's knife and held Dominique close. We probably should have fastened seat belts, but the kid needed the comfort more than a seat belt. I felt gross because my clothes clung to me in strange places. Dominique fell asleep. I might have joined her in taking a nap, but I couldn't stop thinking. I don't believe the thoughts were very coherent, but my mind needed to spin its wheels.

We traveled in silence for quite a while, except for some soft instrumental music Varick put on for us.

I broke the silence with a soft, "Thank you, for what you did back there. You were amazing."

"It needed doing," Varick said, sounding uncomfortable with the praise.

His answer made me chuckle.

"What's funny?"

"Nothing," I answered. "It's just something Jillian would say."

"It's something we all hold to," Varick explained.

His statement made me sad. I let it linger for about half a minute before asking, "Do you ever wish life was … normal?"

I sensed a smile in Varick's reply. "Normal is the status quo. Days like today are normal for me." I thought he'd leave it at that, but after a few beats of silence, he continued, "My abilities make me work physically harder than the others, but they are no better or worse. The normal you refer to will probably always elude us. When I accepted this, I stopped wishing for that version of normality."

Letting the conversation lapse, I drifted into musings about how Dominique would fare after today. Like Jillian and me, she'd survived a life changing event. I recalled how confusing the first few days and weeks were after our kidnapping and wished I could spare Dominique the painful flashbacks and moments of panic that would mark the coming days.

When we stopped moving, I glanced out the window, expecting to see we'd arrived at the hospital. Instead, I saw the happy, sun-like symbol next to large letters spelling Walmart.

Before I could question Varick, he said, "You both need new clothes, and I think we all need some food."

My stomach rumbled in agreement at the word *food*.

Varick handed me my purse, and I shifted to move Dominique aside.

"You should probably stay here, but I haven't enough cash on me to get everything we need. I think this qualifies as supplies and emergency travel expenses."

Remembering my recent swim, I agreed with Varick's assessment, so I handed him the thick envelope he'd given me a few hours—and seemingly a lifetime—ago. He quickly counted out a few hundred dollars and handed the envelope back.

"I'll try to be swift," Varick promised.

The slamming door woke Dominique, so I explained where we were and Varick's new mission. She informed me she needed to use the restroom but agreed it could wait until we got new clothes and could safely venture into public. I distracted her with news of her mother's improvement.

To our pleasant surprise, Varick returned within fifteen minutes bearing wonderful gifts. He opened the door by me, pitched three large bags onto my lap, and mumbled something about waiting outside. His behavior baffled me until I saw that two of the bags held a full set of clothes from socks to shirts to shorts and everything that goes underneath. I laughed at the mental image of Varick strolling around Walmart in every unmanly section.

Dominique climbed into the way back row of seats so we could have some privacy as we changed. Varick had included one of his ever-present knives, so I quickly broke the seals and cut the tags from the clothes. It took some complicated maneuvering to strip off the wet clothes and wriggle into the new ones, but the comfort of a warm, fresh shirt that didn't reek of chlorine nearly brought forth tears of joy.

I'm fairly certain Nadia gave Varick a shopping list because the third Walmart bag held two new deodorants, hand sanitizer, two hairbrushes, a handful of travel-sized tissue packs, a package of hair ties, a container of Advil, kid-sized sneakers, gauze, non-stick pads, and a fresh compact in my usual shade.

I wondered why he'd purchased two hairbrushes until I started attacking the tangled mess of my hair. After beating the hair into some semblance of order, I pulled it into a ponytail and used one of the hair ties. It wasn't the most glamorous hairstyle, but it sure beat leaving damp hair clinging to my neck. The last task before disembarking was tending the nasty cut along Dominique's upper right arm.

When Dominique and I finally stepped out of the SUV as new women, we found Varick leaning against the front passenger door looking exceedingly bored. Dominique wasted no time in seizing my hand and bolting for the store with one destination in mind. I glanced back to explain, but Varick waved me on with a laugh.

"I'll be in the food section," he called.

That's exactly where we found him a few minutes later. He hadn't bothered to get a cart or a basket, so his arms brimmed with food stuffs. I caught a box of granola bars as it tumbled from his arms. Two more boxes teetered precariously, so I plucked them off the pile and gave them to Dominique to hold. She insisted on getting something sweet, so I threw in a box of donuts. Varick shook his head at that and rolled his eyes. He'd picked up things like bottled water, apples, bread, cheese, salt free rice cakes, and peanut butter.

Back in the truck, Dominique attacked the donuts, I inhaled a granola bar, and Varick consumed an apple. With our hunger thus held at bay, I used a lighter to clean one of Varick's knives so I could slice the block of cheese into consumable chunks. Next, I cut an apple into slices for Dominique to dip in the peanut butter. Varick munched on rice cakes and ate a few slices of cheese. I made a cheese sandwich for myself then had half a chocolate donut for dessert. All in all, it was a pleasant meal.

Eating took about fifteen minutes, during which time my brain was blissfully occupied by the tasks of preparing, distributing, and eating food. When that ended, I checked the backseat and saw that Dominique had fallen asleep again, donut box clutched to her chest like a teddy bear. She looked incredibly young. My bemused smile faded at the intrusive thought that someone had just tried to murder this beautiful child.

"She'll be all right," Varick said, sensing my shift in mood. "Young children brush off scares easier than most people."

"Why did they do it?" I whispered, still watching the rhythmic rise and fall of Dominique's gentle breathing. "It makes no sense. Even revenge against Christy doesn't compute after all this time. Why wait?"

"People can hold in hate for a very long time," Varick replied. "Once they find a target for their problems, the plan to right the perceived wrong overshadows everything, including reason."

I sighed, wanting to argue but knowing he was right. After turning around in my seat and studying Varick's profile for a short while, I asked, "Is this what you do when you take jobs from Nadia?" I waved toward Dominique.

Varick shot me a sidelong look before confirming, "Some of the time. Does the knowledge make you more or less inclined to join us?"

"More."

We said little else the rest of the trip back to the hospital. Now we're killing time in the parking lot while Varick and Nadia plan the best way to sneak us inside. The security around here has tightened up significantly. If I didn't think it vital to get Dominique in to see her mother, I'd vote for finding a hotel and returning tomorrow.

One would expect me to welcome the down time, but it's only given me more time to notice how sadly out of shape I am.

The Sore One,

Danielle Matheson.

Chapter 31
Hopefully Not Goodbye

ITEM 166: Malia's second letter to Jillian
Item Source: Jillian Blairington

Dear Jillian,

You will soon see what I've done, but here, I hope to explain the why. Nadia told me what you did for Dominique. I'm glad you saved her, though I wish you hadn't strained your Gift to accomplish it. I should like to have a companion, a friend, a sister in this time of need. Nadia has her own battle to fight right now, and I'm not going to let you awaken in time to involve yourself in the coming conflict.

I argued fiercely with myself over this. As a general rule, I do not usually apply my full Gifts to family or friends. I have made an exception for you in this instance. You need a deep, uninterrupted sleep. I am letting you relax and preventing you from sensing my concerns about the coming evening.

Michio and I are finished with the work we came to do. He, too, is resting. I am proud to have aided in this miracle you and Michio started. It is a triumph to cherish for the rest of our days. Besides our family, only Christy and perhaps Dr. Ketterman will remember these events. Christy is spending some time with her mother. The phone call from her aunt shook Christy to the core. I have given her some subtle help, but I believe time with her mother will fortify her emotions more than I can.

I'm sorry you didn't get to meet Dr. Ketterman. He is the staff doctor assigned to Susan Kilpatrick during her stay here at the hospital. From the many ways he's gone out of his way to help us, I suspect he's

169

one of Nadia's contacts. He had the nurses order extra food for the room as we could not buy any ourselves. I have saved some for you. Sorry it will be cold when you awaken. Danielle took the majority of our funds with her on the mission to save Dominique. Dr. Ketterman has promised to see Susan and her daughters to safety as soon as Varick and Danielle can bring Dominique.

They—Varick and Danielle—will not like my plan any more than you will, but I would rather risk your ire than your lives or freedom. I can handle many things, but not a role reversal. Mine has always been the role of captive. You know this very well. What you do not know is that the only type of training I consistently failed at is the one where multiple lives hinged on my decisions. Varick may not like such exercises, but he can make those decisions. Nadia tends not to find herself in such situations. Even Dustin has succeeded a time or two where I have not.

The reasons for the rift between the Guardians and Dr. Devya matter little. Perhaps our government has simply tired of waiting for us to grow up and intends to press us into service. More likely there are one or two ambitious people somewhere along the chain who believe they can turn this power struggle to their own advantage.

Michio cannot fall into their hands. His Gifts rely heavily upon the nanomachines he controls. The Guardian scientists will start out by studying him, but their patience will not last forever. When that well runs dry, they will take his Gift by force. The Gift is so much a part of him that I think he will perish without it. This is the heavy truth I must press upon my mother.

I have contacted Varick and Danielle and explained my intentions. As predicted, Varick did not like my reasons or my plan, but he was the first to accept them and helped to convince Danielle. For her part, Danielle understands my desire to protect you and Michio. She even volunteered to help with my new mission. I have not come to a decision about her offer yet, but I am inclined to accept her aid.

Surely you can understand my deep abiding fear for Michio's life, but you may wonder why I fear for you as well. Dr. Devya's training exercises may sometimes be unpleasant, but at least he understands your capabilities and limits. In comparison, the Guardian scientists will be like toddlers trying to fathom the depths of theoretical calculus. Toddlers destroy things that frustrate them. The analogy may be simplistic, but I cannot risk being right and doing nothing.

I hope I am not giving you the impression that I intend to

surrender. I am not giving up. There is far too much living to do to consider that option and my distrust of the Guardians runs far too deeply for me to put much hope in their promises.

While I am in a confessing mood, I will share with you one of my deepest fears. I have no wish to become the Guardians' prisoner either as I believe they would use me to strike at Nadia. Her Gift is perhaps Dr. Devya's greatest success. Should he succeed in depriving the Guardians of Nadia, they will do everything in their power to persuade her to break free. You have seen my dreams. I do not need to define such things to you.

Do not worry for me. I know you would help me bear this burden if I asked, and that is precisely the reason I will not ask.

Complete success will mean we get to go home and live in peace with our families. Partial success means we get to flee in the hopes of one day being truly free. Failure means either death or imprisonment.

Regardless of the outcome, thank you for the long conversations and loving support throughout the short time I've known you. This is hopefully not goodbye, or at least not a long goodbye.

Your loving sister,
Malia Karina Davidson

Chapter 32
The Crazy Plan

ITEM 167: Jillian's eighty-third post-kidnapping journal entry
Item Source: Jillian Blairington
The long nap helped, but my head still hurts. Guess it don't help that I'm cross with Malia. She left me here with a cold meal and a crazy note about a plan I probably wouldn't like. She's right about the not liking her plan part. It's complicated, multi-phased, and might work, but that ain't the point. Malia helped me rest while she wrestled with her inner demons alone. That's not how this relationship is supposed to work. Nana would say I'm being as silly as a snake wearing a tutu, but even Nana's a big fan of families fighting their battles together.

The first part of Malia's plan involves getting Varick and Danielle to safely deliver Dominique to her momma's room. The second part consists of Dr. Ketterman smuggling Christy, Dominique, and their momma out of the hospital. The third part has Varick and Danielle escaping with Michio and me. All parts have Malia monitoring everything through Nadia. The fourth part has Malia drawing Dr. Robinson's people to her and convincing 'em to not bother pursuing us. I understand that persuasion is one of Malia's Gifts, but the chances of her convincing an army's worth of government people to up and go away ain't very high.

The first part of my plan involves eating the cold food saved for me. It's a nicely breaded chicken breast with green beans and plain penne noodles, no garlic powder or butter or anything that would remotely help it along. That's probably why I've been avoiding it for the past half-hour.

The second part of my plan will consist of me putting myself into a working sleep and monitoring the rest of Malia's plans. She's getting my help whether she wants it or not.

The third part of my plan will hopefully be me shaking my little sister and giving her what-for about trying to keep me out of it. Nadia's telling me the first part of Malia's plan is starting, so I'll eat at least the chicken, turn on the thought recording thingy, and start plan monitoring.

***

I'm not certain how many plans were considered and discarded for sneaking back into the hospital, but the one decided upon seemed simple enough. Varick carried Dominique right through the front doors with Danielle hurrying along like a worried momma in hot pursuit of her family.

The dream state let me see 'em with Nadia's illusion intact like a ghost image superimposed over their bodies. She didn't make many changes, but Varick's new, scruffy beard and Danielle's full complement of pricey jewelry made 'em both look older. Their outfits also looked classier than the real things. Varick still wore all black, but the illusion turned his cargo pants into expensive dress slacks. Nadia left Dominique's clothes alone but altered her features so nobody could peer at her directly and remember what she looked like.

The soldiers standing near the doors eyed 'em suspiciously, but their expressions didn't change much when they spotted a man limping in beside his wife. I guess the soldiers are supposed to glare at everybody. Varick carried Dominique until they got in the elevator. Then, the illusion shifted. Varick set Dominique down and the girl grasped Danielle's hand. The new illusion had shifted Dominique's hair and eye color so they matched Danielle. They exited the elevator looking more like sisters than mother and daughter.

For her part, Dominique skipped down the hallway straight to her momma's room. She opened the door so forcefully that the noise knocked me up a few sleep levels. I recovered about the time Danielle and Varick stepped into the room and shut the door. This time, I was ready for the loud bang and blocked it out.

Danielle rushed to me and reached to wake me up, but Varick caught her left hand.

"Don't wake her." He spoke softly, but his voice held command.

"Why not?" asked Danielle, too surprised to be offended.

"She's working. She's probably even listening to our conversation."

"Why would she bother?" Danielle wondered, eyeing me strangely. Her focus allowed me to see myself, which I can honestly say was odd.

"She's watching over you," Varick replied. "Did you not feel her at the house? I felt her for a time."

Danielle appeared thoughtful. "I did feel … something." She glanced over at the happy reunion taking place on the other side of the room and lowered her voice. "But I thought her Gift only affected dreams."

Varick smiled. "To Jillian that was a dream."

"But it actually happened."

The smile widened. "She does not dream like other people. She can see events as they transpire, and though her control might not be like Nadia or Malia, she can occasionally shape these dreams."

Danielle's attention fixed on Dominique and she murmured, "That's explains it."

Varick's smile dimmed. "Yes, that is what happened, but Jillian pays a higher price than the others." He leaned over my sleeping body and tucked a bottle of Advil into my right hand.

The thought made me want to laugh, but the dream translated that into an amused smile. That explained the headache, but it suddenly occurred to me that I didn't know why I'd never suffered such a setback like this before. Experimenting, I wished Danielle would raise the question.

Danielle turned toward me like I'd tapped her on the shoulder.

I repeated the request, slower this time.

"I think Jillian wants me to ask you something," Danielle murmured.

"It's possible. What would she like to know?"

"Why did she get a headache this time?" Each word came out of Danielle reluctantly, but I was pleased all the same.

"I'm not sure, but I believe the other times you've changed a dream like that Nadia or Malia were present to help you," Varick answered, speaking directly to me.

"Malia was present this time, too," Danielle pointed out, voicing my sentiment quicker this time. "Why would her presence work at other times and fail now?"

Varick thought carefully before attempting an answer. "Malia's work with Michio probably prevented her from helping you with such a dramatic shaping event. You'll have to be mindful of that when working alone."

"Doesn't she always work alone?" The question was purely Danielle's idea, but I still wanted to hear Varick's answer.

"Their Gifts were always meant to work together," Varick said. "They reach out to one another unconsciously, but Jillian doesn't always need the extra support. She mostly shapes the dreams of others, which happens more naturally."

Nadia's voice broke into our thoughts simultaneously. *You are correct, Varick, but the discussion must wait until another time. You and Danielle must first get Christy's family to Dr. Ketterman and then get Michio and Jillian out of the building. I need her to continue sleeping. Malia needs us.*

Chapter 33
The Easy Way?

ITEM 168: Danielle's forty-ninth letter
Item Source: Danielle Matheson
Dear Dr. S.,

If I want to hang around Jillian and her siblings, I'm going to have to get used to strange conversations. One of my friends said her sister would talk to anyone who asked her questions while she's asleep. Kayla referred mostly to "yes" and "no" questions though. The conversation I just had with Varick and sleeping Jillian went way beyond "yes" and "no" questions and answers.

Varick and I snuck into the hospital with Dominique Roman using the front door of all things. Spy movies give you the impression that sneaking around involves more complicated maneuvers. That part came later, but at least the late afternoon started off normally. It's also appropriate that Varick and I talked with Jillian. The Roman sisters deserved some time with their mother. Michio slept on the spare cot. Only Malia was conspicuously absent. If I hadn't had pre-warning on that score, I would have panicked, but Malia thoughtfully informed us of her "barking mad" plan, as Varick phrased it. I'm still waiting on Malia's response to my offer to help.

Dinner consisted of granola bars, apples, cheese, rice cakes, and anything else we had left over from our Walmart raid. I thought we'd have to throw half of it out, but the worry of the last few days gave us great appetites. I saved two granola bars for Jillian, but we cleaned up the rest pretty thoroughly. She ate them in about four seconds when she woke up for a brief break. We didn't get to talk much because she went back to sleep almost immediately after swallowing the snack.

Naps are wonderful things. Even I took one, but I think mine was half intended to stave off boredom. Though I can't vouch for the others, I believe I can sympathize better with police officers on long stakeouts and soldiers stuck in trenches eons ago. Waiting stinks. We needed to wait until dark, which didn't happen until around eight o'clock. On the bright side, we had food, access to a "loo", and the company of friends, albeit nervous company.

Varick's a bad influence on my vocabulary, but he does know how to cheer me. "It's time." His announcement ending the wait got an immediate reaction from everybody who was awake.

I jumped out of my seat and went to wake Dominique who'd finally dozed off in the last hour. Christy's mother nodded solemnly. Christy smiled nervously at her mother, gave her hand a hard squeeze, and then backed away to give Varick room to approach.

Varick slipped into the space Christy vacated and scooped her mother up as if she weighed no more than Dominique. The war against cancer had drained much of the vitality and extra weight from Christy's mother, but she still couldn't be defined as a small woman. Christy steeled her expression, but I knew the sight of her emaciated mother pained her more than it did me.

I wondered what illusion Nadia had placed over Christy's mother. To my surprise, I got a flash of thought like a niggling memory. A closer look at Christy's mother revealed the same youthful face Dominique had first worn as we walked into the hospital. Suddenly, the subtlety of Nadia's first illusion made sense. The disguise she'd given Dominique when we entered was the face her mother possessed as a child. Nervousness gnawed at my insides, but I grabbed my purse and hurried after Varick. We took the elevator and exited, striding right across the lobby and out the front doors.

One of the guards nodded stiffly at us as he pressed the handicap button to swing the doors aside. Dr. Ketterman waited for us with Nurse Keili. He opened the back door of his white Mercedes and let Varick put Christy's mother into the back seat. Varick took the front passenger seat and I took the seat next to Christy's mother. With a wave to Nurse Keili, Dr. Ketterman hopped in his car and drove off. He headed toward the exit but then looped around toward the staff parking lot like he'd forgotten something.

Varick and I wished him luck and disembarked. We took the emergency stairs up to the roof and snuck into the hospital. My heart rate didn't return to normal until we entered the room that had so recently been Christy's mother room, but the reprieve was brief.

The original plan had Christy and Dominique traveling with their mother, but we'd forgotten three things. One, the original plan would leave behind a lot of luggage. Two, Christy's car would have to be abandoned in the parking lot. Three, Nadia's illusions tend to be strongest if she's familiar with a person. Therefore, if Varick and I were present, the scene could be changed a lot easier than if Christy and Dominique traveled alone.

This second trip down was a little more arduous than the first because I had to lug two suitcases, Jillian and Malia's. Michio, thankfully, didn't have a suitcase of his own, as his things were stuffed in with Jillian's belongings. I can't complain though because Varick hauled the two heaviest suitcases, Christy's and mine. Christy helped her sister with her bag, and Dominique carried a few Walmart bags stuffed with garbage. Some nurses would straighten the room for us, but we didn't want to leave too much behind to be tracked.

Whatever happened to doing things the easy way? I thought we'd take the elevator down and walk out like last time, but Varick reminded me that there was no record of Christy and Dominique entering the building today. Instead of going down like normal people, we went up to the roof, climbed down each miserable flight of stairs, and hiked around to the parking garage. Even hurrying, the trip took us almost ten minutes. After we reached Christy's car and loaded it up with luggage, our last task became to convince Christy to carry forth her part of the plan.

"I want to stay and help," Christy insisted.

My aching arms wanted to strangle my friend, but I didn't have the energy. "Couldn't that sentiment have come up a half-hour ago?"

Before Christy could answer, Varick said, "This is helping." He took the last bag of garbage from Dominique and tossed it into the back seat. Then, he swept her up and loaded her into the front seat, making sure all her limbs were tucked inside before shutting the door.

"I mean really helping," argued Christy.

"You have to pick your mother up at the rendezvous," Varick reminded. "Protecting Dr. Ketterman's identity is a huge help."

"Won't the agents remember his car?" I didn't really want to argue in Christy's favor, but curiosity got the best of me.

"They've seen enough cars out there today," Varick said. "Besides, I'm not sure we really saw his car."

"How will I know it then?" Christy wondered.

"You will know him," Varick replied. When Christy still looked skeptical, he continued, "Listen to Nadia. She will show you the way."

Christy took a few more minutes to convince, but at last, she reluctantly got into her car and drove away. Moments later, Varick and I looked down to see Christy exit the parking garage. I held my breath, but the gate swung open like magic as Christy approached. She paused a moment to chat with the guards and then pulled out. I did a double take then because it looked like her car was continuing out the exit like normal, only all its lights ceased working and it actually went left.

"Where is she going?" I murmured.

"Perhaps heeding Nadia's directions was poor advice," Varick mused. "She tends to take liberties with driving directions."

"Why are Christy's car lights not working?"

"Malia," Varick answered.

"You have very … willful and inventive sisters, Varick."

Chuckling in agreement, Varick led the way back to the hospital, up those irritating stairs, and to the home away from home.

The final trip down proved to be the most difficult. This time, I carried Michio who clung to my back like a little monkey. Varick took Jillian in a fireman's carry. We would have looked like an odd procession if anyone saw us, but I think Nadia's illusion that round consisted of blending us into the shadows. That explains the "wait for dark" instruction. I still say the last trip gave us the most trouble because we had to pause to let patrols walk by far more often than the previous trips. Michio was good as gold and silent as a breeze, but he got heavy. Dylan and Katy are way past the piggyback ride stage of life, so I'm out of practice.

To be fair, it's been a long day. They say it ain't over till the fat lady sings, but I think she's got laryngitis today. This day might never end. I'll soon be off to help Malia. Varick's grumpy, but he's agreed to stay with Michio and Jillian and keep them out of trouble.

He put up a last minute protest, but the semi-ease with which Varick agreed tells me he's worried. "You've done more than enough to help us, Danielle." Varick's tone mixed persuasion and plea. "This scheme could go either way."

"Will I improve Malia's odds by being present?"

"That's not the point."

"It *is* the point because it means I'm going." I started rooting around in my purse for car keys, but on second thought, I handed the whole bag over to Varick. "This has my keys, just in case." I couldn't bring myself to be more specific, but Varick picked up on my meaning. "They need you," I said, referring to Jillian and Michio.

"I will see them to safety," Varick assured. He frowned but accepted my purse. "And if Malia's plan goes sideways, I'll be there."

It occurred to me that I should talk him out of that, but besides not wanting to waste my breath, I understood his need to protect. That is after all the very meaning of his name and the nature of his Gifts.

I can now cross out "write Dr. S. an email from a creepy spot in a parking garage" from my list of things to do. Yippee.

The Brave or the Foolish (only time will sort the difference),
Danielle Matheson.

Chapter 34
Malia Plays Pied Piper

ITEM 169: Jillian's eighty-fourth post-kidnapping journal entry
Item Source: Jillian Blairington

Malia's plan seems to have worked out perfectly so far. That should make me happy, but I can't help thinking it's about time for a disaster. Danielle and Varick escorted everybody out over the course of a few hours. They even carried Michio and me.

I've gotten a better handle on switching between real-world dreams. Nana says to always enter a day expecting to let it teach ya something new. Today, I learned I could host a few real-world dreams at the same time. The skill strained my Gifts, but it's a fair price to pay to track multiple siblings and situations.

Danielle just left to help Malia. Varick and Michio are still here with me in the parking garage. My older brother chose a corner spot behind one of the government SUVs. Soon after Danielle left, Varick set Michio up by one of the wheels and let him play games on Danielle's iPad. He made sure the sound was off but the light doesn't make much difference 'cause the garage is pretty well lit.

I wondered why we didn't go to Danielle's car right away. It would be more comfortable for everybody and have less risk of somebody spotting us. Eventually, I remembered that the government has people watching Danielle's car. It's a mite disturbing that their file on Danielle contains that information.

Curious, I stretched my dream sense above my body until I sensed the second level up in the parking garage. Recalling that Danielle had parked on the roof, I quickly moved up two more levels.

My connection to Malia and Nadia let me feel the government agents before I spotted their white van parked two rows over from Danielle's Honda Accord. They must have a camera mounted on the front of their rearview mirror 'cause I couldn't spot people.

Letting that dream fade to the back of my mind, I checked on Malia's progress. Her daft plan has had her wandering the hospital halls under various illusions Nadia provides. It surprised me that Nadia would agree to help, but I guess the logic follows my reasons for helping. My main contribution so far has been to make the government people sleepy. That might sound silly, but lack of sleep dulls the senses, making Malia's plan easier to enact.

So far, my little sister has led Dr. Robinson's people on a merry chase all over the hospital. I don't think the administrators are real pleased with that, but they don't gripe too loudly. The plan's strange enough that I feared somebody with a cell phone would try and record it, but Malia assured me she's taken measures against that sort of thing. If Malia missed anything, I'm sure Dr. Robinson's people caught it 'cause they've brought some serious equipment with 'em.

More news vans have rolled in. I can't decide whether the publicity's good or bad. It should keep Dr. Robinson from doing something drastic, but it also brings us mighty close to discovery. I eavesdropped on the news people, and thankfully, they don't know much. They're simply saying "the hostage situation is ongoing" and that there are an awful lot of government people present. You can say lots about government people, but they sure know how to stonewall news people.

Since the government couldn't shut down the hospital, Malia found willing people to aid her in confounding the attempts to find us. I don't know everybody's story, but the help has come in many forms. I need to be clear that nobody's helping against their will. Some volunteered 'cause they owed Nadia a favor. Some just wanna do right. Others see a profit in it. I think a journalist slipped in, but hopefully, Nadia will deal with him in her own time. Still others just enjoy confounding government people.

Whatever their reasons, the volunteers have hidden in closets, patient rooms, stairwells, and other dark recesses. Some of the nurses went about their business as usual. What made 'em different is the fact that they let Malia fit 'em with one of our physiological profiles. Apparently, some of the government's fancy toys are machines attuned to our heartbeat and brainwave scans. Though the readings are sorely out of date, the machines are smart enough to adjust and extrapolate. That means they use old data to guess what our profiles ought to be now.

If it had been my plan, I woulda had Malia break the government's machines so they can't have our profiles, but she's right to believe that would only be a short-term fix. They would send more people with new machines later.

I've never really seen Malia's Gift like this. It's neat to see, even if it is also creepy and scary. I can't imagine how much concentration it must take to reach out to a person and change their emotional state.

Nadia's part is twofold. She works with Malia to change a person's vital signs so they echo the profile of Malia, Michio, Varick or me. Nadia also makes the soldiers and agents believe that they've seen one of us, so they pursue the decoys. Most of the decoys have been caught by now, but there are still a few left. Soon, we're gonna have to decide to activate another wave or let the plan proceed to its next phase. Unfortunately for my nerves, that decision belongs to Malia.

Electronic mastery is another part of Malia's Gift that she's using rather freely tonight. I must admit it's the part about her plan that I like best. A few special decoys—doctors, nurses, pharmacists, janitors, and other folks with access to restricted areas—have led a good number of government people into traps. Like all great traps, these are simple. The decoy walks into a restricted area, the government person follows, and the electronic locks shut down, trapping everybody. Fail-safes are supposed to keep the locks permanently open if something disturbs 'em, but I don't think the designers prepared for Malia.

I suggested drawing Dr. Robinson into a trap, but it's another one of those short-term fixes Malia ain't fond of. We kinda like having Dr. Robinson as our chief opponent. I know that sounds strange, but Malia's connection to her gives us an advantage. If we send the government people packing, they will return with somebody else. Dr. Robinson may be trigger happy and keep designing stuff that gets one of us poisoned, but in her way, she's devoted to keeping Malia and Michio safe.

Dr. Robinson's down in the cafeteria 'cause that's where the government people set up their operational headquarters. The location also happens to be one of the few spaces large enough to store their collection of decoys and other detainees.

I feel bad for the agent they sent in earlier 'cause he played the part of a hostage-taker. When Dr. Robinson's people took control of the hospital, they subdued and arrested him. He's being held in one of the rooms nearby while they pretend to question him. That means different agents move in and out of the room, staying for various amounts of time. They changed his handcuffs so his hands can be in front of his body, but he's been wearing 'em for hours. Handcuffs ain't exactly made for comfort.

As I considered helping the undercover agent sleep, I felt drawn to the main cafeteria. Following the instinct, I let my consciousness connect to the disturbance that caught my attention.

Malia stood a few feet away from Dr. Robinson who was deep in discussion with some of her people. Over her casual clothes, Malia appears dressed in loose fitting gray slacks and a classy red blouse. Her features reflect Nadia's projection of what Malia will look like in about fifteen years. I agree with the image, especially the eyes. Generally, I'd describe Malia's dark eyes as timid, guarded, or reserved. The older version of Malia possesses eyes that hold a lot more confidence, strength, and cool intelligence. They're eyes that tell ya they've got a message you'll want to hear.

A hush fell over the crowd of decoys, agents, and unfortunates caught in the mix. One agent rushed from Malia's side to whisper in his boss's ear.

Dr. Robinson studied Malia carefully and nodded absently to the agent. She issued some quiet orders to her men, and two agents moved to flank Malia. After another long look, Dr. Robinson said, "My men tell me you wish to speak in private. I am under orders not to negotiate with you, but I will hear what you have to say."

"Not quite in private," Malia replied. "I would like one witness."

Chapter 35
A Different Sort of Miracle

ITEM 170: Jillian's eighty-fifth post-kidnapping journal entry
Item Source: Jillian Blairington

Danielle's role in Malia's plan made more sense after the request for a witness. A few quick orders solidified the arrangements, and soon, two more agents escorted Danielle to the room where the others had brought Malia.

Danielle had made a fine decoy of me, but she'd only managed to dodge three agent patrols. The fourth pair caught her rather quickly 'cause she wasn't in the mood to run. I'd been nervous for her, but I figured she'd have a nice time-out with the other decoys then be released in a few hours. Nadia had fitted her with two illusions, the one of me and one altering her features so she didn't look like herself.

Until the conversation got underway with Dr. Robinson, I liked having Danielle there 'cause it made my job much easier. My mark on Danielle gave me an anchor to focus on so the dream wouldn't shift away without my permission.

A sharp breath from Danielle told me Malia hadn't prepared her for the disguise. Her eyebrows shot upward, but she merely said, "That's some growth spurt."

Malia let a faint smile play across her face. "It is for the people out there more than anything else. They would not understand a child's request to speak with a powerful government agent."

"You do think of everything," Danielle complimented.

"Not everything, but hopefully enough. Are you certain you wish to be here?"

"The more you ask that question the more nervous I get," Danielle pointed out. "Is there something you're not telling me?"

I missed Malia's answer 'cause I got the feeling there was another conversation happening outside the door, so I moved my attention there.

"I strongly advise against this, Dr. Lynchberg," said an agent. He sounded familiar, so I added the visual element. The speaker was Mr. Sanders, one of the agent men who had inspected Dr. Devya's lab. "These children are dangerous. At least let me or Smith accompany you."

"Your protest is noted, Sanders. Now, get out of my way," said Dr. Robinson. I didn't care that everybody called her Dr. Kathleen Lynchberg, she would always be Dr. Karita Robinson to me.

A moment later, the door opened and Dr. Robinson stepped through alone, closing the door firmly in Agent Sanders's face. She stared at the door for an extra second before facing Malia and Danielle.

An oval conference table took up most of the room. The agents had seated Malia in the center chair and Danielle two chairs further down, away from the only entrance or exit. Both Malia and Danielle wore handcuffs. Since there weren't too many places to put their hands, they kept 'em folded neatly on the table.

Silence tried to take over, but Malia chased it away with a pretty grave statement. "They will betray you soon, Mother."

I figured the next logical question ought to be *Who?*

Instead, Dr. Robinson stepped forward and carefully placed her fingertips on the conference table's smooth, dark surface. "Is this warning from you or Nadia?"

"Both," Malia answered. "Nadia sensed it first, but I can confirm their dark intentions. They will call you with a pretense of urgency, ambush you, and place the blame on Varick. They would have done it already, but they're having trouble locating Varick."

Idly tapping the fingers of her right hand, Dr. Robinson said, "You know why I am here. Why would you tell me this?"

Malia cast off Nadia's illusion, returning her features to their normal age. Her voice also changed from the rich fullness of a confident woman to one more suited to a preteen, but the words were typical Malia, which is far more mature than any preteen. "You know the answer to that. You've also known somebody would make a move soon. The only mysteries left were who intended you harm and how they would carry forth their plans."

Dr. Robinson looked like she was measuring Malia's words. "What do you propose I do with these errant individuals?"

"Turn their plan against them," Malia advised. "Allow us to help you. If you stay with me, you'll be safe."

"Let's find out." Dr. Robinson unclipped a cell phone and poked a number.

"Agent Sanders speaking."

"Come in, please."

The door opened and Agent Sanders walked in and stood a half-step behind Dr. Robinson.

Malia's disguise was back in place.

Without turning to face him, Dr. Robinson addressed the man. "My daughter thinks you intend to kill me, Sanders. Well done."

Her response confused me and Danielle, if I read her stunned expression correctly. I couldn't tell what Malia was thinking. She kept a much tighter hold on her facial expressions.

"Thank you, ma'am," responded Agent Sanders crisply.

"Tell Smith he's a fool for that part about framing Varick. I told you to be subtle."

"Apologies, ma'am. It won't happen again."

"Good, you're dismissed."

Agent Sanders departed, and both Danielle and Malia took on their normal appearances.

As the door clunked shut, Danielle cleared her throat. "I take it this was a trap, an intricate one."

"I knew at least one of them would answer a threat to me," said Dr. Robinson.

"That is so twisted," Danielle muttered.

"There is another threat, a real one," Malia insisted.

I drew a small measure of hope from Malia's calm tone.

"Not from Smith or Sanders," assured Dr. Robinson.

"No, not from them," Malia agreed. "An agent named Adams and a few others I do not know."

Dr. Robinson's frown told me dropping Adams's name had scored a point. She looked annoyed by the prospect of a plot she hadn't blessed. "I will have the matter investigated."

"I was not sure about the Smith-Sanders plot, but I am certain a threat exists," Malia said. "Before I left Dr. Devya's compound, we encountered a group called Katharos. You and the Guardians threaten Katharos as much—or more—than we do, Mother. That is why

Danielle is here."

"Why am I here?"

"To protect us," Malia answered. "Nadia could not find out much about Katharos, but their ideals are clear enough. They fight for purity and natural order, as their name suggests."

"You're being naïve if you believe such a group would spare us for one girl," said Dr. Robinson. She took a moment to text something to one of her people. "Fanatics do not care about collateral damage."

"These do," Malia countered.

Her serious tone brought Dr. Robinson's head up from her phone. "What else do you know?"

"Have you ever used this room alone?" Malia inquired, instead of answering.

Dr. Robinson considered the question carefully, then answered, "No, but I'm long overdue for a break. I kept putting it off because there's far too much to do."

Malia fired another query. "Did you have it swept?"

"Of course. My people searched for listening devices as well as—ah, I see what you mean."

"I don't," Danielle snapped. "What are you getting at, Malia?"

"There is a small bomb under this table," Malia announced. She sounded like finding a bomb under a table was an everyday occurrence.

Danielle moved her chair back so fast she nearly tipped over backwards.

"Do not fear it," said Malia. "I have disabled the detonator. It cannot harm us."

Dr. Robinson dropped to her hands and knees and peered under the table. I followed her line of sight and spotted the bomb just as she did. For a moment, I thought she'd crawl under the table to retrieve the bomb, but she only grabbed a corner of the table and hauled herself up. "You have my attention, Malia. What do you wish and what can you tell me about this new threat?"

"How did you know a bomb would be there?" Danielle's question to Malia came out shaky.

"She can sense electronics and identify their intent," Dr. Robinson explained.

"Their intent?" Danielle repeated.

"Bombs feel malevolent," said Malia. She pushed her chair back, ducked under the table, and emerged a moment later with the tiny bomb. "This one has a short kill radius."

"How much of a radius?" Danielle asked, as curiosity briefly overcame fear.

Dr. Robinson took one look at the bomb. "Four feet, maybe five. This room and its inhabitants would have died, but I think the walls would have absorbed most of the blast. Are there other bombs?"

"I have disabled four others today," Malia reported. "I cannot say if I caught them all, but your sensors should be able to pick up any I missed. They didn't spread them around very widely for fear of killing innocents."

Nodding like the explanation worked for her, Dr. Robinson tapped more orders into her phone. When she looked up again, something had softened in her dark eyes. "Thank you for the save. Now what is your proposal?" In response to Danielle's questioning look, Dr. Robinson explained, "Today's events confirm that Malia and Nadia have given the problem much thought. Therefore, there must be a proposal that required a personal presentation, or I would have received a phone call."

I'm used to that sort of logic from Nadia, but it surprised me coming from Dr. Robinson. It really shouldn't have surprised me, seeing as our mommas musta been picked for the project for a reason.

"My wish is this: return to your bosses and convince them of the threat Katharos represents," said Malia. "My request is this: carry the message that we only want to be free, but that we will help fight this new threat."

"Do you speak for all of your siblings?" asked Dr. Robinson.

Malia lifted her chin as if she'd expected the question. "I speak for Nadia and myself, but I'm certain Varick and Jillian will also help. Aiden and Michio are too young for a conflict of this nature. And while I do not know where Dustin will stand, I know he will protect Cora and Dr. Devya in whatever way he deems best."

"That assessment sounds accurate," noted Dr. Robinson. She fell silent, thinking very deeply. "My superiors will take a great deal of convincing, but I believe I can manage it. Our relationship with Dean and his people is also in need of repair and this might mend those bridges." Her eyes focused on Malia. "I can make no promises, but I am in favor of your deal. We can—"

A few shouts, some screams, and a gunshot suddenly demanded our attention.

Chapter 36
The Director Answers a Challenge

ITEM 171: Jillian's eighty-sixth post-kidnapping journal entry
Item Source: Jillian Blairington

Normal people duck when crazy people fire guns, even warning shots, but Dr. Robinson drew her gun and contemplated the door which shook 'cause somebody was frantically pounding on it.

"Director, these men would like to speak with you." The nervous voice belonged to Agent Smith.

"Stay behind the table," Dr. Robinson instructed Malia and Danielle. "And take off the handcuffs." She pressed her back against the left side of the doorframe and slowly reached for the handle.

Her order confused me 'cause the fear buzzing in the next room made me forget Malia's talent for lock picking. Not waiting to see if Danielle and Malia followed Dr. Robinson's advice, I shifted my attention to the main room. The decoy crowd still sat in their chairs, but their posture had stiffened significantly. Around the room, government agents squared off, pointing their handguns and rifles at each other. Since it was my dream, I asked Nadia to identify those loyal to Dr. Robinson and had 'em light up with blue auras. Automatically, I transferred this information to Malia.

"Get her out here right now!" demanded a man holding a gun on Agent Smith.

"I'm trying," barked Agent Smith. "You're not helping me think. Back up."

"You don't need to think. I want Director Lynchberg out here in the next ten seconds or you're dead."

"I'm here," said Dr. Robinson. "What can I do for you, Adams?" She leveled her gun at Adams who still had his weapon pointed at Agent Smith.

"Where's the Experiment?" asked Adams, filling the last word with scorn. His harsh inflection made the word a title.

"This is a very public forum to be having this conversation. We should speak in private." Dr. Robinson spoke in a crisp, businesslike tone that hid her tension.

"This is the perfect forum," argued Adams. "You can't hide this! There are dozens of witnesses!"

"Witnesses to what? What are you after?" Dr. Robinson's questions came out with genuine curiosity and confusion.

"The government can't hide its dirty little secrets forever," declared Adams. "We will expose you. We'll expose everything!" Keeping his gun steady on Agent Smith, Adams twisted his head and shouted, "Sykes, get that camera over here."

A man eagerly ran up holding a small digital recorder. His last two steps faltered as he frowned down at his camera. He stopped running and fiddled with some buttons before shaking the thing. He let out a frustrated grunt and grumbled, "It's not working."

Adams hissed a curse then flung Smith aside and pointed his weapon at Dr. Robinson. "Bring the little witch out here."

"Threatening an eleven-year-old girl is not going to help your cause," Dr. Robinson pointed out. "Your precious witnesses are only seeing two agents having a violent disagreement. Are you sure you wish to change that dynamic?"

As Dr. Robinson and Adams entered into a staring contest, I searched for an opportunity to intervene. The memory of the painful fallout from making Dominique faint made me hesitate to use that part of my Gift. Adams's grip on his gun looked tight enough to squeeze the trigger before anything I might do could take effect. Besides, there were at least another half-dozen standoffs around the room. Any move on my part would get somebody killed.

"I'm twelve now, Mother," said Malia, sounding incredibly young.

My first thought was: *When did that happen?* And my second thought was: *She's very good at setting impressions.* I couldn't see Malia from the current perspective, but since she wasn't shouting, I guessed she stood almost directly behind Dr. Robinson.

"Mother?" repeated Adams, managing to sound both disgusted

and intrigued.

"Your files are woefully inadequate if they neglected that fact," Dr. Robinson said, throwing in a hint of mocking over the disdain.

"No matter. Now I have two reasons to kill you," Adams muttered.

"Why do you hate us?" Malia asked, playing up the frightened kid tone. If we ever have normal lives, Malia should take up acting. She peered around Dr. Robinson, looking even more waiflike than usual. She lightly touched the back of Dr. Robinson's shirt, and then bent her head away from Adams, like she couldn't bear to look at him.

I felt a surge of something charge through the dream.

As Adams's gun dropped toward Malia, Dr. Robinson stepped forward, forcing the man to backpedal or shoot her. His hands trembled and sweat broke out across his brow. Panic entered his eyes as he stumbled backward. He stared hard at his gun like it had betrayed him. "What did you do to me?"

I didn't get Malia's answer to that question 'cause my dream connection snapped as someone shook me awake. My eyes sprang open and fixed on Varick.

"We've got to go. Get up." Varick already had Michio pasted across his back. Danielle's purse had been draped over Michio's shoulder like a bandolier.

"Hurry!" encouraged Michio.

"The war's about to move out here," Varick explained. "We must move up."

It didn't sound like a great plan to me, but Varick wasn't in a discussing mood. He'd already scrambled over the low cement wall and started climbing up one of the columns that connected each floor of the parking garage.

"I can't follow you up there."

"Then hide. I'll be right back."

"Hide!" I spat the dumb advice out but ducked down anyway as the sound of running boots echoed through the garage.

My options weren't great. Running would get me caught and hiding would only delay getting caught for a short time. Parking garages don't leave many options when it comes to hiding. I rolled under the truck and listened hard.

"Are you sure she said they'd be in the parking garage?" asked a man's voice.

"For the infinite time, yes," said another man. His next words

192

didn't sound right for a government agent. "Call the woman and ask her yourself."

"How does she know?" asked the skeptical man.

"How should I know?" retorted the scornful man. "The brats probably told her themselves. Everybody trusts a nurse."

I wanted to know which nurse they were talking about, but I couldn't concentrate enough to ask Nadia.

The footsteps drew closer. To distract myself, I entered a light sleep and followed Varick's progress up the side of the parking garage. He'd made it to the top and vaulted over the side. Michio hopped off his back, and Varick picked him up the normal way before sprinting for the white government van watching Danielle's car.

As Varick drew within ten feet of the van, he suddenly halted and set Michio down. Three agents scrambled from the van and pointed their guns at Varick.

"Keep him safe," Varick ordered. Without waiting for an answer, he turned around and dashed back the way he'd come.

"Halt!" cried one of the agents.

Instead of complying, Varick vaulted over the concrete railing and jumped.

I had to snap myself awake and concentrate to keep from screaming. A hard thud announced Varick's arrival, but I didn't want to look. A fall from that height shoulda flat-out killed him.

The two men I'd been listening to raced toward my position.

"Over there!" cried one man. I think the speaker was the skeptical man, but I couldn't tell for sure.

The other man's feet planted themselves firmly as he entered a shooting stance. Worried for Varick, I rolled out from under the car and kicked the man's right leg hard. His surprised cry cut short as he scrambled to stay on his feet. A bullet hissed out of his gun and pinged off the ceiling, but I was more concerned that the guy would fall on me. It occurred to me that I should worry about the gun being silenced, but I was busy trying to get up. I made it to my knees as the assailants overcame their surprise enough to start redirecting their guns.

Varick appeared from the darkness like an avenging shadow, slamming into the man I'd kicked, driving his head hard into the truck's hood. The other guy couldn't decide whether to shoot me or Varick, and the indecision cost him the chance to do either. A swift kick from Varick sent the gun flying off into the night, and a short, confusing fight later, the second guy collapsed next to me with a groan.

"Did they hurt you?" Varick asked, reaching to help me stand.

Taking Varick's hand and shrugging off his concern, I said, "Are you sure Michio's safe?"

"Nadia vouches for those agents," Varick replied. "We should go help Malia. Her plan has a few flaws."

Before he could rush off, I needed to know something. "Who knew we'd be here?" I waved to the unconscious men at our feet. "They said a nurse told 'em where to find us."

"We can deal with that later," said Varick. "Malia's in trouble."

"I thought she wanted us to stay away." It wasn't really an argument, but the night's events weren't exactly unfolding in a predictable pattern.

"Things change." Varick boosted me over the concrete wall, hopped up and over himself, then started jogging toward the hospital. On the way, he explained what he had in mind.

Since most of my breath went into running, I couldn't argue much. Varick's plan made sense, but it felt like he wanted to dump me in a safe place. When I told him as much, he agreed. This made me mad, which fueled my energy as we charged up the stairs to the roof. After sneaking into the hospital, we wound our way through the eerily empty hallways until we reached that closet the Pendletons had stuffed Danielle and Christy in many hours before.

Pushing aside deep misgivings, I stepped into the closet, and said, "You'd better not forget me."

Varick solemnly vowed not to forget me then shut the door and locked it.

Chapter 37
Not Our Real Enemies

ITEM 172: Jillian's eighty-seventh post-kidnapping journal entry
Item Source: Jillian Blairington
Since sleep wasn't gonna come naturally, I knocked myself out the hard way, taking only enough time to get comfortable on a giant box of lab gloves before passing out.

Queen Elena appeared before I could sink too deeply into sleep for her to reach. She wore the familiar blue dress and her sparkling crown. The multicolored jewel representing Michio winked in and out like a warning beacon. Queen Elena launched into an explanation before I could question her. "Jillian, you will soon need to defend yourself. Do not fear to use your full Gift in that endeavor. I apologize for not anticipating this possibility. The Darnell boys are here in the van with Michio. He will do what he can to thwart them, but they have already betrayed your location. If you can safely defend yourself and help Varick and Malia, I would much appreciate it."

Queen Elena vanished as abruptly as she had appeared. Her message took about seventeen seconds to deliver 'cause she spoke faster than usual, which is saying something for Nadia.

Thinking dark thoughts about Dario and Koresh Darnell, I sank my consciousness into a level ideal for working.

Nadia's voice called to me from afar. *Do not judge the boys too harshly, Jillian. They are not our real enemies. Be swift and safe.*

Wanting to follow the "swift" part of her advice, I clamped down on a grumpy thought about her definitions of enemies and concentrated on finding the dreams I needed to capture.

195

The hallway immediately outside the closet that hid my sleeping form was obviously closest. Finding the hallway empty, I cycled that dream to the back of my mind, leaving a mark on it to alert me if something changed.

Since my marks on Varick and Malia were far newer than the one on Danielle, I searched for my friend next. The cafeteria dream opened, revealing a strange standoff. Dr. Robinson and Agent Adams had both lowered their guns, but they still clutched the weapons tightly like they'd love to raise and fire 'em if given half a chance. The intensity I felt rolling off Malia in waves said she wasn't giving anybody that chance, but I also felt her energy beginning a slow, scary decline. Unfortunately, I wasn't the only one noticing the strain on Malia.

"When I break free, I will kill that abomination," Adams declared. His face contorted as he tried to break free from Malia's influence.

"My daughter's misguided sense of mercy is the only thing saving you right now," Dr. Robinson said. She seemed resigned to Malia's grip on her emotions, but her alert eyes said she too was fighting that hold. "Who do you think she's going to release first?"

I got the feeling their verbal duel had been raging for most of the time I'd missed and would continue for another few minutes, so I switched my attention to the parking garage. I'd forgotten to mark Michio, so my attention wandered restlessly over the top parking deck until I spotted Danielle's car and used it as a reference point. The three agents stood outside the van chatting nervously.

In another moment, I moved my consciousness through the van and found an all-out brawl in progress. One of the Darnell boys had both arms locked around Michio's waist, trying to pull him off his brother. Michio kicked, scratched, bit, and screamed like a wildcat, twisting his body and using his head to batter the boy holding him from behind. The other Darnell boy alternated between trying to grab Michio's flailing legs and trying to duck his wild punches.

I considered alerting the agents outside, but I figured Michio was holding his own for the moment. I marked the van with the same sort of alarm I'd left in the hallway so I could find it in a hurry if Michio got into serious trouble. I'm a big believer in fair fights, so before I left, I tapped Malia's Gift long enough to pull on the Darnell boys' emotions. Nothing huge, just a tug to calm 'em down and slow their reflexes. After all, the fight was two-to-one and they were both a couple of years older than Michio.

196

I rechecked the standoff as Varick arrived. He wasted no time getting to Agent Adams and knocking the man down with a punch, after disarming him, of course. Danielle threw him a pair of handcuffs, and Varick applied 'em to Adams's wrists.

A giddy, insane laugh bubbled out of Agent Adams. "You'll never stop us! My men will find the other child."

Varick pressed the man's face hard against the floor. "Call them off."

The crowd of decoys looked on with interest, but they were too far away to hear much of the conversation. Only a few of the agents remained in the room. I wondered where the others had gone.

Adams laughed harder. "I can't!" He gasped and laughed some more. "The little freaks have stopped talking to me."

"You are a hypocrite," stated Dr. Robinson.

"What is he talking about?" Varick demanded.

"We have some recently acquired additional assets out in a van in the parking lot." Dr. Robinson glared down at Adams in disgust. "Apparently their arrival wasn't a well-kept secret."

"Go," commanded Malia. My sister leaned heavily against the door frame with Danielle propping her up. "Jillian." She fought for the second word.

"What about Jillian?" Danielle asked nervously.

Yeah, what about Jillian? I echoed silently.

Adams's giddiness had subsided to malicious chuckles.

Dr. Robinson fixed Varick with a serious frown. "You'd better get back to wherever you left her. Most of his men slipped out while we were negotiating. Some of my men went after them, but they're going to proceed with extreme caution."

Varick took a second to shove Adams's head against the floor one last time and got up.

"I'm coming with you," said Danielle.

"Stay with Malia." Varick didn't look back to see if Danielle would heed the order.

My alarms simultaneously drew me toward the hallway dream and the van with Michio. Frustrated, I peeked at the hallway and saw both sides filling with armed agents. A quick check with Nadia confirmed 'em as hostiles.

Do not fear to use your full Gifts, Nadia reminded. *I am with you.*

A few quick instructions let me set up a second alarm for the hallway dream. Then, I checked on Michio. He stood near the van's back doors glaring at the Darnell boys who warily occupied the other side.

"We can do this, Dario," encouraged one of the blond boys.

"What's the point?" asked the other boy. Even if his brother hadn't identified him, I woulda pegged him for Dario 'cause I remembered him being the gloomy one. "Agent Adams will be caught, and they'll probably kill us for helping him."

"You always think everybody's out to kill us," complained Koresh.

"They *are* out to kill us, Kor," Dario insisted.

Figuring Michio had won his match, I moved my attention to the fight rolling my way. I thought the agent men would grip the door handle like civilized people but the nearest man aimed his gun at the door. Fear nearly froze my brain solid, but the desire to not die kicked the fear aside long enough for me to reach for the guy about to blast the storage room door. Lacking time for finesse, I crashed down on the man's consciousness like a tidal wave, driving him into a deep sleep. He collapsed. The fellows behind him eyed each other nervously, but I wasn't in a mood to see if they would decide to run or fight.

Moving to the next two in line, I reached to knock 'em out. One lurched forward, blocking my attempt with a wall of panic. His hand landed on the door handle and sprang the trap I'd left there. He fell backwards with a surprised cry. The third man fell back, screamed, and scuttled down the hall like a crab. The fourth man in line got off two shots at my door before Varick tossed the fifth assailant on top of him. Before they could rise, I knocked 'em cold.

Varick approached the door cautiously. Without reaching for the handle, he called, "It's safe to come out now. Is it safe to enter?"

With considerable effort, I roused myself, went to the door, and knocked three times to let Varick know he could safely enter. He promptly unlocked the door and met me with a smile. "Nice work."

I blinked up at him as my eyes adjusted to the hallway light. "Is it over?"

"I hope so," Varick answered. He pulled me into a brief hug then ushered me down the hallway.

A tremor ran through the floor, but I dismissed it as a figment of my overworked imagination.

We raced down to the cafeteria and found it mostly empty. "Where'd everybody go?" I wondered. I was so busy scanning the emptiness that I didn't spot the mess right away.

Varick dashed toward the conference room I recognized from my dream. Only this time, a thin cloud of smoke wafted from the doorway. I didn't have time to wonder why the fire alarm hadn't gone off. I stumbled after Varick and finally spotted Malia and Danielle kneeling over a body. My steps faltered, drawing me forward with a halting gait. Danielle held tightly to Malia, and both girls had tears streaming down their cheeks unchecked, making me fear the worst.

Varick skidded to a stop inches from the fallen form, exchanged a few words with Malia and Danielle, and sprinted for the door. I watched him go and fought off the urge to break down and cry.

Chapter 38
The Only One Who Can Save Her

ITEM 173: Danielle's fiftieth letter
Item Source: Danielle Matheson
Dear Dr. S.,

If the government knew I was writing to you about these events, they'd shut both our accounts down for good. I regret how much that makes me sound like a paranoid conspiracy theorist, but perhaps the nosy government lackeys who screen emails have read on and know that I fully support their cover up.

The official story will say that agents Smith and Adams sacrificed their lives saving innocent bystanders from a terrorist bomb. In truth, Smith idiotically loosened Adams's cuffs and paid for it dearly.

I wanted to go with Varick to help Jillian, but he was right about Malia needing my help. The kid could barely stand let alone walk. I'd planned to help Malia to one of the conference table chairs when Agent Smith barged past escorting Adams.

"Not in there!" shouted Dr. Robinson.

Smith either didn't hear or purposefully ignored her in favor of arguing with Adams. A lot happened in the next few seconds. I'd just begun changing directions to lead Malia to a quiet spot when a hand seized my right arm and yanked hard, flinging me to the floor. Malia, who had been clutching my arm, landed on top of me.

A flash nearly blinded me. Confused shouts were abruptly silenced as a wave of heat hit me, followed quickly by a muffled boom. I slammed my eyes shut and clutched Malia close, rolling on top of her to provide some protection. I ended up rolling further than I'd meant to roll and landing on my back facing the doorway.

At first, I thought Dr. Robinson had weathered the event unfazed, but then, I noticed how heavily she leaned on the doorframe. In slow motion, she crumpled to the ground and landed in a sitting position facing me. She looked sad, weary, and shocked. The next detail to sink in was the deep scratches and dark smudges along Dr. Robinson's face and arms.

Malia squeezed me hard, making me fight to breathe. She tried to twist her head and see, but I caught her head and held on firmly.

"Don't look. Don't look. Don't look." I'm not sure how many times I whispered the order to Malia while ignoring the advice myself.

The government men snapped into action. Agent Sanders issued curt orders left and right. Two agents rushed forward to lay Dr. Robinson flat on her back in front of the doorway and press towels, napkins, and ties to her left side. The others hustled the bystanders away from the scene. Their efficient movements told me they had an emergency protocol in place. Strangely, the agents ignored us.

It wouldn't occur to me until later that the agents' swift actions actually almost killed their boss.

Malia eventually pushed away from me and crawled over to her mother. Having nothing else to do besides watch over Malia, I followed. One glance at Malia's face told me she was shunting her own emotions aside. She settled on her knees next to Dr. Robinson, closed her eyes, and placed both hands on the woman's right arm. Maybe I imagined it, but I thought Dr. Robinson relaxed. I didn't have long to ponder the possibilities. Malia slammed into me and bawled like a kid who'd been through a traumatic experience. That's how we were when Varick and Jillian showed up.

When Varick skidded to a stop, Malia said one word. "Michio."

"Right you are," Varick said. He cast a concerned look in our direction but sprinted to fetch Michio.

"Hurry," I whispered. I had no voice and very little strength, but I managed to hang on to Malia as she sobbed. Sympathetic tears mixed with frustrated tears as I silently begged Dr. Robinson to not die. Her death wouldn't be fair. Malia had fought too hard to save the woman from her own schemes.

Dr. Robinson's strong pull, the fall, the hard landing, the flash, the explosion, the heat, and all the rest moved through my head on loop. Varick had saved me earlier in the day by talking down that heart-broken maniac, but this was different. This lady had literally placed her body between us and a bomb.

Jillian plopped down beside us and placed a hand on my knee. Both of my arms still held Malia tightly. Sooner than I thought possible, Varick returned, tearing through the cafeteria with Michio riding on his back. Two towheaded youngsters ran in his wake. Coming to an abrupt halt, Varick swung Michio down to a soft landing beside Dr. Robinson. My purse thudded to the floor behind Michio.

"Will she live?" asked one of the boys. Deep scratches marked his face and it looked like he would sport a black eye soon.

"It's bad," confirmed the other boy. He too appeared to have been in quite a scrap.

Aside from a mussed up mop of black hair, Michio looked perfectly fine. He didn't have a scratch on him, so I didn't know he'd been in a fight with the two boys until Jillian told me later.

"I'll keep everyone out," Agent Sanders promised. He motioned for the other agents to step away so Michio could approach. After a moment's hesitation, Sanders added, "Call me if something changes." Shoulders slumping, the man left, waving for the two blond boys to follow him out.

Varick stood guard over us as Michio sat down and placed his hands over Dr. Robinson's wounded side. I hugged Malia tighter and gripped her shirt hard so I wouldn't reach for Michio. Malia's sobs had abated to occasional hiccup-like spasms. She'd already soaked through a whole pack of travel tissues and thoroughly drenched my new shirt. My mind skipped to the time when Dr. Robinson held me back while Michio healed Jillian from a close encounter of the lead kind.

Time meant little to us as the color slowly returned to Dr. Robinson. Part of me wished not to watch, but the sight was too fascinating to look away. From time to time Michio's delicate fingers would pinch around a metal fragment and pull it out, letting it drop to the ground next to him. At other times, he would gently trace the path of a bloody scratch or gash and it would obediently close.

Malia eventually shifted to a more comfortable position in my arms. She and Jillian held hands. I think they both joined the healing effort. Though I couldn't tell you what Jillian did, I got the feeling that Malia was slowing the blood flow, so Michio could close the wounds.

Incidentally, blood flow is how the agents almost killed Dr. Robinson. The natural reaction to any huge wound is to stop the blood as quickly as possible. Unfortunately, much of what the agents used in their initial efforts got thrown away when Agent Sanders chased them off. If the blood had pooled around Dr. Robinson, the miracle boy might have been able to direct it back into her.

Besides the improving color, our first clue that the healing might actually work came from Dr. Robinson's lips. "My boy."

The weak words perked up everybody. We inched closer. Dr. Robinson's shirt looked like a rag pile reject full of burns, holes, and long rents, but the skin beneath looked perfect.

"My beautiful boy." Dr. Robinson slowly raised a hand, but she didn't move to touch Michio. Instead, she studied her clean fingers with amazement. Unshed tears made her dark eyes sparkle.

I was amazed, too. She'd had no small amount of blood on both her hands and clothes mere moments before.

My eyes went to Michio's hands which were also clean, and I marveled at how his Gift had grown since the last time I'd witnessed such an event.

"She'll need more blood," commented Varick, ever the practical voice. I caught a note of hesitation but couldn't work out a reason for it.

Michio nodded, ready to cry. "I'm sorry."

Varick hugged him. "It's not your fault, Michio. You did your part well."

Suddenly, every eye fell upon me. A cold feeling washed over me, as Malia withdrew her gentle touch upon my emotions.

"Well, we're in a hospital," I offered lamely.

"Let me go," whispered Dr. Robinson, smiling weakly. "That was my idea."

Nadia clarified the situation. *You are the only one who can save her, Danielle. As a safeguard against foreign governments obtaining our genetic codes, our blood has been modified to break down if it leaves our bodies for more than a set time if it's not treated with a stabilizing chemical. We may donate to each other, but not to others. Nobody, aside from a few select agents, even knows Dr. Robinson was near the blast. I have seen to that. We cannot request a blood transfusion without raising awkward questions. Michio's Gift must not be discovered.*

"Does my blood match?" I whispered the question seemingly to the air, but everybody knew I was talking to Nadia, even Dr. Robinson. I couldn't muster the brainpower to remember my own blood type, let alone track what would be a match to me.

It does.

"Then, what do you need me to do?"

Lie down beside Dr. Robinson. Michio will do the rest. Thank you for understanding. We are all in your debt.

It took a moment to rearrange people, but eventually, I did as Nadia instructed. Michio squeezed his tiny body between Dr. Robinson and me. Once settled, he took my left hand and pressed it firmly against Dr. Robinson's right hand. Malia held my right shoulder with both of her tiny paws. A brief, intense pain ripped through my left hand, like someone wearing razor blades had given me a firm handshake. It disappeared so quickly I thought I'd imagined it.

My head felt light and darkness crept into my vision.

Close your eyes and rest, but try not to fall asleep. It will be over soon.

Following the advice, I concentrated on breathing in and out. A warm hand picked up my free hand and squeezed. Since the hand was too large and rough to belong to Jillian and Malia still clutched my shoulder, I concluded it must belong to Varick. My lightheaded state didn't let me think about that, so I simply enjoyed the comfort and tried to maintain a relaxed state.

"Done!" Michio cheered.

Another brief flash of pain zipped through my left hand and the process was indeed over.

Varick fetched everybody a round of orange juice, and in about fifteen minutes, I felt almost human again. Agent Sanders raided the coffee cart for some stale bagels we consumed for a midnight snack.

The next few hours passed in a blur of frenzied activity. Dr. Robinson wasn't exactly up to skipping about the room doing her force of nature impression, but she managed to direct the show from a non-blown up conference room. Much to my amusement, Dr. Robinson wore an illusion provided by Nadia for the rest of the evening. That kid somehow managed to match every crease, stain, and shadow that had ever touched the woman's outfit, sans bomb damage, of course.

A nameless random agent eventually took pity on us and fetched a bunch of blankets. Varick and Michio curled up on two blankets, while Jillian and Malia each fell asleep using me for a pillow.

As you might have guessed, I couldn't sleep very well, so I decided to use Malia's hands-free, thoughts-only typing toy to flood your inbox again. Cheers. (You can blame Varick for that British-ism.)

The Temporary Insomniac,
Danielle Matheson.

Chapter 39
How Was Your Trip?

ITEM 174: Malia's thank you letter to Danielle
Item Source: Danielle Matheson

Dear Danielle,

Words of thanks seem inadequate when compared to the enormity of the gift you have given me and Michio. My mother too sends her heartfelt thanks and an apology that she cannot convey these thanks in person. The nature of her position means much of her communications do not remain private. A file already exists on you, but my mother has promised to see that the file stays secure.

My siblings and I have been richly blessed to have you in our lives. The last few days have given me great insight into your beautiful soul. I understand now why Jillian counts you such a close friend. If you'll grant me the privilege, I should very much like to count you as one of my friends, not merely the friend of my sister.

Jillian's Nana says that accepting thanks with good grace is as vital as giving it in abundance, so I acknowledge your high praise of our work with Susan Kilpatrick. Jillian and Michio did most of the work, but I won't deny my own contributions. Thank you for the opportunity to cultivate new friends. Dominique will be fine in time. I am keeping in close contact with her, and she has Nadia and Jillian to watch over her thoughts by day and night, respectively, should she wish.

I felt your concern for the two blond boys who accompanied Varick when he ran in with Michio. I don't know if you ever had the pleasure of making their acquaintances. Their names are Dario and Koresh Darnell. Jillian might have mentioned them, but that was her

205

first real meeting with them as well.

My mother's people will see that the Darnell boys—or Lanier's lads, as Nadia refers to them—receive proper training and have their physical needs met. Nadia and I will track their emotional needs and lend what aid we can. My personal feelings for the boys could not be more mixed. It's very likely we will someday find ourselves at cross purposes with the Darnell boys again, but Nadia insists they are not our enemies.

The wounds Michio inflicted upon them are already mending. I doubt the boys expected to encounter such resistance from Michio. While I regret that the conflict turned into a fistfight, I am proud of Michio's ardent defense of Jillian, for the Darnell boys were directing our foes in finding her.

Varick has spoken with Nurse Keili and determined that the betrayal was not malicious. The government infiltrators questioned her about our movements, and she saw no reason to deny them the information. I cannot tell you how greatly relieved I am at this news, for I cannot predict the lengths my brother will go to in order to protect us. Incidentally, I believe you now rank among the "us" so far as my brother is concerned. Varick would protect a perfect stranger, but there's always an extra measure of fervor to protection provided to family and friends. You have many times proven yourself a friend. I would say more, but it is not my place.

The fact that my mother needed saving was partially my fault. Jillian insists my guilt is foolishness and that only Agent Adams—and perhaps Agent Smith—ought to bear the blame. But the fact remains that I should have taken the time to dismantle the assassin bomb completely. I let the knowledge that it would have a small blast radius lead me to dangerously underestimating the bomb. Although Aiden would have been better for disassembling the weapon, I could have done it if I concentrated on the task. I thought disabling the detonator would be enough. That mistake nearly cost my mother her life and caused you pain in the process. For that, I am deeply sorry.

Before I close this missive, I would like to explain why you might have felt me withdraw when the issue of saving my mother came up. My Gifts were meant to support people, but like all powerful tools, they can also be misused. Though my formal training in the art of manipulation would probably have resulted in you drawing a favorable conclusion, my conscience could not bear the strain. Imposing my will upon others is something I try to avoid wherever possible. I did not want you to think the decision to help was ever anything but your own free gift to bestow.

Yours truly,

Malia

***

ITEM 175: Varick's second letter
Item Source: Varick Allard Ayers

Dear Dr. Sokolowski,

Nadia has gone silent. She prepared me this time, but the silence is deafening. The fact that she suspects a longer sleep than usual would not normally worry me. I would attribute the fear to a lingering reaction to the time she spent in a coma. My sister is not used to mysteries that baffle her, so she finds the unknown cause of the coma especially terrifying. However, in light of the recent events, I know something is wrong.

I have asked Jillian to take over the duty of checking in on Anastasia until Nadia can return to full strength. I will try to do my own check eventually, but I must be cautious. Few people understand a man shadowing a couple and their newborn baby. Logic says I should leave Anastasia's fate solely to her new parents, but instinct tells me enough of the wrong folks already know about her connection to us.

As advised, I have reached out to Danielle. I needed to write her in thanks anyway. I do not know where the coming months will send me, but if possible, I plan to join her at college and keep her safe. The small campus ought to provide its own brand of safety, but it will not take much for the troubles facing us to spill over into her life.

I considered trying to drive Danielle away and make Jillian cut ties with her, but you are right in saying I need a friend and Danielle needs a protector. Jillian would never stand for the strategy anyway. I'm afraid Danielle's fate has become linked to ours, so I've asked her if she'll let me teach her some self-defense.

I regret that the men who intended to harm Jillian escaped by the time the real agents arrived. I should have informed them sooner, but I needed to get Michio to Dr. Robinson as quickly as possible. In hindsight, I suspect I had enough time for both tasks, but in the decision-making moment, I went with the safe choice.

Michio's secret is safe due in no small part to Malia's plan. The fact that the plan worked makes it no less barmy. I'd expect something like that from Nadia, but Malia should be the predictable sister. Jillian's probably the most straightforward, but even she supported Malia's

207

efforts. What could I do? I had to help, or they would have gone forth without me. At least Michio has been a good enough fellow to not tell me what to do.

Christy's mother decided not to press kidnapping and attempted murder charges against Mr. and Mrs. Pendleton upon the conditions that they enter grief counseling and submit to a psychological evaluation. I delivered the terms in person. My chat with the Pendletons went exceedingly well. I don't think they will bother Christy's family again. The family has drawn tightly together. In time, perhaps I will reach out to Christy, but Dominique and Susan need her full attention right now.

Jillian has been avoiding the video game training exercises I created for her. I think the last one unnerved her, but she'll recover. Malia will talk to her about it. The dungeon scene featuring Malia is true to the algorithms predicting her behavior. Jillian must accept this. I need to prepare her for situations that may arise. She must learn how Nadia, Malia, Michio, Dustin, Aiden, and I will react to danger. The knowledge could one day save her or us. It is too important to let slip even if it is painful to watch. Will you speak with her about this?

If I am called away unexpectedly, I will have somebody take over the duty of safeguarding you and your place of business. Thank you for everything you do and have done for my family.

Your servant,
Varick Allard Ayers

***

ITEM 176: Malia's third letter
Item Source: Malia Karina Davidson
Dear Dr. Sokolowski,

The recent events have given me a better understanding of Jillian's insistence upon numerical means of distinguishing our parents. As I cannot bring myself to mimic Jillian's method, I have taken to calling my adoptive mother, Mrs. Carol Davidson, "mom." My biological mother, Dr. Karita Robinson, has forever been "mother" to me while Cora shall keep the British spelling and pronunciation of "mum."

Cora is not a trained scientist, but she has invested herself in Dr. Devya's work as much as, or more so, than many of the scientists. As far back as I can recall, Cora's role has always been caretaker. While we had an endless stream of tutors and trainers, Cora remained a constant in our early lives. She taught us to speak, read, write, and think about the world outside our compound. As such, my mum probably knows me best.

One of the more pleasant consequences of our recent experiences has been to start a relationship with Mother. Dr. Robinson had always kept her distance, even during the years she worked for Dr. Devya. As I told Jillian, my relationship with Dr. Robinson is complicated. Aside from physical characteristics, which largely passed unaltered from her to me, we share much in the way of internal drive and manner of thinking. This is a sobering realization for she has made many decisions I do not agree with or fully understand. Nadia keeps reminding me I am not my mother, but the lesson has yet to truly sink into my heart.

The first question Mom (Mrs. Davidson) asked me when I got home almost struck me dumb with its ordinariness. She asked, "How was your trip?"

To be honest, I did not know how to answer her. On the long car ride home, I had convinced myself to say nothing, but the open invitation cracked my resolve. My Gifts allowed me to recover quickly enough to supply a satisfactory, if vague, answer hinting that our trip was successful.

Mom knows I have not told her everything, but I detected no hint of condemnation, only a sense of patience and support. I need some time to sort through what is safe to tell her. She knows a little about my Gifts already, but I am leaning toward being more open on that front. I have already told Mom and Ann that their prayers for miracles were answered. Mom assured me she did not need to know exactly how. I may tell her anyway, but I'm grateful she's not pressing the point.

Nick was visiting when we arrived late yesterday afternoon. He picked me up and whirled me around twice, claiming that he had a lot of catching up to do with bothering me. We shared a large meal of spaghetti and meatballs with plenty of garlic bread. Danielle, Michio, and Jillian fit in as naturally as they did before. They're staying the night so they can start fresh tomorrow morning. We shared some news from our trip, but my family largely steered the conversation away from that topic.

Ann called to check on me after dinner, so I went into the family room so I could hear her. When I came back, everybody surprised me with a birthday cake. I didn't know how any of them knew my birthday had passed until I recalled reminding my mother of that fact in Danielle's presence. Jillian probably heard me say it, too. Marina and Joy had both worked on the cake, and their efforts were appreciated by everybody. Marina and I have a tennis date tomorrow. I could get used to this "normal family thing," as Jillian called it.

Harsh as my training could be, I am grateful it was not in vain. What I did to prevent my mother (Dr. Robinson) and Agent Adams and their respective forces from killing each other was directly from a training exercise. I suppressed their will to fight. The method's flaws became clear when Agent Adams sent his men away to find Jillian. Once their intent changed from killing my mother's people, I could not prevent them from leaving, for fear of losing my hold on those who remained in the room. I shall have to rethink that strategy.

I am all right. Thank you for asking. The guilt fades a little each moment I am home. Our mission was a success, though not a complete success. I could certainly have done without the bomb exploding, but I can say I learned much about my limits, my siblings, and my priorities.

As always, thank you for taking the time to listen.

Yours respectfully,

Malia Karina Davidson

Chapter 40
Moving Day

ITEM 177: Jillian's eighty-eighth post-kidnapping journal entry
Item Source: Jillian Blairington

We're finally on our way home, and even though I got a good night's rest, I'm gonna take a nap. Today's moving day for Dr. Devya and his people. Malia's momma, Dr. Robinson, will try to smooth things over from her end, but I don't think Dr. Devya wants to take any chances.

Dr. Devya doesn't trust the government to keep its word even if it promises to leave him and his alone. Can't say I blame him much for the strong distrust given the size of the force that showed up at the hospital. Nadia wouldn't tell me exactly how many people showed up, but I'm guessing it neared a hundred between the cops and government agents.

It's a miracle only two people died when that bomb went off. I feel bad for their families. Agent Smith, whose real name was Casey Andrews, left behind a wife and two baby girls. I dunno about Agent Adams's family 'cause his government record was false, but Nadia thinks he might've had a wife too.

Malia blames herself for letting the bomb explode, but I keep telling her she ain't responsible for Agent Adams's actions. He planted the bomb or at least had it planted. All Malia did was prevent it from killing her, Dr. Robinson, and Danielle. Not even Nadia knew there would be a manual way to set the thing off, and she usually knows just about everything.

I should check in with her soon. Nadia said she'd let me know when I should join her this morning. I think she wants me to witness

211

something again. I keep trying to guess what it could be, but Nadia ain't exactly predictable. The last major thing she had me witness, last night in fact, was Anastasia at her new home with her momma and daddy. The way her new parents gazed at her with love, devotion, and awe told me things will be all right for her. Maybe her Gifts will return one day, but she'll do fine without 'em.

There's Nadia's signal. I'd better see what she wants.

*****

I drove myself into a working sleep expecting to have one of my dreams form whatever scene Nadia wanted me to witness. Instead, I felt the invitation to one of her dreams, so I followed it and found myself in the throne room. Normally, the throne room's mostly empty, but this time, it was packed wall-to-wall with Nadia versions and guests.

A few were reading or writing, but most were keeping busy other ways. Three of the girls raced around the throne room perimeter with a boy who looked like my friend Jimmy Denson. One Nadia expertly biked in and around the other figures. Another rolled by on one of those mini-scooters Nana doesn't much care for. Another whole flock of 'em played tag. A few quiet ones played chess in one corner next to one working on a jigsaw puzzle. One Nadia even shot arrows up at a target mounted on one of the chandeliers. Bits of the target paper rained down on a young Nadia playing piano.

Most of the girls appeared to be teenagers, but a fair number of smaller children were also present. I blinked, thinking Nana woulda had a fit if she saw this place.

So much was happening that I could hardly focus on any one thing. A soccer ball flew at my head. The ball woulda smashed my jaw if Naidine hadn't appeared and caught it. She tossed the ball back to a half-dozen Nadias wearing blue and white soccer uniforms with neat numbers stitched in white letters across the front. Most of the numbers said eleven but a few said twelve or thirteen. They waved thanks and started playing again.

Nadie raced up wearing a green dress that coulda doubled for one of Nana's table cloths except for the part around the middle which looked like a wall paper border made of pink whales swimming in a white sea. Having been trained by Michio, I stooped and met Nadie's fierce hug. Even though I'd been prepared, her running start threw me off balance. Naidine steadied my shoulder.

"Hello, Jillian," said Nadie. "Thank you for coming." With her message delivered, Nadie wriggled out of my grasp and ran off.

"We should probably go someplace with less ... activity," Naidine suggested. She casually placed a hand on my left arm and tugged me out of the flight path of a remote controlled helicopter.

Though still staring around in wonder, I let Naidine usher me out of the throne room, through some long hallways, and into a quiet garden. Here, we passed another dozen or so versions of Nadia basking in the sunshine, reading, knitting, or singing softly. When we moved past the garden, we found more Nadias dancing, fencing, jousting, climbing the castle walls, or practicing martial arts.

As I prepared to ask Naidine where she was taking me, I spotted two large horses tethered to the lowest branch of an apple tree.

"We riding today?" I asked.

"If you do not mind," Naidine replied. "I find it relaxing." She unwound the reins holding the big brown mare to the tree and handed 'em to me. "Do you remember how to mount a horse?"

Shrugging, I said, "I'll cheat if the horse doesn't behave herself."

Naidine held the horse steady for me as I mounted. Then, she untied the large black horse standing ready for her.

"Guess we'd better dress the part," I said. "English, Western, or fantasy?"

"Fantasy," Naidine responded, humoring me.

"Commoner, soldier, or royalty?" I asked next.

"I leave royalty things to Elena," said Naidine.

"You're no fun," I mock-scolded her. Snapping my fingers, I changed her clothes to something better suited to a fantasy setting. In keeping with Naidine's gloomy tastes, I imagined her in a sleek, black riding outfit with silver threads wound throughout the shirt. Shiny black boots, a silver belt, and a deep blue travel cloak completed her outfit. For myself, I imagined simple brown pants, brown boots, and a loose white shirt. I woulda gone with blue except I needed to balance all the black Naidine was wearing.

Once I'd had my fun, Naidine set a brisk pace for our horses. At first, I had to concentrate to make sure I didn't fall off, but eventually, I settled into a rhythm that allowed me to enjoy the breathtaking view. Nadia sure can imagine places well. The land we passed through was mostly grassland, but distant mountains and wispy cloud formations made for a beautiful, slow sunset featuring mainly yellow, orange, and red.

The sunset occupied my attention so thoroughly that I didn't even notice my horse had slowed to a trot.

"I would like you to meet somebody," Naidine announced. She dismounted, removed the horse's bridle, and let him wander off.

I watched her until she came over to help me dismount and set my horse free. I wanted to ask who I was gonna meet, but if Naidine had wanted to tell me ahead of time, she would have done so already. I wondered how we were gonna meet anybody this far into nature, but that was just me forgetting this world existed in Nadia's head. She could have us meet on the moon if she took a shine to the idea.

Naidine started walking in the same direction as we'd been riding. About three minutes later, she stopped, and said, "Jillian, please meet Tea Time. She is rather famous around here for her fine selection of teas and her timely advice."

As she spoke the odd name, a fancy outdoor patio set materialized. Three big white wicker chairs with comfortable looking flower cushions sat around the table, shaded from the bright sun. A dozen more cushions lay scattered about the set like little islands of flowers abandoned in a sea of green.

I wondered how the sun could be so bright when we'd just watched a lovely sunset, but here again, my rational thoughts didn't fit the world. In dream time, this could be a completely different day.

In the center wicker chair sat a spry looking older lady with large glasses and wavy white hair. She smiled at me in a way that made me feel welcomed. Slowly, I drank in enough details of her features to recognize her, but I still didn't believe it right away.

"Nadia?"

The lady's smile widened as she gently corrected, "Tea Time." Her voice was Nadia's slowed by age to something close to a normal pace. "The children call me that because I have a fondness for tea. Sit down and join me in drinking some and I shall explain further. You too, Naidine, dear."

I thought the lady must be older than I'd initially guessed 'cause the table was completely empty when she first spoke. By the time she'd uttered "dear" though, a platter of light pastries had appeared right next to the pole holding up the umbrella. A matching tea pot, saucers, plates, and tea cups also showed up a half-second later. Tea Time gripped the handle of the steaming pot and poured three cups of sweet-smelling brown liquid.

Not recognizing the smell, I asked, "What kind of tea is it?"

214

"Whatever kind you wish, dear," answered Tea Time. "I have raspberry while Naidine prefers mint."

Carefully lifting my tea cup, I cautiously smelled it 'cause it looked way too hot to test. As the steam filled my senses, I caught a hint of the sweet, tangy, fruit-filled flavor. "Pomegranate," I concluded.

"A fine choice," Tea Time said. She continued to pour more cups of tea.

"Who else is coming?" I wondered, blowing gently on my tea to speed the cooling process.

"Will Her Royal Highness join us?" asked Naidine. She spoke so mildly that I couldn't tell if she was being sarcastic or serious.

Tea Time didn't have that problem. She placed a wrinkled hand upon Naidine's perfectly smooth one, patted a few times, and said, "I thought you girls had sorted your differences." With a heavy sigh, she continued, "But I see now that you are back in your color of choice. Would you like to talk about it?"

"Yes, but later. We must brief Jillian right now," Naidine answered.

"You are quite right," Tea Time agreed. She patted Naidine's hand one more time before turning to me. "I apologize, Jillian. I am so easily distracted these days. You are sure to have questions, but first, I promised an explanation for my name."

"Why don't they call ya 'Nana' or 'Grandma' or something like that?"

"Well, for one thing your Nana is the only Nana necessary, and I have always believed 'grandmother' or any variation thereof is a title to be earned," answered Tea Time. "The children initially suggested a title such as 'Wise One' or 'Ancient' or even 'Wisdom,' but these do not fit me."

Naidine looked amused. Crossing her arms and leaning back in her comfortable wicker chair, she let a smirk play across her face. "You said 'Ancient' made you sound old."

"And so it does," confirmed Tea Time.

"What's wrong with 'Wise One' and 'Wisdom'? They sound respectable," I pointed out.

"That is it precisely, Jillian. Both titles are respectable to the point of being presumptuous," said Tea Time.

Seeing my raised eyebrow, Naidine interpreted the statement. "She will not let us call her by a title she feels is arrogant."

"If it's true, it ain't arrogance," I argued.

Naidine and Tea Time both chuckled, dipping their chins ever so slightly left in identical gestures. I don't even think they noticed.

"A title like 'Wisdom' is a heavy burden to bear as it sets very high expectations, but I am always happy to help the children as needed." Tea Time paused to hold a tea cup out to her right side, seemingly to the air. When she let go, the cup vanished. She repeated the maneuver eight times and each cup disappeared. One by one, the cushions surrounding our table winked out like somebody had deleted 'em. "There, that was easy. Where were we?"

"What just happened?" I demanded.

"Tea Time served tea," Naidine answered dryly. She picked up her cup of mint tea and took a sip. "I did mention her teas were popular."

"Ain't the others gonna stick around?" I wondered.

"They have decided to leave the discussion to Naidine and me," explained Tea Time. "Would you prefer I summon them?"

I shrugged. "I'm okay with either. I didn't want 'em to feel left out."

"I think we can handle the summary," said Naidine, sounding grave.

"Why am I here?" I sat up straighter.

A new wicker chair appeared, holding a projection of the real Nadia. "You are here because I do not wish to be alone right now." One didn't have to hear her soft, unsteady voice to tell she'd been crying. Her sad eyes looked the part perfectly and her purple blouse had darker splotches where tears had fallen.

"She is frightened." Anger crackled behind each of Naidine's words. She abandoned her tea cup and balled her hands into fists.

My eyes asked the next question, but I whispered it too 'cause nobody was looking at me. "Why are ya frightened?"

Tea Time's expression turned distant. She gazed in my general direction but didn't really see me. She sighed. "The procedure for any move involves secrecy, but this is the first move since the Dark Time."

"The coma," Naidine clarified.

"What's that mean?"

"If you would like to see the answer for yourself, drink the tea," instructed Naidine. "If not, then stay with us and we will explain."

After taking a long look at Tea Time, Naidine, and finally Nadia, I lifted the tea cup in a toast and drained the whole thing. Nana woulda been horrified by my lack of manners, but I knew I shouldn't waste a second.

I dunno what Tea Time put in that tea, but it washed me right back into my own head and slipped me effortlessly into a real-time dream. I found myself in Nadia's room. It's bigger than most of the other dorms 'cause she's used to sharing. The extra space made it seem lonelier. Nadia sat on her bed, wearing the same jeans and purple blouse she'd worn when I saw her at the tea gathering. Her knees were tucked in close, held in place by her clasped arms.

The door chimed merrily and slid aside. Cora entered with Dr. Carnasis a step behind. They each carried something, but I didn't pay the items much mind.

Nadia looked up and dashed away the last of her tears. "I take it that is Father's final answer," she commented, waving toward the small medical case in Dr. Carnasis's left hand. "Thank you for presenting my case to him."

"I'm sorry, Nadia," said Cora, sounding like she meant it. "He thinks it's safer this way." She put a set of gray scrubs next to Nadia. "Would you like some privacy to change?"

"It does not matter," Nadia replied. She pulled off the tear-stained purple blouse and put on the plain gray, lifeless shirt. In a half-minute, she had fully changed. Solemnly, she folded her regular clothes and placed 'em at the foot of her bed. Then, she resumed her original seat. "I am ready."

"Lie down," instructed Dr. Carnasis. She sounded resigned, but her hands quickly went about the business of cleaning a spot on Nadia's right arm and preparing a needle for the injection.

"How long will it last?" Nadia inquired.

Dr. Carnasis and Cora exchanged a quick, uncertain glance.

Cora knelt down and picked up Nadia's closest hand. "We will wake you as soon as possible, I promise." She wrapped both hands around Nadia's fingers and held 'em tightly as Dr. Carnasis stuck the needle in the clean spot on Nadia's arm.

Nadia had watched the injection, but as soon as it was over, she leaned her head back against her pillow and stared up at the ceiling lights. The drug took hold quickly, sinking Nadia down into a deep sleep. I reached out to see if she would dream, but I felt only blankness.

As I was about to panic, Nadia's voice spoke. *Jillian, if you hear this then my preparations have worked, and you will have access to the throne room. I do not fear sleep, but I believe they intend to keep me unconscious for quite some*

217

time. That will severely limit my abilities. Naidine and Queen Elena should also be in the throne room. Please visit often. I do not like where events seem headed, and I will only be able to lend aid if I am kept apprised of the situation. If you are willing, that is the task at hand. Give Varick and the others my love. Farewell.

As there didn't seem to be anything more to see, I started to close the dream, shutting down the visual elements first.

The dream shifted by itself, and I heard a man nervously whispering, "It's too late. We're moving out right now, and they won't tell us where we're going. I had to pull in every favor to get to drive one of the trucks and not land on the blackout crew." He paused to listen, so I guessed he must be on a phone. "They put the girl under, but I don't know if I can deliver her now. Devya's paranoid." He listened some more. "Yeah, I got it. You worry about your part, *brother*. If the boss has you go for the kid, know that he's not going down easily." A slightly longer pause ensued. "I've got another angle I'm working on. I'll be in touch when I know more."

The dream slipped away before I could get the visual elements back or hear if the man said anything else. Given what I'd just witnessed, I guessed that the man was talking about Nadia when he referred to the "girl," and I think the "kid" who wouldn't go down easily must be Varick. The other "angle" the man talked about made me nervous.

My brain felt fuzzy, so I woke up to chat with Danielle. I'd have to return to these troubles again, but I wanted her take on the mysterious phone call.

Epilogue

ITEM 178: Carla Wittier's sixth letter
Item Source: Dr. Carla M. Wittier
To Dr. Stephanie Sokolowski:

Jillian's latest entry is indeed worrisome, especially that last conversation. The man on the phone certainly sounds like he intends trouble. I believe fears for Nadia's safety stand justified.

I'm having a hard time picturing the factions in play. Dr. Robinson and her agents represent the wishes of the United States government. Dr. Devya and his scientists seem to want a clean break from whatever bonds the government has placed on them. This Katharos group seems unaligned with regard to the previous two factions. Since the last group tends toward the most violence, I fervently hope that the man on the phone works for Dr. Robinson.

I had suspected Danielle might face danger, but I could not imagine how much danger. It is best that she spend some time away at college and not dwell on the troubles brewing for Devya's Children.

It does my heart good to hear your positive report on the situation with the Roman sisters and their mother. The teamwork involved in that miracle is nothing short of amazing, but if I had to attribute success, I would call it a victory for Malia. She has blossomed in the Davidson household.

Jillian appears to be handling her stress and worry better these days, but life tends to want to get complicated for her.

I agree that Varick stands on the least stable emotional ground. The others have much stronger support systems, and he will suffer the most from Nadia's renewed silence. It's very clear he hates the idea of not being able to locate her. He is a loner, but his strong connection to

219

Nadia has always kept him well-grounded. I cannot predict how he will react to this new threat.

Your suggestion that Varick stick close to Danielle is ingenious, but the question remains: will the friendship be enough to keep him from doing something rash?

Please do not hesitate to contact me day or night if you hear something about Nadia or one of the other children.

Kind regards,

Carla M. Wittier, Ph.D.

October 13, 2014

Dear Reader,

Thank you for reading Jillian and Danielle's third adventure. If you enjoy the series, you can always help by connecting with me on social media, joining my email list, and leaving positive reviews.

Tell your friends and family that they can get a free kindle copy of Ashlynn's Dreams from Amazon. I'm always willing to give out review copies of the other ebooks in exchange for honest opinions.

Look for the audio versions narrated by Kristin Condon. Ashlynn's Dreams is currently available and Nadia's Tears Winter ~2015. (If you can't afford it, check in first, I might still have free codes.)

Email me any time. I'm always happy to hear your thoughts.

Sincerely,

Julie C. Gilbert

Connect with me

Email: devyaschildren@gmail.com
Facebook: www.facebook.com/JulieCGilbert2013
www.facebook.com/pages/Ashlynns-Dreams/137395832945727
Twitter: @authorgilbert
Pinterest: www.pinterest.com/julie20201/
Blog: http://julie20201.blogspot.com/
Goodreads:
www.goodreads.com/author/show/4111900.Julie_C_Gilbert

Made in the USA
Middletown, DE
10 April 2015